Rag and Boyd

The Elfstone

Rag and Boyd: The Elfstone

Helen L Brady

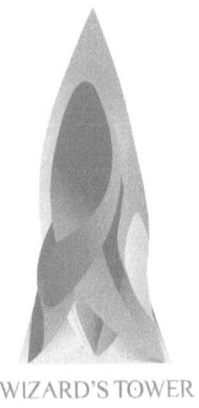

WIZARD'S TOWER

Wizard's Tower Press

Rhydaman, Cymru

The Elfstone
A Rag and Boyd Novel

Text © 2025 by Helen L Brady
Cover design by Charlotte Mouncey
Book design by Cheryl Morgan

The section header character is from the Cianán Ùrfont by
Feòrag NicBhrìde

Previously published By Conrad Press, 2022

This edition published in Great Britain
by Wizard's Tower Press, January 2025

Paperback ISBN: 978-1-913892-94-4

http://wizardstowerpress.com/

Contents

HELEN L BRADY

Praise for Rag and Boyd: The Fabulous Zoo

"Engaging characters, a captivating storyline and enough suspense, thrills and humour to keep you gripped."

"This book took me to a new world through its playful narrative voice and ability to merge fantasy with a believable story."

"What really elevates this is the delightful cast of characters and creatures, vividly realized with marvellous descriptive prose."

THE ELFSTONE

For Ann, being my very first cheerleader and long-time supporter.

And Amaka for critiques and encouraging me to write better.

ς

PROLOGUE

The prosperous red brick and timber Tudor farmhouse and its sprawl of newly thatched outbuildings snoozed in the mid-summer sun. The rickety, hand-made wooden ladder belonging to the thatcher was still leaning against the ragged ends of the roofing straw, waiting for him to return and tidy them up. At the foot of the barn wall, fat chickens clucked sleepily as they settled down, round and brown as bread loaves, to doze in the dusty, dried earth that lapped up against the tawny bricks.

Penry stood nearby among the small grove of narrow-trunked young oak trees that provided a shelterbelt for the buildings and watched the farm. No adults were in sight, only a little, brown-haired boy in a crumpled doublet, his hose dusty at the knees from crouching down and dropping pebbles into the stone horse-trough; he appeared to be counting the ripples. Penry sized him up; the boy was maybe a hand-span smaller than he was, probably a mite sturdier, but then mortals of that age often were. As an alfar-born child he'd remain slender for many years to come; a more muscular body would only develop with his warrior training... if he chose that path. Still, Penry felt confident that in a knock-down fight, he could win. He looked down at the large, near-transparent stone, the delicately rippling surface almost silky, in his hands—now was the time to see if this thing worked.

Penry replaced the stone in his jacket pocket and slowly approached the dry-stone wall that divided the woods and open meadows from the farmyard. He was careful to keep in the shadows where possible and he knew his footfalls were silent—to the boy he would suddenly just appear, as if by magic.

'You can come closer,' the boy said.

Penry halted, one foot in the air, and wobbled a little before he recovered from his surprise and stood firmly on both feet. The boy twisted around to look at him, 'Who are you?' he said, not seeming at all alarmed.

Penry lifted his chin, 'I am Pentagaron... er... Penry to you! And I am the fifth son of the Great Alfar, Dark Lord of the North Country.

The boy frowned, 'You don't sound Scottish.'

'No!' said Penry, 'it's not that north country!'

'That's good,' said the boy. 'My mam says the Scots Queen is a scarlet woman and a traitor to our Good Queen Bess.'

'Who?'

"You're not from around here are you?"

Penry scowled, he had been hoping for shock and awe from the young country boy, not polite conversation. He tried again. 'I am come to claim sovereign rights over this household and this portion of ground.'

'I don't think you can do that.' The boy stood up and came closer to the wall. 'This is Grandma's house and we're only here because my mam has taken to her child-bed again.'

'What?'

The little boy sighed, 'Don't you know nuthin'? When a mother needs to farrow, the other children get sent away till the new baby comes.'

Penry wrinkled his nose, 'The beasts 'farrow'. Is she giving birth to an animal?'

'Nooo! Though it sounds like it. We should be going home soon to a new brother or sister, and I must be a good boy and help look after Gilbert and Joan, so my Pa says.'

This was not going as Penry planned. He shook his head, waved his hand to silence the chatter... then took from his jacket pocket the knapped, crystal Elfstone; its sharp edges glistened the startling blue of a butterfly's wing where the sun struck it. Penry grasped it awkwardly in his fist, waving it in front of him. He had trouble holding it, because although it fitted an adult's hand it was too big for his. He sliced extravagantly at the air in front of him with the tapered edge, but nothing happened. He tried again, his slashes getting wilder the more effort he put into it.

'What are you doing?' said the boy, watching with interest. 'My name's Will by the way. That stone's pretty—Mam would like that. Do you want to swap it for a chicken? I'll let you have a fat one.'

Penry growled with frustration. He tried to change his grip on the slippery surface of the crystal axe-head so he could hold it with both hands. Another slash made the air ripple for a moment with a glow of colours.

'Yes!' shouted Penry triumphantly, stepping closer to the dry-stone wall and slashing again even harder. It wasn't clear if he tripped or if something tripped him, but suddenly Penry fell forward—the stone slipped from his hands, launching itself over the boundary wall. It bounced, flipped and rolled in the grass just as another faint ripple of rainbows ran through the air, reaching down to the ground. The bending colours flicked up and over the stone, which came to rest against a tussock of coarse grass.

Captivating, vivid blue... the slightly tapering crystal lay quiet and still, winking in the sunlight—it looked like a slice of pressured ice, stolen from beneath a glacier, and now forever immune from melting. Will stepped forward and picked it up. He weighed it in his hand; it felt heavy, heavier than a normal stone that size.

'Give that back!' shouted Penry.

'Are you sure you don't want a chicken for it?' said Will hopefully.

'A plague on you and all your chickens! Hand me the stone! My father will kill me when he finds...' Penry fell silent for a moment when he thought about it and that that might actually be true... 'It was a gift to my father from the Fair Folks' Queen. It is not yours to keep.'

'Aye, and I think by the sound of it, it wasn't yours to take, was it now?' said Will taking a step backwards.

'Give it back. I command you to give it back to me!' shouted Penry.

'Come and get it then.'

Penry tried to scramble up the stone wall, but the invisible Veil that divided Penry's world from Will's, swept and rippled like the deep folds of an enormous curtain and forced him back. Penry pushed forward against the implacable barrier, which gave a little under his fists but could not be torn, pierced or broken by them.

Will watched the little alfar becoming wilder and more desperate in his fight against something Will couldn't see. All he could see was a skinny little manikin with long black hair that fell loose around his shoulders, dressed in funny grey and black clothes with lots of shiny silver buttons and buckles to his sleeves and hose.

Penry came to a stop, breathing hard and only a little way away from panic. He swallowed hard. 'Look here... Will. How about we make an exchange—what can I give you to throw the stone back to me?'

Will considered. 'You must want this very bad—is it so valuable?'

'It was a gift of tribute from the Fair Folk of Arden to my father, cased in a casket carved from the teeth of the great ocean beasts, and lined with golden sea-silk woven by mer-folk.'

'Yes,' Will nodded to himself, 'that sounds expensive.'

'Give it back!' howled Penry.

'Alright' said Will, 'but I want a pile of Marchpane, gilded with gold-leaf—all on a solid gold platter!'

'Marchpane?'

Will nodded vigorously—he loved the sweet almond paste.

'On a golden plate?'

'Yes' said Will, 'I think that's fair.'

'Hold on. Stay there and let me think,' said Penry, stepping sideways into the shadows and backing away towards the concealing thicket of oak saplings. Looking back, he could still see Will standing patiently, turning the Elfstone over in his hands, the boy even gave it a polish on the sleeve of his linen doublet.

Penry had an idea. He gathered up some dead twigs and quickly wove them together, placing large green leaves and dandelion flowers on top; then he picked as many butter-cups as he could find and heaped them up. Carefully he carried his construction back towards the wall, murmuring the phrases for a simple glamour he hoped would hold long enough to pass the trick off to the mortal boy. As he stepped from the shadows, the sun glistered brightly off what looked like a sumptuous stack of marzipan sweets gilded with real gold leaf. The vision was a little unsteady and flickered in and out of focus, but Penry hoped it was enough to fool the lad.

'Here—Marchpanes and gold,' Penry announced as he reached his side of the wall.

'God love us!' gasped Will.

'Now—you hand me the stone and I'll give you this golden platter.'

Will held the stone up to the sun to admire it one last time. 'All right—you put the platter on the wall and I'll give you your trinket.'

'No. You give me the stone first.'

'We count to three and do it both together,' said Will. 'One, two, three...'

Penry put the plate of glamoured buttercups down; they wavered slightly but still looked like luscious golden sweet-meats. Will tried to put the stone down beside the plate, but it felt like he was pushing against something strongly resist-ant. The harder he pushed, the more his hand holding the stone rebounded, not only that, the 'something' was sweep-ing him backwards step by step, away from the wall.

'Hurry, hurry,' shouted Penry.

'I'm trying. I—can't—push it—through.'

'Try harder!'

'I am!' Just then, Will noticed the pile of delicious marzi-pan sweets was nothing but yellow buttercups and leaves.

'You wanted to cheat me!'

'No!' said Penry, 'Yes—because you're nothing but a stupid mortal and that stone is mine! Mine! Mine! Mine!' Penry was jumping up and down with rage. 'It's mine, and you're a thief!'

Will folded his arms and looked stubborn, 'Am not.'

Just then somebody from the yard called Will's name, he turned his head at the sound. 'I have to go.'

'Nooooo, give me the stone!'

'Later. I have to go.'

Penry screamed in frustration.

'You can't get to it, and neither shall I,' said Will, 'see, there's a gap in the wall down at the bottom behind the grass. I shall put it there and hide it, and I'll come back soon.'

'I cannot see you!' shouted Penry.

Will stepped forward with an effort, crouched down, then came up empty handed and pulled two small dark stones out from near the top of the wall. 'Look, I'll mark it with these, and there's an acorn sprouted there as well so I know I can find it again.'

'No, nonononono...!'

A voice came from behind Penry. 'Little Master, has this mortal boy seen you?'

It was Penry's nurse-gard, come to find him, drawn by his shouts and her master's thrall laid on her to be ward to his son. The tall alfar-maid glided towards them; gowned in greens and soft greys it almost appeared that she'd stepped out of one of the tree trunks of the nearby wood. Will stood still, open-mouthed, as the Green Lady approached them.

'This will not do Pentagaron, your father is waiting for us to leave.'

'But... but...' stuttered Penry.

'But me no buts!' She turned to face the child across the wall: 'Boy—you shall fall asleep.'

She pointed at Will and fluttered her fingers in a complex gesture, 'And everything you thought you saw and heard will be but a dream.'

Will blinked, yawned, and slowly sank to his knees and over to his side, and by the time he had curled up in the sun-warmed grass he was fast asleep. A voice called Will's name again from the other side of the barn.

'Come Penry, we must go immediately, or your father will be angry.' She clasped Penry's hand and swiftly drew him away.

While young William Shakespeare, curled up in the long grass... dreamed of beautiful fairies and mischievous sprites.

ʕ

CHAPTER ONE

Spring's changeable weather had settled to become summer sunshine... punctuated now and again by some
tremendous thunderstorms that blew in from the west of
course. Rag and Boyd both missed their old school-friends'
company, but they were beginning to get used to the rhythm
of life now they lived up here in the remote north-west of
Scotland with Uncle Wulf. And there were so many things
they couldn't talk to their old friends about, or say what their
new life was like, that they both drifted away from the online
forums they used to use.

The shock of their mother's sudden illness and rapid
death was beginning to fade, especially since their father,
once missing and presumed dead had now been returned to
Wulf's castle. The adventure of that rescue—which even they
had to admit had been foolish for them to attempt alone—
the dangerous discoveries it had involved had begun to be
part of the ongoing strangeness of their new world. Apart
from worries that their father's ill-health was barely improv-
ing, this rural life was their new, and very busy, normal.

Schooling had started; the post-mistress from the village
a few miles away came up to the castle twice a week in her

post office van to teach them Maths. They had English Literature and Language lessons from a retired teacher who also lived in the village.

Today they were on their way home from their English lessons. The Long Brothers, Peat and Russ, two of the clan of broons that lived and worked at Uncle Wulf's castle had driven down to collect them, and once they'd left the public roads, Boyd was having another go at driving the enormous old shooting-brake car. He was having trouble with the gear changes, particularly as this stretch of road was very winding. The screech of metal as the gears crashed together was enough to put Rag's teeth on edge.

'No, no!' Peat said, 'put your foot right down on the clutch and lift it gently... no, gently. Feel for...' The gears meshed again with a screech... '...the bite,' said Peat.

'Awwww...!' Peat's brother Russ moaned aloud, his usually handsome young face screwed up into a wincing frown. 'I think maybe that's enough, Boyd. Either the car's going to give out or I am.'

'Sorry,' Boyd spoke through gritted teeth, 'I'm nearly... there...' The gears crunched again as he slowed for the next hairpin bend.

'Yep. That's great. Pull over...'

'Now?'

'Yes, lad, just over here,' said Peat

Boyd guided the car to a juddering stop. Russ sighed with relief.

'You're getting the hang of it, Boyd,' said Peat, 'but maybe we'll keep the practise for the straight bits first... Hop out and I'll take over.'

Boyd reluctantly got out of the driving seat and opened the rear door to change places with Russ and slide in beside his sister.

'I still think if he can learn to drive then I should as well,' she said.

Peat slid over into the driver's seat, pushed his dark hair back from his face as his brother climbed in, slamming the car door after him. Peat started the car up and pulled away smoothly, 'All in good time, Morag m'dear, all in good time...' The good-looking young broon easily negotiated the next bend and slowly gained speed as they bumped down the track.

'If we had a smaller car, I'm sure I'd be able to manage it better,' said Boyd, 'This one is very heavy to steer.'

'All the better to build some muscles on you,' said Russ with a grin, he looked over to the back seat and winked at Rag—who was getting used to the two dark-haired brothers' amiable little jokes and bantering ways.

'But if you did have a smaller car then I could have a go too,' she said.

'We've told you, lass,' said Peat, 'when you can reach the pedals on this one, then you can have a go at the driving.'

Rag leant back in the seat and folded her arms tightly over her chest.

'Ah don't look like that,' said Peat who could see her face in the rear-view mirror. 'Ecru has a load of herbs for you ready in the still-room when we get you home. And Boyd, you're to help Gam in the glasshouse—and both of you—don't be late for your archery practise this afternoon.'

That was the one good thing about home-schooling—they'd found other lessons were practical to the point they didn't feel like classwork—it was just stuff they were learning to do from the other broons at work in Uncle Wulf's household, which apparently varied, but at present numbered twelve.

Botany was gardening and herb-lore with Gam and his wife, Ecru—who created a whole pharmacy of salves and tinctures in her large still-room between the glasshouse and the kitchens; she coached them in preparing and preserving herbs and foodstuffs.

Biology ranged from water management to animal husbandry on both sides of the Veil that divided that strange Otherworld from their familiar 'mannish' world. They helped in tending to all sorts of creatures, from the normal farm animals, to the often weird and unfamiliar beasts of the Otherside—through to butchering rabbits, plucking chickens, and gutting fish. Rag didn't mind the fish, but she was still squeamish about the rabbits.

'Design and Technology' was repairing fences, gates, and woodwork with Tan and Sandy, with the occasional bit of plumbing and building maintenance. There was also sewing, repairs, and the making of new garments with Sienna, and her twin sister, Sepia; the sisters also did leatherwork, making harnesses, bags, boots, and things. They had some basic cookery lessons—which came under both Chemistry and Survival Skills, according to Hazel's assistant cook, Fallow—a younger, rather pretty, fair-haired version of Hazel, who seemed very fond of Peat.

Uncle Wulf set them History tasks to read about in the library... though both of them found a quick search of Wikipedia to be a useful shortcut! Geography lessons concentrated on map-reading and also included geology, understanding the landscape, and how to find their way without a compass—which might be with whichever broon they were outside with at the time.

They also learnt about Astronomy, and had begun horse-riding, archery, and some basic defence moves with sticks and staves, and for Boyd, with blunted practise swords—'just in case...' according to Peat. Rag insisted she wanted to learn 'proper' sword-fighting too, so Fallow was given the job of being her fencing-master, which initially made Rag sulk because Boyd was taught by Russ... who she secretly had a crush on... until she saw Boyd's scraped knuckles and bruised arms—Russ and his brother did not give any quarter to their pupil!

Working and learning filled their days, and in the evenings they had books they were expected to read, poetry to learn by heart—Broonie, the Broon—chief among the household broons, had once been a bard and was unforgiving when they stumbled on a line. There was a whole selection of musical instruments in the music room for them to try out, though neither had settled on one to take-up seriously. They were encouraged to learn strategy games like chess and backgammon from the selection always ready in the drawing room.

They were busy, day and evening, with tasks about the farm and Keep, and with the animals in the enclave on the Otherside. But they made time every day to visit their father, going separately so he had more time with them. Lachlan was not well. Sometimes he knew them and would smile weakly and try to follow what they said, at other times he drifted in a dark, foggy place among shadows that could make him suddenly cry out. This frightened Rag, but Hazel was generally around when she visited her father, and would gently take the girl out of his room—often having to wipe away Rag's tears. The little broon did her best to reassure her, but Rag could see her father wasn't progressing well, and nobody could, or would, tell her why.

Muirdoch, the fearsome shape-shifting Water-horse, was slowly recovering from his own injuries sustained during their father's rescue. He was keeping to his human form, having developed a nasty wound infection and septic fever to begin with, which had confined him to his rooms next-door to Uncle Wulf's in the Otherside of the Keep. However, according to Russ, the Water-horse must be getting better and starting to heal properly, because he was becoming more and more bad-tempered whenever his dressings had to be changed.

One morning, when Rag and Boyd were doing their chores near the unicorn's pen, this situation came to a dramatic head. From the Keep, somewhere above their heads, they suddenly heard an angry bellow, swiftly followed by a tremendous splash. They looked up towards the castle walls where a double-doored set of windows stood wide-open behind a stone-pillared balcony. They briefly glimpsed a flash of white diving from the balcony, before the sound of another large splash came from behind the high garden wall, soon followed by angry shouts and the noise of thrashing water.

Shortly afterwards, The Broon hurried out and planted himself, feet apart, arms folded across his chest, standing guard in front of a painted wooden door set in the grey stonework. From the other side of the tall sturdy wall they could hear more violent splashes... raised voices... and after a few minutes silence... sudden laughter. Broonie glared at them and waved them away to continue their chores. Soon after that, Russ and Peat appeared grinning from ear-to-ear, though they hid their smiles as they walked past Broonie, who glowered at them.

'What was that? What's going on?' asked Rag.

'Come away, and we'll tell you,' said Peat, 'but not in front of Broonie.'

They walked down towards the next paddock—Russ and his brother could contain themselves no longer. They burst out in howls of laughter.

'What?' said Boyd.

Russ was holding his side to ease his ribs from the pain of laughing. 'Oooh... Oooh... See it was Hazel took your man's breakfast up as usual, and he said he didn't want porridge, he wanted bacon—and then he took the whole tureen and threw it up the wall. Some hot splashes hit Hazel and she screamed, and the Laird came running in to see what was to do. Apparently, he took one look at all the mess, opened up the glass doors wide—picked Muirdoch up in both arms and threw him out the window!'

'No!' gasped Rag, 'that's two floors up!'

Peat nodded vigorously, 'He did. Hazel saw it. Then the Laird strips off all his clothes and dives out after him, stark naked. That's why Broonie is guarding the door to the pool garden. And all the lasses are forbidden from working in the rooms above it on this side. Broonie says if he finds any of them have been peeking out the windies, he'll tan their hides.'

'There's a pool, a swimming pool?' said Boyd.

'Oh aye,' said Russ quietening down and wiping his eyes, 'his lordship had it made years and years ago when Muirdoch first came here.'

'A proper pool?' said Boyd, staring up at the surrounding wall. The splashing noises of vigorous swimming drifted into the air, along with more laughter.

'Yes, it was when one of the dragons came visiting— before we came to live here,' said Peat. 'The broons had dug out a great big pit and lined it with clay brought from over the glen, then the dragon blew fire all over it—fired the clay hard, like rock. They diverted a wee brook and the pipes from the glasshouse boilers discharge into it too so the water's warmed. It overflows down into the loch when it gets too full.'

'Nobody mentioned there was a swimming pool,' said Boyd. 'I'd love to go swimming in a proper pool with warm water.'

Russ clapped him on the back, 'I'm sure the Laird will agree to that—just not today, eh?'

Russ escorted them down towards the feeding hoppers. Another louder peal of laughter and the sound of more splashes drifted over the garden wall. Boyd turned his head to look back and sighed longingly, then followed Rag, who had hurried after the Long Brothers, towards the feeders and their next set of chores.

Later that evening at supper, the table in the small dining room was laid for four people. Rag and Boyd had taken their seats when Uncle Wulf and Muirdoch joined them, both of them looked cheerful, and although Muirdoch still favoured one leg he now moved with more of his character-istic easy grace. After the meal, Gam came to clear the table and Wulf told him they'd take coffee in the day-room across the hall; it was a small cosy room, with only two sofas and a couple of armchairs, when compared to the much larger formal drawing room. Contrary to its name, it was more often used in the evening when anyone wanted somewhere comfortable to read quietly.

'We should talk about what's to become of your parent's house,' Wulf began, as they settled into the chairs.

'I don't want to sell it!' said Rag immediately.

'No. That is not my suggestion,' continued Uncle Wulf, 'while Lachlan is still... ill, it will be impossible for you three to live there.' Wulf raised a hand to stall further interruption. 'So I propose we bring everything you decide to keep up here. We can arrange for any furniture you especially want to be stored, or brought here by a removal company, and the house itself can be rented out rather than left empty.'

Boyd frowned, 'It was our home...'

'It still could be,' said Rag.

'Yes, it still could be, but not yet,' said Muirdoch, 'your father is still thralled, he's not well enough to leave us.'

'How long will it take? For him to recover?' Boyd asked.

Wulf and Muirdoch exchanged glances.

'But he will recover—won't he?' Rag said, looking from one to the other of the two.

Uncle Wulf nodded slowly, 'Yes, I do believe he can, but... time is another matter.'

'And do you not think of the Keep as home? All the broons say you seem to enjoy your life here?' said Muirdoch.

Boyd was surprised Muirdoch had even asked about them—he'd always seemed quite aloof the few times they'd seen him in the weeks since they bought their father back—but then, he thought, both the horse... and the man-part of *Each Uisge* must have felt increasingly confined hobbling around in his room... never mind his bird aspect!

Ecru had mentioned to Boyd when they were mixing salves that to begin with, though everything had seemed well, Muirdoch quickly developed a raging fever from his wounds, which had turned bad, and that had made them heal slowly. Something which left Muirdoch increasingly frustrated, and probably accounted for the outburst of temper this morning, thought Boyd, suddenly aware that Rag was talking.

'So how are you going to get there? What will you bring back—can I go too?'

'I thought it would be better for you both to go. You and your brother can choose what you want to keep with you here. And decide what you want to be stored if you don't want it now.'

'I want my mother's paints and pictures,' said Rag

Uncle Wulf nodded, 'Of course.'

'And Dad's books and papers,' added Boyd.

'Absolutely. Everything you think he will eventually want, you should bring back with you.'

'But that's a lot of things, we can't carry it on our own,' said Rag.

'Of course not, child—Russ and Peat will drive you down in the car, and you can fill it.'

Boyd nodded, 'Yes that should do it.'

He smiled at the thought of reclaiming the things from his old bedroom—until another thought swiftly followed— did he still want them? And just thinking of that made him feel disloyal to his mother's memory, and his father—it had been their home too. He frowned at his own thoughts.

"When are we going? Rag demanded, 'Soon?'

'In a day or two when I have made the necessary arrangements,' said Uncle Wulf.

'Cool!'

'Umm,' began Boyd, '…it is a very long drive… is there any other way to get there?'

Muirdoch snorted with laughter, 'Already. He will be wanting a Pegasus-pony next!'

Wulf raised his eyebrows at Muirdoch, and gave a tiny shake of his head, before turning to Boyd. 'Other means of transport… would leave you on the wrong side of the Veil when you got there, and having a unicorn cut an entrance for you… might be more noticeable than we would like.'

'Oh—I suppose…' said Boyd.

Rag interrupted him, instantly alert. 'What are Pegasus-ponies? Are they flying horses? You have flying horses? Really?'

Muirdoch avoided catching Wulf's eye, and busied himself with the coffee tray. Uncle Wulf heaved a sigh, 'Yes, there are such creatures, and no, you cannot have one—not yet anyway.'

'But I could have a flying pony? For real?' Rag bounced in her armchair.

Wulf raised a hand. 'Not until I am satisfied you can ride well enough.'

'Oh, I'll practise—every day. I really will, Uncle Wulf!'

'Ummmmm— we shall see. That goes for you also, Boyd.'

'Actually, I'd prefer to have driving lessons—and is it alright if I use the swimming pool, please?' said Boyd, looking across at Muirdoch.

Uncle Wulf smiled, 'that can be arranged. In the meantime, if you want to go upstairs you are free to leave us. I will tell you both more about our arrangements very soon.'

Rag and Boyd got up to leave; Rag was still fizzing with excitement at the thought of her own flying horse.

'Goodnight Uncle Wulf. Goodnight Muirdoch—thank you,' said Boyd. Muirdoch inclined his head slightly and smiled.

'Night!' Rag called, already out of the door.

Once they'd left, Wulf rang the servant's bell; shortly afterwards Gam scratched the door and entered. He gave a small bow.

'Gam—ask Russet and Peat to come to me now.'

'Here, laird?'

Wulf nodded, 'Yes, send them up straight away.'

Muirdoch stirred his coffee cup. 'You noticed the boy still wears that gold torc about his arm?'

Wulf nodded, he checked the pot to see if there was more coffee.

'Will you speak to him?'

Wulf shrugged, satisfied there was another cup left. 'When the time comes. I believe the torc has settled itself on him.'

'You're not worried?'

'Too soon to be worried, perhaps a little concerned, but… to him it is simply a bracelet he found. I shall leave it that way, at present.'

A soft scratching at the door interrupted them.

'Come,' said Wulf.

The door opened, Russ and Peat entered, evidently having quickly brushed their long, unruly hair as it lay flatter than usual. They both gave Wulf a small bow.

'Good,' said Wulf, 'I have a task for you—come closer.'

The brothers walked over to where Wulf sat.

'I have your loyalty?'

'Aye, lord.'

'Always, lord.'

Wulf smiled and nodded. He held out his hand, and in turn each of them bent formally to brush their lips against his knuckles and the heavy, engraved gold seal ring he wore.

'I trust both of you to defend me and mine…'

'Of course, lord,' said Peat quickly, 'with our lives.'

'I hope not this time, Peat of the Broons,' Wulf smiled, 'but I do ask if you will take on a wardship for me.'

'Laird?' said Russ.

'The day after tomorrow I wish you to drive Morag and Boyd to their old home so they may collect their possessions. They will be in your charge. You know they are precious to me, as were their parents. Will you bear my ward upon you while you are their Gard?'

The brothers gave each other a quick glance before both of them placed their right hands to their chests and bowed low.

'Aye lord, we accept,' said Peat.

'Aye, that we do' added Russ.

Wulf nodded in acknowledgement of their pledge. 'Bare your left fore-arm and take turns to kneel before me.'

The brothers rolled up their sleeves, Russ looked apprehensive, but Peat winked at him encouragingly, and then knelt before Wulf, holding his bared arm out. Wulf took Peat's arm and laid it wrist upwards over his knee. He took off his ring, turned the inset seal over to reveal a tiny razor-sharp shard embedded in the underside. He pressed his fore-finger onto the shard, and bright blood welled up from the cut. Then he pressed the still bloody barb into the middle of Peat's forearm, and murmured a few words under his breath. Peat hissed at the sharp pain. Wulf withdrew the ring, and with his bloody fingertip, swiftly drew a complex, knotted pattern above and below the tiny cut on Peat's forearm. The alfar blew along the fine crimson trail laid over the muscle; it vanished instantly.

The broon looked down and could see the now pearl-white pattern twisting slowly just beneath his skin like a pale serpent. Peat bowed his head once in acknowledgment and stood up, moving aside so his brother could take his place at the laird's knee.

As they walked back to the kitchen's sitting room, Russ rubbed hard at his forearm.

'It doesn't hurt,' said Peat.

'No,' said Russ, 'but it itches.' He pulled his sleeve up to look at his bare arm; the pearly pattern beneath his skin gently swirled in mesmerising knots.

'Well stop scratching and it'll keep still.'

'Easy for you to say,' mumbled Russ.

'Och away! Stop scratching—and I'll get wee Fallow to be a good lass and sneak us a drop of whisky each,' said Peat.

'Oooh. Fine thought!' said Russ, cheering up at the idea.

'And, my wee brother, you're always saying you want to get out an' about a bit more... Now's your chance!'

'How far is it anyway?'

'Oh a dare say it'll be a good few hours' drive,' said Peat.

'And how far is that?' said Russ... before they were enveloped by the light and warmth of the kitchen-parlour where the other broons were relaxing after finishing the chores of the day.

ζ

CHAPTER TWO

In the middle of England, the same red-brick and timber farmhouse basked again in the midsummer sunshine; it sagged a bit, the bricks had flaked and the roof was mossy... but then it was about 450 years later! Otherwise, thought Penry, it hasn't changed that much. Though its surroundings had—the oaks that were once verdant on both sides of the divide had all gone on that side, not a stump remained, and the approach to the old farm was now surrounded by dark, smooth-surfaced roads, rows of houses... and lots of people. He knew they couldn't see him through the Veil; the more attuned ones might have a feeling of being watched, but they wouldn't see who by.

Penry circled the grounds, looking for the right place— behind the barns, but slightly to one side. There should be a wall... then he saw it, and he remembered what the boy had said 'there's an acorn shoot...'

The shoot was now a 450-year-old oak tree, and it's spreading roots and expanding girth had demolished a sub-stantial piece of the original dry-stone wall. What remained had been re-built to curve around the trunk, before it ran off to border a grassy area, before colliding with a tall hawthorn hedge that ran across its path.

Around him on his side of The Veil, the land was grassy Common lightly studded with trees, the grass kept short by the wide-horned cattle the villagers grazed there; big, white beasts that stood as tall as he was at the shoulder. Nobody was in sight, which was a good thing; he didn't want to be seen by the village folk, they would question what a young svartalfar was doing here, especially one alone. Their houses were some way away and Penry had thought it unlikely he'd be seen, and even if he was—he was sure he could talk his way out of any problem. Or, if it came to it, he could summon his personal Gard—the one he'd been very careful to 'lose' before he came down here. A mixture of persuading, cajoling and insisting on having his way, had forced one of his father's men to bring him here using the warrior's Vortex to instantly transport him.

He found a combination of silky smiles, veiled threats, and easily-forgotten promises got him most things he wanted, at least when he was outside the hearing of his Gard—who, very unreasonably, thought privileges needed to be earnt! In getting what he wanted, he modelled himself closely on his father; even if he was the fifth and youngest son, he would make his father proud. Which is why he had returned here, determined to retrieve what he'd lost all those years ago.

He could still remember his father's curses when they'd returned to the first of the mountain fortresses to rest the Pegasus mounts overnight—they were strong fliers, but needed a break every few hours. His father had called for the casket so he could inspect the tribute from the Fair Folk—the one he'd cajoled from them with silky smiles, scarcely veiled threats and empty promises. He was furious to find the ornate ivory casket was empty.

Penry had hidden, quaking with fear that he might be discovered, but his father had never even considered that the babe of the family might have taken it. He was sure one of the fairs had stolen the stone away before they left the convocation. He raged and cursed, then dispatched his own guards to retrieve his 'gift'. Using the Vortex to get there and back, they returned an hour or so later, their hands and armour spattered with blue fair blood, to report that The Court was gone and the few stragglers they had caught had denied everything, right until their painful end.

The Svart Lord was incandescent with fury, even the Guard-Captain kept his eyes on the ground, but ranting, raging and throwing the furniture around didn't bring the stone back, even if it relieved his father's temper. At that point, Penry certainly wasn't going to volunteer any information as to its whereabouts. The atmosphere of the remaining journey home was prickly with his father's barely contained anger—everyone had performed their tasks as dutifully and swiftly as possible so as not to raise his father's wrath again.

Penry gave an involuntary shiver at the memory—never since, well almost never, had he seen his father so enraged. It was only quite recently that he had discovered the rarity and true importance of the curious crystal and what it could do, and why his father had wanted it. Knowing the real power of something that as a small child he only thought of as a pretty plaything had made him concoct this plan to get it back—and prove to his father he was as good, if not better, than his brothers. He'd show them! He was pretty sure he could find the hiding place, although having seen how things had changed... but it should still be there. All he needed was for someone to invite him across...

The main attractions provided to visitors to the old farm seemed to be away from this side of the barns, which was good. He could study the remains of the wall and work out which way the oak tree had grown—these stones, so he'd heard, reached for the light, it wouldn't have let itself be buried too deeply, at least that's what he hoped. He stood among the shadows of the remaining trees in his Otherworld and watched carefully for somebody to come by.

Mackenzie was bored. It was hot, and she'd had enough history for one day. Coming on this Performing Arts trip while her mother did the Climate Change conference had seemed like a great idea. Her mother as chief representative for the United States of America had to be there every day for meetings, consultations, and whatever else they did. She'd told Mac that even at 15, there was no way she could stay at a London hotel on her own for a whole week, but if she went to Warwickshire with her performing arts group on this student exchange Summer School thing, why then afterwards they could have two whole weeks together and go to Paris AND Rome! And it had been sort of ok to begin with, but staying with the English family in their tiny house, in their tiny spare bedroom, had lost its gloss. She was getting bored with them, and bored with Shakespeare; she preferred modern plays, or even better, parts in movies or TV. The other girls might think it was dreamy to play Ophelia or Juliet, but if she had to, she wanted to be Puck, or Portia, or maybe Henry V—and she had a suspicion that some of them thought she wasn't 'right' for playing Shakespeare, even after they'd been to the theatre in Stratford and seen black actors making up half the cast.

The others were absorbing the atmosphere 'Wow, do you think Shakespeare could have stood, like, right here?' Or they were trying to flirt with the only two male, costumed guides that were under 50. Mac had found a couple of the women talking about family life in Elizabethan times interesting, but she didn't care about the farm animals, so she'd wandered off to look for a wifi signal and somewhere to sit down.

It was a hot, sunny day and this patch of shaded grass looked like a good spot for some 'me-time'. She was just choosing between full sun or dappled shade when she suddenly noticed the spiky-haired guy standing in the shadows. She could have sworn he wasn't there a minute ago. He was weirdly dressed in black and grey, with long hair spiked at the front almost like an anime character; she'd have missed him if he hadn't waved to attract her attention. She sighed—she did not want to be instructed about anything else that happened on Elizabethan farms! He was smiling, so she had to smile back... and, on closer inspection, he did have a rather cute smile.

'Hello.' Penry approached the old stone barrier, where a wild rose was doing its best to get its roots deep between the rocks and make even more of the wall fall down.

'Hi,' said Mac.

'Are you visiting?'

'Yeah, with my friends—are you... working here?'

'Me? No, no just passing through, same as you must be,' said Penry vaguely, adding with a winning smile, 'I like your shoes.'

'What, these? These are last seasons, but my mom is going to buy the new Nikes when we're in Paris'

'Ooooh... ' said Penry, not understanding but still smiling encouragingly.

'You sure you don't work here? Only your clothes are... a bit...'

'Really? Yes, I suppose. My family—they're quite independent. You could even say *out of this world*.' Penry smiled at his little joke.

'Oo, I get it, that's cool. I like Alternative, especially that sort of Goth look... stuff ...but, you know how it is—my mom, her job, she says I have to make a good impression.'

'Your mother has an important job?'

'I guess.'

Penry continued looking into her eyes and smiling, making Mac feel quite a bit warmer than the air temperature should have made possible. A flush crept into her brown cheeks making them quite rosy; she looked down, noticing that although this Emo-kid wore boots they weren't DMs, but something more sort of historical looking, like riding boots or something. And he was so pretty! She found herself wondering what his long, shiny black hair smelt like...

Penry pushed his glamour as hard as he could. It wasn't a proper thrall to have her completely under his will, he wasn't strong enough to achieve that yet, but he wanted her to agree to what he asked—it was part of his plan to get through the Veil that divided their worlds.

'What's your name?'

'Mackenzie, but everyone calls me Mac.'

'Hello Mac, I'm Penry.'

'Penry—that's unusual.'

Penry gave a thrilling little laugh, designed to send shivers down her spine. 'Well Mac, we're an unusual family.'

Mac could feel herself grinning like a fool, but he was really, really cute.

'We have lots of old traditions—did you know it's always considered very rude to enter a property without being invited? You'll need to ask me in if you want to meet me properly.'

'Really? I thought that was vampires and stuff.'

'Sorry?'

'Never mind.'

'Anyway,' Penry continued, 'to cross the wall, you have to invite me over the threshold. And to show you mean it, without wishing me harm, you need to make a welcome gesture—by spilling a drop of your blood.'

'Shut up!'

'It's true. I have seen it done—you have to pierce your fingertip, just a little, and leave a drop of blood on the stone—it placates the gods of the boundaries.'

'That sounds gross, I'm not doing that. Was it in a video game or something?'

'It's how you formally invite me to join you. It is sort of a game, but this wall is a threshold and I can only cross it to meet you if I'm summoned by blood—otherwise it is... bad luck. And you wouldn't want me to have bad luck, would you?'

Mac laughed, 'You're crazy!'

Penry pouted. He put his hands on the wall and leaned forward, with another big smile.

'Let's play the old game—you know you want to. And there's all this Shakespeare play-going stuff around you. You'll act the part beautifully.'

Mac folded her arms and considered; this was sort of ridiculous, but he was cute and he made her laugh—why not?

'So—what do I do?'

Penry bestowed his most alluring look upon her—and Mac didn't even realise she gave a big sigh.

'See? There's a rose here just waiting for us—use a thorn to prick your finger and wipe the blood onto the stone and say after me... "Come to me, Come now to me..." '

Mac winced as she pricked her finger; the blood welled up darkly against the paler brown skin of her finger-tip. She repeated his words solemnly, after all—this was just like acting a part.

'...Bound in blood, stone, leaf and tree... As my will so mote it be,' said Penry

'...As my will so mote it be...' Mac repeated. 'Is that it?'

Her blood had left a crimson streak on the wall—that rapidly faded, seemingly absorbed into the stone even as she watched.

'Wow,' she said.

'Let's see if it works, shall we?'

Penry found toe-holes and climbed the wall. He stood on the top, reached forward experimentally, and then jumped. For a moment Mac thought she saw a flash of colours rip through the air around him, but she put that down to the sunlight flashing off the many silver buttons on Penry's jacket. He landed on the thick grass with scarcely a thud.

'I'm here!' he said triumphantly.

'Yeah, you sure are. So that was all some D&D role-playing shtick?'

Penry just smiled and nodded, not knowing what she was talking about, but happy to go along with what she wanted to believe.

'Well, um... it certainly is warm today,' said Mac, 'Hey—why don't I buy us some ice-cream? There's a booth in the yard.'

'That would be welcome—do you mind if I wait here for you?' said Penry. 'I'll just sit under that oak tree.'

'Sure—do you like chocolate or vanilla?'

Penry gave another dazzling smile—it was beginning to make his face ache. 'I'll have whatever you have.'

Mac barely suppressed a giggle as she turned to go. She walked a few steps, and suddenly it felt like she was trying to walk through glue. She struggled to put one foot in front of the other. Penry watched her and walked quickly to her side—strangely with him nearby, her next step rather than being a great effort, abruptly let her take an effortlessly long stride which unbalanced her. Penry was at her side and caught her as she staggered. Mac blushed to the roots of her carefully combed hair. *What a dork*, she told herself crossly.

'It must be the sun,' said Penry. 'Here—come and sit down with me for a moment in the shade.'

He guided her to the foot of the huge oak tree.

'Let's just sit here—you must be tired—very tired.'

Mac yawned. 'See you are tired—even sleepy,' said Penry soothingly, 'just lean back against the tree for a minute. That's it—you are safe with me.'

Mac's eyelids fluttered, she could barely keep them open—but she struggled to stay awake.

'Oh wow,' she yawned again. 'Maybe... we could just sit here a little... while...'

'Yes, of course we can—you must be so tired. All that walking around... In the hot sun... making you sleepy...'

Mac's eyelids slowly drifted closed again, and stayed closed.

ᔑ

CHAPTER THREE

Morag stared out of her bedroom window, and suddenly thought this might be for the last time. The once familiar view of rooftops and chimneys, and to the side, several streets away, the tops of trees surrounding the modern block of flats... it all felt a bit odd now. As if she knew it from a distance. It was her home... but not. At least, thought Rag, it had been their home until some months ago, and then everything had turned upside down.

Their mother had died so suddenly after that short illness. Then they'd been sent to live with the mysterious Uncle Wulf they had never met before, at his castle in the Highlands of Scotland. Their father had vanished some months earlier and nobody knew where he was, or even if he was still alive. Rag felt glad she'd refused to give up hope—she knew her daddy was still alive. Boyd had struggled between thinking their father must be dead or he'd have come back for them, and being angry that he hadn't. Then they'd eventually found out where he might be—and who with—and what he had been doing... That was a whole new revelation.

Even Rag could see now that the two of them setting off to find him themselves had been rash—but she didn't regret it. The strange Otherworld they'd found a way to cross into was a place where they very quickly realised they didn't know the rules. Back then, they had no experience at all with the strange peoples and fabulous animals that lived there. But they were learning—all the time.

She could hear Boyd in his bedroom across the landing; they had the two attic rooms at the top of the house, below them were their parent's bedroom, the spare room, and the large room that was their mother's studio and their father's office. She heard his door shut and her brother's quick footsteps going down the tight curve of the stairs. She picked up black bin-bags of clothes and followed him downstairs. They had arrived late the previous night and made do with blankets, makeshift beds, and food from a late night takeaway. She knew Russ and Peat were eager to be packed and away by mid-morning if possible. It was a long drive back home to Scotland.

The door to the office was open. Rag could see Boyd at their father's large old-fashioned bureau, staring inside the opened drop-down flap at the interior and the pigeon holes stuffed full of papers. She dropped her bags and walked into the room.

'It feels strange doing this,' said Boyd, 'like I'm intruding.'

Rag went to stand beside him.

'I don't know what to take,' he said.

'All of it,' said Rag. 'We don't know what Dad wants, or needs.'

Boyd nodded, 'If the house is going to be rented... I suppose we have to.'

He had some big shopping bags and a couple of packing boxes and began to lift out papers and place them inside, keeping the bundles in each section together. Rag wandered over to stand beside her mother's small antique writing desk, the one with all the little drawers, some even had secret drawers inside. She brushed her finger tips across the curly patterned wood.

'I want this,' she said, 'Mum always said I could have it.'

Boyd paused from unloading the big oak bureau and looked across the room. 'Uncle Wulf said we could have some of the furniture sent up by a removals company. They are going to come in and pack Dad's library.' He looked down at the bureau. 'I think Dad would like to have his own desk— for when he's better.' Although both of them knew that didn't look like it was going to be soon, neither of them said so.

'Yes,' said Rag, 'and his chair, and everything else in here.'

Boyd frowned for a moment, but then shrugged, 'If they are coming up to Scotland in a van they might as well fill it up. We can tell Auntie Carol we want everything from this room packed. Uncle Wulf can find a room for Dad to have all his things around him at the Keep—for when he's better.'

'I think Dad would like that,' agreed Rag.

'But we need to take his papers away. We don't know what might be in them—here, take that bag and start emptying the drawers.'

Rag pulled out a drawer and put it on the floor and began to gather up the various papers, pens and oddments. One flat tin rattled so she opened it, inside was a strike-a-light, a modern one that looked unused. She fingered the deeply etched metal cylinder—it felt sharp, eager to make sparks... so it seemed to her. She glanced over at Boyd whose attention was elsewhere, then quickly closed the tin and put it in her pocket. 'Dad won't mind,' she thought, 'and I can give it back when he wants it.' She carried on emptying the drawers.

Boyd in the meantime was closely examining the large sturdy penknife he'd found. It had a long, folded steel loop, and a short, wickedly sharp, curved blade with a loop on the top big enough to put his finger through, plus a steel marlin spike, as long as his thumb and fully a quarter inch square at

the base—this tapered to a very sharp point, and folded up
to one side of the metal handle with the blade on the other.
One end had a large ring with a strong, bright blue nylon
lanyard threaded through it. It fitted nicely into his hand,
and almost before he even thought about it he pushed the
sailor's knife into his trouser pocket. He glanced at Rag; she
was busy filling a bag and wasn't looking at him. He almost
took the knife out and put it in the packing box, but thought,
'it won't hurt—and a folding-knife can be useful. I'll put it
back later,' and even as he thought it, he knew that was a lie.
He wanted it—he could whittle wood, make holes, and cut
the feed sacks open... and Russ and Peat had small knives for
doing stuff like that... which made him feel justified.

They carried on emptying the desk in silence.

Morag and Boyd walked carefully down the steep front
steps of their old family home carrying big, heavy-duty
shopping bags. Rag plonked her bags down on the pavement
beside the big old-fashioned car.

Russ and Peat were packing cardboard boxes into the
open back. They'd driven the grand shooting-brake down
from the Highlands, bringing Rag and Boyd for what might
be their last visit for some time—apart from, it looked like
they would have to do it all over again!

Outside the low, front gate, Uncle Wulf's huge, vintage,
mainly wooden, car was parked awkwardly, filling the narrow
pavement that formed a compact, circular path outside their
house and its close neighbours. The tall, narrow building was
one of a number of equally tall houses dating back 200 years.
The near-identical painted facades of the homes all had
front doors of varying colours, with steep stone stairs, leading up from neat front gardens that were divided from the
sharply curving pavement by low walls. Beyond, in the centre of the circle, was a large private space of grass and mature
trees shared between the residents, kept secure behind a high

wrought iron fence with a padlocked iron gate. It was quiet here, peaceful... even though the bustle of the town was only a couple of streets away.

Rag looked around and smiled, but thought... *I'll miss being here, but I don't think it's really my home anymore.* Now they had their father back with them in Scotland, living in another place didn't seem so bad. She walked to the open front door to collect more boxes and bags.

Boyd was deep in thought and feeling equally conflicted about coming home, only to leave it again so soon. He stood in silence until his sister had passed him on the path, waiting to hand his box to Russ. His dark curls fell forward over his face as the broon stooped to work out how to fit as many untidy, bulging boxes as possible into the cavernous back of the shooting-brake; he had the concentration of an expert Tetris player. As he stood back to eye up the remaining space, Russ noticed the glint of the thick band of gold on Boyd's wrist, peeking out below his sleeve.

'Does the Laird know you have that on?'

Boyd shrugged,' I don't know. I suppose so... he hasn't said anything.'

Rag arrived back to dump another bag on the pavement beside them. 'I thought you said that it was made of gold. That's too valuable to wear all the time.' She turned and walked back to the house.

Russ took the box Boyd held out, eyed the space and made his decision, only to have the box refuse to fit by a tiny margin.

'What's in here?' asked Russ.

'Letters, papers, and that one's more of Rag's soft toys,' Boyd replied.

Russ whacked the box with his fist, flattening it into the right shape to fill the gap, 'There,' he said with satisfaction, 'knew it would fit.'

Peat approached them with a large basket of paint brushes, tubes and boxes of paint, and some thick sketch-books. 'Aye, but you can't fix everything with your fists, brother.'

'I can give it a try,' grinned Russ.

Rag returned and placed another box carefully on the pavement. 'Well don't try with this one, it's full of glass. You should take that off you know,' she said to her brother, pausing for a moment before walking back up the path.

'I can't. Since that Salt Woman gave it a polish and wrapped it round my wrist, I can't get it off. I've tried.'

'Can you not?' said Russ.

Boyd shook his head, 'If I try pulling it, it just seems to get tighter, like it's hanging on.'

Russ nodded, '...that would be the way of it.'

'What?' said Boyd.

Russ shrugged as Peat staggered down the steps with a weighty trunk, approaching them in time to hear their last few words.

'Show me,' he said to Boyd, 'Ah yes.' He took Boyd's wrist and turned it over and back, taking a good long look. 'If it fits, it fits. They don't come off easy—just push it up under your sleeve for safe-keeping. Not that it's going to fall off.' Peat returned up the path to the open front door.

'Ever?' Boyd called after him.

'Ever,' said Peat over his shoulder.

'Ever? Really?' Boyd addressed Russ.

Russ shook his head, '...as like as not that thing is dragon made. ...She warmed it up did she? Brought it back to life?' Boyd nodded. 'There you go, lad, it's picked you.'

Boyd frowned 'But...what do you mean... back to life?'

'Ask the Laird, laddie, I'm not fly with all these things—I can't tell you what and why, but things like that are special.' He turned away and carried on shoving boxes in the vain hope of creating more room.

Rag appeared with two pillowcases stuffed full.

'Just how much more of it is there?' Russ grumbled when he caught sight of her.

Rag dumped them and walked back towards the house, 'Lots!' she said over her shoulder.

Russ sighed and leaned against the back of the vehicle. 'It's no good. We'll have to make two trips.'

'But it's such a long drive—isn't there any other way—you know—to... get here?' said Boyd as Peat came back to the car and the growing pile of boxes.

Peat shook his head, 'That wee pukis can dive down here and fetch stuff, but it's only a few things at a time.' Peat returned to the house to try and discover what else Rag was intent on packing.

While they were off looking for their father, the little cat-like dragon Rag had adopted, a pukis, a creature who loved to collect and hoard as much as his grander cousins did—he'd sensed Rag's loneliness and magically flitted between the worlds to bring up to Scotland some of her beloved toys and mascots. Even Uncle Wulf didn't know exactly how the pukis did it, it just could. Uncle Wulf was considering how useful it might be to try and train the pukis to deliver messages across the Veil, if it could be trained— rather like an extra intelligent homing pigeon perhaps...

The boxes were piling higher on the pavement. Auntie Carol, their next-door neighbour, bought out a tray with mugs of tea and a plate of biscuits.

'My—the only way you're going to get everything in is if they strap you two to the roof!' she said with a laugh, before leaving the tray with Boyd.

The tea was welcome, and it gave them a few moments to chew biscuits and look at what they wanted to take, and the lack of space they had to put it. Eventually Boyd spoke up.

'Russ—if Rag and I caught the train back to Scotland—you and Peat could fill up all the footwells and the whole backseat. Then you could do it in one trip. Auntie Carol is going to supervise the removals people to pack the furniture before the letting agency take over. She'll lock up with her spare key.'

Peat frowned, 'Oh we couldn't just leave you here, the Laird wouldn't have it!'

'We'd be fine,' said Boyd, 'the train station is only a 15-minute-walk from here. Rag and I will stay together—we just change trains in Birmingham, ok probably in Glasgow too, but Uncle Wulf could speak to that solicitor of his, Mr MacLeod. They could get us a hotel for the night if it was very late when we arrived.'

'It would be hours on the train—you sure you and your sister could make the journey without killing each other?' said Russ with a grin.

'We're not that bad!' said Boyd. 'Well, I'll promise not to, how about that?'

'I do not know about this,' said Peat shaking his head. 'Your uncle was very particular that we stayed close.'

'I could ask Uncle Wulf—Auntie Carol would let us use her landline.'

'It would save us another drive,' said Russ, he sat down in the open back of the car. 'I mean, I wouldn't mind if we could have used the Hippogriffs to fly down...'

'They can't carry more than a couple of panniers at a time. And we'd have been on the wrong side! Anyway, I thought you were dead keen to have a road trip and get out o' the Keep?' said Peat.

'Aye, well that was before I had to sit on my bum for the best part of 10 hours!'

'We stopped for breaks. And you got some sleep when I drove.'

'Brother, coming back in a few months is one thing, driving home, then all the way back down here tomorrow, and then driving overnight again to get back to the Keep is quite another!'

'We could maybe drive down the day after...' said Peat doubtfully.

Russ gave him a look that said... you know that's not going to happen—the Laird will want it done with.

'Yes... I know,' said Peat nodding agreement with a sigh. They both knew that Wulfric Kennetson expected tasks set, to very quickly become tasks accomplished.

'Why don't we just ask him? Peat, you can come with me when I telephone him, I'll go and ask Auntie Carol,' said Boyd.

'Ask Auntie Carol what?' said Rag teetering down the steps with another two full-to-bursting bags of 'stuff'.

'We're going to see if we can go back by train so Russ and Peat can have more room to load everything in the car,' said Boyd, already walking towards Auntie Carol's front door.

'That's an awfully long journey, and we have to change trains—that's why we flew up there when Miss Skipton escorted us to meet Uncle Wulf.'

'I know,' said Boyd from Carol's front door, 'but I'm sure they don't let unaccompanied under-sixteens fly anymore— but nobody will check on the train.' He went into Carol's house when she opened the door, with Peat a few steps behind him.

ς

CHAPTER FOUR

It had taken some persuading and many assurances that they would stay together and come straight back without delay before Uncle Wulf agreed to them catching a train. He had asked to speak to Peat privately as Boyd went to give Rag and Russ the good news. As Russ took another bag off Morag he said to her very seriously, 'But if you kill your brother on the way home—I'm not coming to bail you out.'

Rag pulled a face, Russ just grinned at her and laughed, 'Oooo, you know I would, hen!' he said.

Rag's cheeks pinked at seeing his beautiful smile. She looked away to hide her blushes. Sometimes when the brothers were working and covered in straw, sweat, or mud and animal dung, she'd forget how handsome they were—then one would smile and their eyes would twinkle, or the light would fall just so on a perfect, serene profile... or that lustrous dark hair... And she'd remember. And it was silly to have a crush on either of them—they barely noticed her, or at best, treated her like their little sister. She frowned.

'Ah—don't take what I said to heart, lass,' said Russ when he saw her face, 'I was only joking.'

'I know that,' she said, and walked quickly back into the house, leaving Russ alone to play luggage Tetris.

Russ suddenly whipped his head up—someone was watching... He looked all around, and finally spotted a figure slumped on the ground under the darkest shadows of the trees in the central garden. It was a big man in travel-worn dark clothes, his face shaded by the hood of his leather coat, but he was definitely staring at the car. Russ slid his hand down his leg to flick open the flap pocket on his cargo trousers that concealed a long hunting knife in a leather sheath. The tall man realised he'd been seen and sat upright. Just then Boyd and Peat came back from Carol's house.

'The Laird is going to telephone back when he's made arrangements,' said Peat. Russ raised a hand in warning and nodded towards the trees. Peat followed his gaze and saw the stranger, who was wearily struggling to his feet as if he was exhausted.

'Boyd—go inside the house and stay there, both of you,' said Peat.

Boyd looked to see what they were watching, and he saw the man walking slowly towards them; as he did, the figure pushed his hood back revealing pure white-blond hair like Uncle Wulf's. He held out his hands to show they were empty.

'Why? What's happening?' said Boyd.

'Not now—go inside until we know ourselves,' said Peat, also reaching down to leave his hand ready against the hilt of a hidden blade.

'Who...'

'Go!' hissed Russ.

The man was nearing the fence and Boyd could see why the Long Brothers were suspicious. This stranger was rough-looking and travel-stained, but a Liosalfar. He looked a bit like Uncle Wulf, but probably younger, even dressed like him, apart from the long, dark green leather coat, and matching cylindrical leather pack, slung across his back by a broad strap that crossed his chest. He had the same height and muscular build, but his white-blond hair was cropped very short at the sides, while the remainder was longer but badly shorn, as if it'd been crudely hacked off with shears. His supple leather coat was loose enough to hide any number of weapons, even if his hands were empty.

Boyd retreated slowly back to the house, while Russ and Peat waited warily as the stranger approached the metal gate that gave access to the private garden. He paused and pulled open his coat to show he had heavy leather gloves tucked into his wide belt. He acted deliberately, not making any sudden movements. He took the gloves and put them on before taking hold of the gate to open it—by yanking the padlock so hard it fell away in two pieces, before he lifted the latch. He took the gloves off and replaced them on his belt as he came towards them; every step seemed a weary effort. He halted a few paces away.

'Well met. I mean you no harm. May I sit down?'

Russ and Peat glanced at each other, Peat nodded.

'I thank you.' The stranger stepped forward and sat on the low garden wall.

Boyd was at the front door, but that wasn't near enough to clearly hear everything that's was being said; he watched the three of them closely. The stranger's dark clothes were crumpled and his soft leather knee-high boots were stained and scuffed; now Boyd could see all the alfar's leathers were actually a very dark green.

Rag came up behind him, 'What's going on?'

'Shhh,' said Boyd, 'Russ and Peat told me to stay out of the way. I'm trying to listen.'

'Who's that?' whispered Rag. Boyd shrugged his shoulders and put a finger to his lips, still watching.

'I am Galad. Would you have seen a young svartalfar around here? He goes by the name Penry?'

'Why would we know a svart? And why are you here?' said Peat.

'He is the Svart Lord's youngest son. At present, I am employed as his personal Gard, but he slipped away from me. He's hereabouts. It must have been the wards laid on you two that I sensed—they bought me here; near enough to ask for him anyway.'

'If you can sense the wards, then you know we're sworn to Wulfric Kennetson,' said Russ. Galad nodded. 'And you still choose to approach us?'

Galad lifted his hand, 'Peace—I have no quarrel with you.'

'Aye well, you had a quarrel with somebody,' said Peat, 'we know of your sort, disgraced—outcast—and now you're the Svart Lord's dog—have you really sunk so low?'

Boyd saw the flash of anger cross the liosalfar's face, saw him visibly tense and half stand, an abrupt movement which made the Brothers step back and reach to draw their knives—then he saw Galad control himself with a conscious effort. Boyd watched him take a deep breath, and force himself to relax and sit down again on the wall.

'As a traveller, may I request some water from your house—freely given?' He spoke mildly.

Peat looked at Russ and nodded. Russ pushed his knife back into its sheath and walked up the path to the door.

'What's going on?' said Boyd, 'Who is he?'

'In a minute. Morag—will you fetch our *guest* a glass of water, please?'

'Yes, but who is he?' she said.

'When I find out, I'll tell you—just know that for a liosalfar to be rough-sheared like that—and to keep it that way— means he's an outcast. He's done something unforgivable in his past, and been punished for it. Now, hen—fetch the water and we'll get him on his way as soon as we can.'

Russ barely took his eyes off Galad, though the alfar continued to sit quietly without moving.

Rag disappeared to get the water. Boyd frowned, 'If he's so bad, why are we giving him water?'

'It's a matter of the household's honour, and therefore Wulfric Kennetson's honour—to refuse the simple hospitality of water to a traveller is bad form. But when he's drunk it, he can be gone!' Russ took the glass from Rag's hands as she returned. 'Still—stay back both of you—just in case.' He walked down the steps.

Rag peered out of the front door, 'Is he really that dangerous?'

Boyd shook his head, 'I don't know. They seem to think so—and he is a liosalfar, same as Uncle Wulf, and you've seen him in a fight.'

Rag nodded, she remembered Uncle Wulf, long knives flashing in the darkness, teeth bared in snarls of fury as he slashed at the terrible thing that had attacked them by the lake when they were lost in the Otherworld. She shivered— yes, she thought, I'm sure this one could be just as dangerous.

Russ handed Galad the glass, 'Freely given of our hospitality,' he said with a perfunctory hint of a bow.

'My thanks to you and yours,' said Galad formally, and drank the water down thirstily. The brothers kept a wary distance and watched him in hostile silence, not bothering to hide their contempt.

Suddenly, Auntie Carol appeared at her front door and shouted across to them, 'Hello there. Is Boyd with you? His uncle is on the phone.'

Boyd heard her and started down the steps with Rag just behind him. Russ raised a hand, palm towards them in a commanding gesture—stay there. Galad looked around at the youngsters, raised his head in an unspoken greeting, finished his water and held out the glass to Russ, who took it back without a word. The liosalfar nodded once in thanks, stood up, flipped his hood back over his head, settled his pack across his shoulder again and strode off, out of the circular terrace of houses and towards the town.

Both brothers let out the long breath of air neither realised they'd been holding; Russ gave Peat a grin and a wink before turning to Rag and Boyd. 'Come on then Boyd, don't keep the Laird waiting.'

Boyd quickly trotted down their front steps and around to Auntie Carol's house.

'Was that another of your Uncle's friends, dear?' she said.

'Something like that,' said Boyd following her into the house.

He glanced over his shoulder, Peat was behind him, he smiled at Boyd reassuringly and said quietly. 'I think that one's gone, he'll not be back.'

Rag hurried forward to Russ, who held the glass out for her to take back. She took it with a small tut of annoyance.

'Well? Who was he? What was he doing here?'

Russ lifted one of the boxes off the pavement and pushed it into the car before speaking.

He turned to face her. 'A liosalfar does not cut his hair, certainly not like that. That was an open disfigurement, a punishment and a sign he should be shunned. Something he's done... was very, very wrong—unforgivable even. And for him to keep his hair like that means he agrees—or he's defiant about it and refuses to accept the judgement. Any way it falls... his looks single him out as an outcast.'

'What could he have done that was so bad?' said Rag.

Russ shook his head, 'I don't know, lass. But it marks him—it means he's dangerous, and not to be trusted. His hands were scarred too.'

'I didn't see,' said Rag.

'Mmmm—they were, and on his neck, and I dare say there were more under his clothes. He's done a lot of fighting, and he wants to show it.'

'Why—and what do you mean—show it?'

'Pass me that bag, hen—all alfar can heal themselves, they don't have to show scars unless they choose to. That one chooses to. He wants people to know about past battles, to be afraid of him.'

'Oh,' said Rag, 'I think that's quite sad—hiding behind what he looks like.'

'No! That one's proud of what he looks like! You steer clear, yer ken?'

Rag passed Russ another couple of boxes in silence.

Boyd came out of Carol's door, 'It's all fixed, Russ. We're going back by train. Uncle Wulf has made the arrangements, and I have promised faithfully we'll go straight home. You can load the back seat!'

'Oooh, thank the stars for that!' said Russ.

ʃ

CHAPTER FIVE

Penry crouched down and stroked the back of Mac's hand gently, but she didn't stir; she was fast asleep. He shifted to his knees and poked between the oak tree's roots with a piece of broken branch—nothing there. He moved nearer the wall and tried again. The third time he dug down and found a large rock just below the surface. He went to find a stronger piece of fallen branch and traced the side of the rock, finding another piece and another—this must be the old foundation stones to the original wall. He found a fist-sized piece of stone that tapered to a cone shape and used that to dig around the rocks, forcing them to the surface. There was nothing here! He was beginning to feel a bit frantic and started hacking at the ground—he couldn't come all this way for nothing.

Penry sat back on his heels. Mac mumbled in her sleep. Penry was worried she'd wake up soon. He crouched down on the ground behind the newly exposed rocks and crept forward making his way up the tree roots gouging the earth to loosen it as he went. He was just beginning to have doubts when he poked deep into the thin soil between the large roots at the base of the oak and he felt something—a tiny vibration. He poked harder, scraping at the dry earth until he could see a natural hollow he could reach into. This could be it! He scrabbled in the soil, digging as quickly as he could— there was just a glint of something shiny. He'd found it!

He grabbed the stick with both hands to enlarge the hole, then reached in, not caring about the earth under his finger- nails. He dug down with his hands—and felt the stone. He quickly grubbed the earth away from around its edges until it finally came free. Penry sat back on his heels and wiped the Elfstone free of dirt, polishing it with his sleeve. A stray sun- beam caught the tapering stone, and an actinic flash of bright blue glittered through the shell-like fractures covering the surface, where the axe had been struck to shape it. He turned it over, admiring the fascinating play of curved crystal lines that blinked electric-blue as they caught the sunlight.

Mac stirred, and Penry hastily stuffed the hand-sized stone into the inside pocket of his jacket. He realised how dirty his hands were and tried to wipe them on the grass and his trousers, quickly picking at his nails to get the dried soil from under them. He was just about presentable as Mac woke up.

'Oh my, I am so sorry for falling asleep like that.'

'Think nothing of it, you were tired.'

'But it was so rude.'

'Don't worry. It has been lovely talking to you, but I think I should be going now.'

'So soon?'

'Your friends will be looking for you.'

Penry got to his feet, and was going to hold out his hand until he saw it was still pretty dirty. He put both hands behind his back and bowed from the waist.

'It was very nice to meet you,' he said with a smile, 'but I must be going now.' He took two steps backwards.

Mac got to her knees, 'But we didn't have ice-cream.'

Penry took another two steps backwards, 'Another time maybe.' He kept backing away, smiling and nodding. Mac scrambled to her feet, she looked embarrassed and didn't know what to say; she hid this by brushing away the bits of dried leaf and twig clinging to her clothing.

Penry was less than a dozen paces away and found it was getting increasingly harder to walk, something was holding him back. He frowned and strained to push his way through an invisible barrier that seemed to have a grip on his body, holding him firmly. He tried leaning into it with all his weight, but he couldn't break free.

Mac lifted her head and saw him straining. 'Are you ok?' she asked.

'Yes—fine.'

She took a few steps towards him, and Penry suddenly staggered, almost falling over.

'Are you sure you're alright?'

'Never better,' said Penry through gritted teeth as he took a few steps backwards, away from her, and suddenly the binding around his body came back.

'OK,' said Mac, 'Maybe I should go then.'

She took a couple of slow steps in the direction of the main yard and Penry felt himself stagger forwards—he couldn't get away, he had to go with her!

Mac turned angrily, 'If you are so anxious to get away, why are you following me?'

'I—I—It was rude of me to be so abrupt.' He gave her another smile that he hoped would charm her, but his glamourie was wearing off and she scowled.

'I should wait with you until you leave with your friends. We can talk—and maybe have that ice-cream you spoke of. How about that?'

59

He smiled sweetly, tilting his head so his long spikes of hair fell across his face and he had to toss his head to flick them back.

Mac considered his seemingly contrite face. 'I'm sorry I fell asleep.'

'I'm sorry too,' said Penry.

'I'd like you to stay if you can—it would be nice to talk. You could tell me about your folks.'

'Oh, couldn't I just' said Penry. 'Let's walk, shall we?'

'Sure', said Mac with a shy smile, 'The gardens are this way, they're really pretty.'

'Lovely,' said Penry.

When Penry walked beside her, it took no effort at all, but when he tried to walk away from her—he couldn't. He tried walking on the other side of the flower beds, hanging back and letting her walk ahead, but when she got a dozen paces away he was forced to follow. He even tried holding on to a wooden column with roses winding around it and let her walk away, but the pull on him was so hard it yanked him after her, and left a splinter in his finger. He was beginning to get more and more flustered as he realised something had gone badly wrong with his plan. Mac thought he was in pain from the splinter. She took out her water bottle from her little rucksack and said she'd wash his hand when she saw how dirty they were.

'Let me look, I can get it out for you. Just need to wash that dirt off. What were you doing?'

'Oh, nothing really—Ow!!!' Penry snatched his hand away.

The metal rim of Mac's water bottle had touched his finger.

'I'm sorry, Penry. Did I hurt you? I must have caught the splinter.'

Penry put his finger to his mouth, before clutching one hand with the other. 'No, no—it's fine, all gone now.'

'You sure?'

'Yes, yes, fine. I think I need to sit down—lots of people and—the sun—it's hot out here.'

'Why don't we find someplace in the shade? We could go back to the coach, we're not due to leave for another hour or so, but I'm sure the driver will let us sit down, and it'll be quiet there. We can just chill out until everybody comes back?'

'Yes—why not?'

Mac guided him towards the car park where the Summer School's coach was waiting. They had to walk between the cars, and the further among the closely parked cars they got, the more nauseous Penry felt. When he accidentally banged his elbow on a vehicle it hurt, a lot—like a flicker of flame running through his arm. He yelped and staggered backwards, colliding with the car behind him, the flickering jolt of pain encompassed his whole body. Penry moaned aloud and landed both hands down on the car's bonnet. He shot back with a howl, his hands already reddened from the hot metal. Whimpering he tucked his hands under his armpits, trying hard not to vomit.

'Oh you're hurt,' said Mac anxiously. 'The cars must be really hot—I bet they've been parked here all day.'

Penry nodded hard, not quite trusting himself to speak in case he was sick, before finally mumbling, 'I need to walk around them.'

'Sure,' said Mac, 'Let's go this way.'

She led them to the edge of the car park. Penry walked on the other side of her, as far from the cars as he could.

When they got to the coach the driver was in his seat reading a newspaper. Mac waved at him and he opened the door; a flood of chilly air whooshed into her face which was blissfully refreshing. She climbed up the steps.

"Oh that is so good! Is it ok if I sit and read my book? I've had enough of all this old stuff and it's hot out there.'

'Alright, love. I'm just going to use the bathroom, I'll be back soon. It's a good hour before we leave, so you make sure you stay back and don't touch anything while I'm gone.'

'No sir, I'll sit right back here.'

Penry had tried to hang back in the shadows, but he was drawn down the side of the coach as Mac walked to her seat. He started to feel really sick to his stomach and reeled around, bent over. The coach driver heard him retching and gave him a hard look before ostentatiously reaching behind himself to make sure the door was tightly shut. Penry scarcely noticed him, he was feeling giddy and lightheaded, but tried to control himself and not vomit again. Mac came to the door and pressed the release button to open it for Penry to get in.

'We don't have to do that whole summoned by blood thing again, do we?' she said.

Penry shook his head. The air-conditioned interior felt delightfully cool and he inhaled a deep breath. The cold air seemed to settle his stomach a little. As he climbed up the steps he brushed against the chrome rail and winced at what felt like a dizzyingly painful static shock. He pulled his sleeves down over his hands to shield himself as much as he could from the effects. Mac led him back down the coach and slid into her seat.

'You can sit there,' she said nodding to the seat opposite. Penry sat down and tucked his feet up off the floor. Mac pulled down her lunch box and got out another flask of water, offering it to Penry.

'This one's still cold—have some, you'll feel better. I think you might have sun-stroke. I had it once; it makes you feel really sick.'

Penry could feel nausea washing through him. He reached to take the flask, then realised it was made of shiny metal under its colourful painted logo. He snatched his hand back, shaking his head hard. The movement seemed to unsettle his stomach again and he lurched to his feet and staggered down the coach.

'Can't breathe, too cold—I have to get out,' mumbled Penry.

Mac was already half on her feet when she felt herself being dragged inexorably after him.

At the coach door, Penry couldn't work out how to open the thing. He was frantically banging his fists on the glass when Mac walked up behind him and pressed the exit button. Penry almost fell down the steps and staggered over to the grass verge and dropped to his hands and knees. Mac tried to stay inside the coach but she couldn't—it felt to her as if a giant elastic band was around her body pulling her forward. The feeling totally freaked her out; she couldn't help herself, she had to go after Penry. Struggle as she might, she couldn't move backwards to stay away from him.

After a few moments she gave up and strode towards Penry, who was curled up on the grass whimpering quietly, one hand over his mouth.

'What have you done?! What's happening to me?' Mac demanded. She couldn't feel the pressure around her body anymore, but she was pretty sure she would if she tried to move away.

Penry rolled over onto his back took several deep breaths and sat up. 'Sit down here for a moment, and I'll tell you—but you may not believe me.'

Mac folded her arms and gave him *the look*. Penry squinted up at her, 'I know, I know, but just sit—and I'll tell you.'

Mac dropped down onto the grass a couple of paces away from him. She glanced all around her to see if anybody was nearby, and then gave him another hard look.

Penry gave her a weak smile, being outside the metal box was a relief; he was debating just how much of the truth he should tell her—and wondering how much she would believe...

S he didn't believe any of it.

'No way! You are not some dumb fairy...'

'Alfar,' said Penry.

'Whatever! There is not some sort of weird... otherworld ... thing out there. It's because I'm American, isn't it? You just think you can take the pee out of me because—"they're all too stupid to know better"—well I'll tell you fairy-boy... I ain't no sort of stupid!'

And with that she got up and stomped back towards the coach—but she couldn't get that far. She turned on him, 'Now you just stop that!' she yelled.

Penry got to his feet, 'If I could I would!' he shouted back. 'This wasn't supposed to happen. I was supposed to find the Elfstone and go straight back before anybody realised I'd gone. Now look at me.'

'At us, bro, at us! Don't you forget that part!'

A couple walking by on the way to their car eyed the arguing youngsters curiously as they passed them.

Penry dropped his head forward, his shoulders slumped. 'No. I won't forget. I just have to work out what to do next. So, can we go and find somewhere a little quieter for a moment, please? Please?'

ᔕ

CHAPTER SIX

Penry was sitting on the grass, legs outstretched, frowning and rapidly tapping his hands against his thighs in a staccato rhythm of uncertainty and irritation. Makenzie stared down at this strange, Emo... Goth kid she'd only just met, her arms folded, *what did he think she was—dumb and dumber?* Aloud she said, 'So you're telling me, you're a fairy?'

'No! I am not Fair! I am Alfar—there's a great deal of difference,' said Penry... princeling of the Svartalfar.

'Whatever.'

They were away from the car park now, in a secluded grassy corner of the gardens screened by shrubs and hedges. Penry made a positive effort to bring his annoyance under control—and to smile.

'Are you going to tell me what's going on? Or I am walking—I am outta here!

'Unfortunately—that doesn't seem likely to happen...'

'I don't care! What is going on?! What is this—some sort of weird, mind trick, hypnosis thing?

Penry shook his head. 'I can't thrall you. Please, Mac—come and sit down for a moment. I'll explain everything. And looking up at you is giving me a crick in my neck.'

He smiled and patted the grass beside him. Mac considered, if nothing else she was curious... and she could always get up and walk away—because, why shouldn't she? And besides, there were plenty of people about to hear her scream—*and just let him even try to start something!* She sat down on the grass, but not directly beside him.

'OK—I'm listening.'

Penry nodded, still smiling, and obviously working out where to start. After a moment or two he began. 'Not everybody knows, but there is another... world, or place...' He faltered to a halt, then tried again, 'We, some of us, know there is a barrier that divides our world from yours, we call it the Veil. It's all around us, everywhere—something that moves like huge invisible curtains reaching from the sky to the ground—it can stretch and fold, and sometimes it tears accidentally, and sometimes it can be opened on purpose.'

He fumbled inside his jacket and took the Elfstone out of his inner pocket. 'This is something that can cut through the Veil.'

He held it out on his palm to show her, but not quite close enough for her to touch. 'This is what I came to find.'

The crystal rested in his hand; one end was shaped to fit comfortably into a fist when gripped, the other flared gently before tapering into a curved, axe-like edge. As the shifting leaves on the branches above them dappled the sunlight, flickering shades of blue played through the interior of the stone. Mac stared at it, entranced. She leaned forward and reached out to touch...

Penry pulled his hand back. 'It—It's very rare and valuable.' But he didn't put it back in his pocket. 'The Queen of the Fair Folk of Arden gave this to my father—as a tribute, though I don't think she wanted to. It was many years ago, I was very young—it was the first time I'd been taken along to an important meeting, all my brothers were there. I wanted to see the stone and hold it. I'd heard the guards talking together in hushed voices so I knew it was special—they said it could cut through to another place.'

Penry stroked the stone with his other hand. 'You must remember what it was like to be very small—no one notices you. So when they were all busy, I snuck through the wind-banners very carefully...

Mac looked puzzled. 'You don't have wind-banners?' said Penry, 'they're sort of like wall hangings, but for outdoors— these are pieces of finely woven silk. They hang lots of them down from tree branches and things, and make rooms with them... Maybe it's just a Fair Folk thing... Anyway, I crept right through the layers to the place where the meeting had been—everybody had left to say the formal speeches of fare- well outside and get ready to leave. I took it out of its special box, and all of a sudden, I could feel something strange, sort of prickly under my skin, and—it's difficult to explain. It felt powerful.'

Mac sat quietly, listening and half beginning to believe his story; he was so sincere.

'I crept out very quietly', said Penry, 'nobody saw or heard me. I went out into the woods, and there I could see glimpses, little wavering flashes of colour floating in the air. So I walked to the far edge of the trees to get to a place where there was more light and I realised I could see a house, and barns and there was a stone wall, but they weren't *here*, they were *there*, on the other side of the Veil. It was almost like looking through water, you know? Sort of blurred and hazy, and because I wanted to see what this other place really looked like, I tried to use the stone to cut a hole through.'

'And did it work?' breathed Mac.

Penry shook his head, 'No. Then I realised there was a boy watching me. He could see me! I didn't think about that, that I might be seen. Anyway I tried again, but this time I walked closer to the wall because that's where the Veil seemed to be hovering. I don't know what happened, whether I tripped or I got caught up in the Veil when it rippled, but I fell and the stone flew out of my hands, and just then the Veil sort of flipped up from the ground, the Elfstone rolled under it and ended up on the other side.'

'So what did you do?'

'I very politely asked the boy to give it back, but he made outrageous demands. He wanted a ransom of gold!'

'Just for handing it back?' said Mac.

'That was a bit of the problem—I tried to get what he wanted and give it to him, but he couldn't open the Veil either. Then he said he had to go because somebody was calling him and he promised to come back. I saw him hide the stone, but just then my gard came and found us. She realised the boy had seen me and she thralled him to sleep and made him forget—she told him that it was all a dream. Then she dragged me away because they were all waiting to leave. I daren't say that I'd stolen this precious thing and then lost it. My father was furious when he eventually found it was missing—he thought one of the fairs had stolen it. He sent his personal guards to find it... but of course they never did.'

'But why did you waste all this time before coming back for the stone?'

Penry shrugged, 'I was very young, it didn't seem important and I pretty much forgot it. But just recently I heard my father talking about it—he's still angry. He was saying how it would be easier for him to extend his influence if he still had the stone. So I decided to come back and look for it. Show him I could be just as useful to him as my brothers.'

'But then you'd have to tell him you took it.'

'Oh I thought of that—I was going to say I recently saw a drawing of Fair Folk fighters in a book and I suddenly remembered seeing a warrior fair among the wind-banners before they were taken down, and how I had seen him creep away and out of curiosity followed him, but he vanished beyond the trees. And knowing someone had stolen the Elfstone, I thought I would go back and see if there was any trace of him.'

'After 450 years? They wouldn't believe that!' said Mac.

'I was hoping he'd be so pleased to have it back my father wouldn't ask too many questions. It was something I'd deal with later—so I thought.'

'And now? Why has this happened? How were you able to—you know—get here... I saw something flash around you when you climbed over that wall!'

Penry nodded, 'You had a glimpse of the Veil. That book—there really was a book with illustrations. It mentioned a summoning charm that a mortal can use to call someone through—that's what happened when you sacrificed your blood to the stone. I think the Veil must have been very thin here again, but that part seems to have moved on now.'

'How's that? I mean this whole thing is crazy—either something is there, or it isn't. And why if I summoned you, can't I get rid of you?' said Mac.

'I don't know. It was a Fair Folk charm; I didn't know this would happen.' Penry sighed, 'The worlds, the "is it there, or not there" part—I don't quite know myself how it works—my lessons haven't got that far. Maybe nobody knows all about it... the Veil. It's difficult to comprehend, but it is everywhere. I heard someone say it was integral—it was always there even if we couldn't see it, because it works at a deeper level of tiny, tiny things—then he started talking arcane, mystical stuff—about infinite particles, entanglements, probabilities and uncertainties, and waves functioning, or something. I didn't understand.'

He gave another of his brilliant smiles and tried to push his glamourie over the girl, 'In fact, it got a bit boring and I stopped listening.'

Mac folded her arms, not impressed, 'Well maybe you should have done and we wouldn't be in this mess!'

Penry was surprised, she rapidly seemed to be becoming more resistant to his charm... perhaps he needed more practise, he thought. He was about to try again when Mac put her hands up, palms towards him as if pushing all these thoughts away.

'Woah—no! You had me going there, but this can't be happening. Is this some D&D weird shit you're peddling? Just what have you been taking? Because this Can. Not. Be. Real. No way.' She said firmly with a shake of her head.

'But it is. And I don't know what you mean by taking—I took the stone yes, but that was years ago,' said Penry.

'No—I mean happy pills, MDA. Are you taking something... something that makes you trippy—something hallucinogenic?'

'No! I'm no shaman and I'm not dreaming. I wish it was not—but this is real.'

Penry stood up; he was feeling better now that he'd been away from that big, metal box on wheels for a while. He tried walking away, but came to a halt; he couldn't move forward and Mac lurched sideways as she was dragged off balance on the grass.

'Hey—don't do that!' she said as she pushed herself upright again.

'Just trying to see whether it had worn off or anything.'

'You said that wasn't going to happen,' said Mac

'It might have.'

71

Mac stood up as well, 'You have to fix this,' she said firmly. 'You have to fix this very soon. I can't take you back with me—my bedroom at the exchange house is so small I only have a single bed, and you are not sharing! Tomorrow I'm going back to London to meet my mom and we're flying to Paris in three days. I am not going to miss that plane.'

'What's a plane?' said Penry.

'What do you mean—it's an aeroplane, you fly in them and go places.'

'You fly? Through the air? I like doing that—my father's going to get me my own Pegasus-pony.'

'You wouldn't like this sort of flying—planes are made of metal, like a bus with wings. It'd make you even sicker, and there's no way to get off.' She paused and rewound the conversation, 'What's a Pegasus-pony?'

Penry looked momentarily disappointed. 'Is every form of transport made of metal?'

'Pretty much.'

'Shame.'

'What is it with you and metal anyway?'

'It's only iron, and things made from iron ore that are really bad. It is difficult to explain—it hurts, but on the inside, and it makes you feel sick to your stomach, and weak so you can't stand—though my gard says he's used to it now, so maybe it's an age thing—and he practises with steel blades all the time. Fairs are affected much worse than alfar, they don't like any metal except gold and silver. Dwarves can handle ore I'm told, at least while they process it—maybe the iron being inside the rock helps—and mannish-kind like you, obviously it has no effect on you. And dragons... I don't think they mind...'

'You are so weird,' said Mac.

'I don't know what you mean,' said Penry loftily. 'But I think I do know a way we can get out of this—but you may not like it.'

'Go on,' said Mac giving him the eye, as in—*whatdya you mean by that bro?*

'We have to go south to Droithglarma... to the Great Tor. I heard my father say it had previously been part of his plan. At each Midsummer Day's dawn, the Veil is stretched very thin over the Tor. If we can get there I should be able to cut the Veil with the Elfstone—I'll go back through and you'll stay here. Free to fly to Pa-ris with your mother.'

'That's Paris—and how do you know that would work? And where's this Droithglarma anyway?'

'It's in the south-west—a great hill that rises straight out of the glass waters of the Droithmere.'

'Wait—do you mean Glastonbury? Wow, I've always wanted to go to Glastonbury.'

'If that's the Great Tor, then you shall—but we can't walk there in three days, and I haven't the means to buy horses.'

'Hold it, back up—this is crazy. I can't run off to Glastonbury with some hippy kid I just met, to cut a hole in an invisible veil.'

Penry had been walking up and down the patch of grass to ease the cramps in his legs, but he still had the Elfstone in his hand; he held it out to Mac. 'We can—we can go there, and do it with this!'

Mac paused; the electric-blue facets of the stone seemed to wink at her as the sun caught the knapped surface. She reached out to touch it and this time Penry didn't back away. Mac's fingers traced the rippled surface lightly—she felt a faint tingle and almost... it was as if the crystal shivered under her fingertips like a living creature. She snatched her hand back.

'Glastonbury...' She licked her lips, suddenly her mouth felt dry, but when she thought about it—there didn't seem any other way that wouldn't get them both sectioned as crazy people. She got out her phone and opened a screen for transport links and train times.

'If we do this,' she said after a few moments, 'the cheapest way is by bus. But it will take over six hours and we have to change buses four times. By train and bus it will be four hours—do you think you can be inside a metal vehicle for that long?'

Penry nodded, 'I have to, if I stay here like this for more than a few days... I will fade away. I think I will die.' Penry paused for dramatic effect. Satisfied that Mac looked suitably worried, he added 'If we take some water with us that should help.' He smiled cheerfully, 'Think of it as a great adventure.'

ʕ

CHAPTER SEVEN

The vintage, wood-panelled car had finally been stuffed as full as it could be, not an inch remained unused, even Russ and Peat would only just be able to squeeze inside.

Rag and Boyd stood on the pavement; each had a small backpack of overnight things and unknown to each other, their father's sailing knife and camping strike-a-light. Boyd has strict instructions to telephone at every change of train to let the household know they were safely on the next leg of their journey. At Glasgow they were to phone the Keep, and Mr MacLeod, who would arrange either transport onwards to Inverness station or an overnight stay, or both. Over the phone, Boyd had assured Uncle Wulf that they would be fine—they had money for snacks and drinks, they each had a book—they'd be fine! And as soon as they reached Inverness, Mr MacLeod would be with them.

Beside the car, Russ and Peat each shook hands with them solemnly.

'You must both be careful,' said Peat, 'don't talk to strangers. Don't go wandering off. Keep together until MacLeod meets you. We're not sure if we'll be back at the Keep soon enough to unload the car and get down to

Inverness to meet you off the train, but I'm sure the Laird will be away as soon as we've cleared the car of the last box and bag.'

'That's ok,' said Boyd, 'We have the reference to collect our tickets at Haverdon station. We'll be fine.'

Russ followed up his handshake to Boyd with a brief bear-hug. 'You'll be ok, m' man?'

Boyd nodded, 'Of course.'

'And if you want to stay safe, keep your wee sister away from bows and pointy sticks. She's getting to be a dab hand with the archery.' Russ grinned and clapped Boyd on the back, before he turned to Morag.

Rag was a little surprised that she got a big hug too; she blushed with pleasure.

'Now, hen—look after your brother—and no fighting!' said Russ with mock seriousness. He stepped back and looked at her closely. 'Are you too hot now in the sun, you look a bit pink?'

Rag shook her head vigorously, and turned even pinker.

'Well, if you're sure—we'll be away then.'

Peat gave his brother a dig in the ribs. Russ gave him a wink before he went to the passenger seat, 'You can take the first two hundred, brother mine. I might have a wee nap,' said Russ, climbing inside and wedging his legs between the many bags in the footwell.

Peat shook his head with a smile, but paused before getting into the driver's seat. 'Just be careful the pair of you. And Boyd—if that alfar turns up again, get out of his way and call the house as soon as you can. That one stinks of bad news.'

'Don't worry, we'll be fine. Safe journey!'

Rag and Boyd waved the old shooting-brake off as it trundled round the tight bend in the circular roadway and turned towards the main street. They started walking towards the rail station.

Only Rag turned to look back at their old house as they reached the corner—*Bye, House*, she thought, and felt surprised with herself that she suddenly saw it as being quite small. She shrugged her backpack firmly on her shoulders and strode after her brother.

Mac's finger hovered over the 'pay now' button on her smartphone. 'Are you sure this will work, Penry?'

'Yes, we will be fine. I cannot stay here like this and neither can you. If we travel down today we can find somewhere to stay for the night, there are sure to be inns for travellers.'

'I guess...'

'We can walk around and see the sights of Droithglarma, er... Glas-ton-bury tomorrow and after one more night at an inn we can find our way to the Great Tor and climb to the summit to wait for dawn on the third day, Midsummer's Day. You said you always wanted to visit there.'

'What I wanted to go to was the festival.'

'Festival? For the Midsummer?'

'For the music. It's one of the biggest in the world and the best known... but you don't know what I'm talking about, do you?'

'We do have celebrations for the Midsummer—music and dancing and bonfires,' said Penry. 'It is a sort of festival, I suppose.'

Mac rolled her eyes and hit 'pay'.

'You are so going to owe me,' she said. 'It's just a good job I've got a link to Mom's credit card—I ordered First Class seats, I thought the extra padding might make it better for you.'

'Thank you. Of course I will pay you back as soon as I can,' said Penry, wondering if he could get that glamour right on the buttercups and leaves appearing to be gold...

'That's it, I've bought the tickets—Mom is going to be so pissed. But are you sure you can manage being on the train?'

Penry nodded, 'I can bear it,' he said and tried to look noble.

Mac sucked her teeth. 'I'm going to leave my Mom a text to say I've been invited to a special field trip.' She tapped away at the key-pad. 'There—I am going with Marie to see a special Midsummer Festival performance. Back soon. Kiss, kiss...'

She poked the 'x' several times... pressed send... then her screen blinked, turned black and died. 'Oh crap, the battery's dead! And I don't have my charger.'

'That's important?'

'Yes. How can I go anywhere without my cell phone?'

'You said we change trains in Birmingham? And that is a large town?—Surely it will have places where you could purchase a ...charger?' said Penry.

'I guess...' nodded Mac. 'I'm sure I saw a sign to the station when we turned into this place on the bus. I think we go that way.' Mac pointed and started to walk away. Penry, of course, followed.

The rail station at Haverdon Spa was well over 100 years old and full of ornamental cast ironwork, there were even ornate iron pillars holding up the roof over its two main platforms; it was also very draughty. Rag pushed her hands deep into her pockets and was glad Peat insisted she wear a thick hoodie to travel in. The local train that would take them into the city pulled in. As the doors opened she saw a boy with long dark hair and odd-looking clothes stagger off and fall to the platform on his knees. A worried looking young black girl followed him and helped him to his feet and got him to lean against a nearby brick flower trough.

'This is us, Rag,' said Boyd.

'Look—do you think he's ok?'

Boyd looked over—a middle-aged man had approached the two teens evidently to ask the same thing. 'No, he's fine. He gets very travel sick.' They could hear the girl had an American accent.

Just then, the boy in black lurched sideways and leant his hand against a cast-iron pillar. He recoiled from it with a yell of pain clutching his arm. The middle-aged man half turned, 'It's ok, sir,' said the American girl, 'he hurt his wrist when he fell...'

The boy crawled across the platform on his hands and knees and vomited over the edge above the tracks. The girl quickly hauled him backwards towards a bench. As soon as he touched the metal arm to pull himself up, the boy screamed and sank back to the ground with a sob.

Rag turned to her brother and whispered, 'He can't touch iron. You know what that means... we should try and help.'

The train bleeped its signal to get ready to go. Boyd frowned.

'Come on. We can always get the next train,' said Rag.

The train doors shut and moments later, it began to move out of the station. Boyd and Rag stood on the platform looking at the two teenagers a few feet away as the girl tried to get the boy to stand up.

'Excuse me,' said Boyd, 'there's a wooden bench over there, you can both sit down.'

The girl looked up and hesitated.

'Let us help you,' said Rag. 'Look, I've got water in a glass bottle; he can drink from that.'

Boyd stepped forward and took the sick boy's arm to guide him; he was chalk white and sweating so much his hair clung in damp spikes to his forehead.

'It's ok, you'll be ok in a minute,' Boyd said quietly. 'No metal here, you can sit for a minute, and then we'll take you outside.'

'But we need to get the train...' The American girl bit her lip in confusion.

Rag handed the boy her water bottle, and Boyd helped him unstopper the leather covering so he could drink.

'I don't think you can get a train—not together anyway.' Rag turned to the dark-clad teen, who gulped down the water. 'I think we know about you, and what you are,' she said. 'Our guardian—he is liosalfar as well.'

The boy looked up sharply and froze. Only when water trickled out of the corner of his lips did he remember to close his mouth. He wiped his chin with the back of his hand,

'What!' said the girl, 'is this a *thing* over here?'

Rag smiled and shook her head. She held out her hand, 'My name is Morag, call me Rag, and this is my brother, Boyd.'

The American girl looked her up and down, but as she opened her mouth to reply, Penry vomited up the water he'd just drunk. Heads turned on the platform.

'Why don't we go outside the station—away from all this metal? And we can talk without attracting attention,' said Boyd.

He bent to help Penry to his feet, Mac grabbed Penry's other arm, 'I'm Mac, and he's Penry,' she said.

Between them they staggered out of the entrance into the carpark and down a concrete underpass leading away from the rail station. At the far end as they emerged into the sunlight, Mac came to a halt and dropped Penry's arm, which let him fall against Boyd, who turned Penry and propped him up, back against the brick wall.

'I think I deserve some answers,' demanded Mac. 'You know about these... elves, fairies, whatever?'

'Not Fair,' mumbled Penry, 'Alfar.'

'No, this is not fair! I know nothing about you—then two more turn up,' snapped Mac.

'We aren't alfar... our guardian is,' said Boyd. 'His name is Wulfric Kennetson and he's the Laird of the Northern Keep, that's in the far north-west of the Scottish Highlands. We're on our way back there—at least we were, but we can get the next train to Birmingham and make another connection to Glasgow.'

'This is crazy,' Mac started to back away from them, but suddenly she was walking in glue again and couldn't get any further. She struggled and squirmed in frustration.

'Arghhhhh! If you two know about this elf... thing... binding spell stuff. Then make him set me free! I want outta here!'

Rag looked puzzled, 'I don't know what you're talking about.'

Boyd interrupted, 'Maybe if we go to the park, it has grass, trees, and no metal—then... is it Penry?'

Penry nodded.

'Right, then Penry can help us understand what's happened.'

Penry was feeling a little better, but decided to play groggy while he thought over what Rag and Boyd had said. He'd heard of Wulfric Kennetson—who hadn't in the North? And he knew his father regarded him as a thorn in his side... and these were his wards... There could be an advantage here—he just needed to think about what it might be.

'Come and help me, Rag,' said her brother. 'The park is just down that way, but the bridge over the river has cast iron supports and we'll have to run or he might collapse again.'

Rag went to Penry's side and lifted his arm over her shoulder. His long hair brushed her cheek as he turned his head; it smelt of fresh summer rain on hot stones.

'Thank you,' he whispered huskily in her ear, and out of the blue, she had an almost overwhelming desire to kiss him.

5

CHAPTER EIGHT

They'd managed to get Penry over the bridge, though the effect of the cold iron made him sag against them like a deadweight. Boyd headed for the middle of the grass, as far from metal as they could get before lowering Penry to the ground. The others sat down around him—trying to look as innocent as any other group of teens in the park enjoying the sunshine. The cars and bustle of the main street was some way away and only the happy cries and giggles of some small children running about nearby broke the silence as they looked at each other. After a few moments, Penry sat up slowly, and shook his hair back; it bounced up into a quiff of spiky quills across his head. He smiled at Boyd, first, 'I thank you for your aid. I had not realised how bad travelling would be while enclosed in metal.'

Boyd nodded, 'That's ok. It's because there's a lot more iron—besides the steel carriage, there's rail tracks, the undercarriage and all that.'

Penry put his hand to his chest and inclined his head, before turning to Rag. 'Thank you also for your aid, I am grateful our paths have crossed.'

Rag smiled shyly and nodded.

'And what about me?' said Mac. 'I helped and now look at us!'

'We need you to explain to us what happened, Penry,' said Boyd. 'Then we can try and help you properly. How did you get to this side of the Veil?'

'Veil?' said Mac. 'You know about this quantum curtain hogwash?'

'Oh it is all true,' said Rag. 'We've been to the other side— where the alfar come from—and all the others.'

'There's more like him? Unbelievable.' Mac folded her arms tightly across her chest.

'Rag, maybe we leave that "the rest of them" bit for now,' said Boyd. 'But Penry, we need to know about you—we may be able to get Uncle Wulf to help.'

'No—no need to trouble your uncle,' said Penry quickly. 'I—we—need to get to Droith... erm... Glas-ton-bury by Mid-summer's Day dawn, then everything can be resolved.'

'It's Glastonbury—all one word. Why Glastonbury?' said Rag.

Penry paused for a moment, deep in thought, then made his decision and reached inside his jacket and took out the Elfstone. The crystal shone ice-blue in the sunlight.

'I can cut the Veil with this if I can be at the top of The Great Tor at Midsummer's dawn. Then I go through, and the binding charm is broken, and everything will be well.'

'That's beautiful,' breathed Rag, gazing at the shining stone, 'My dad gave me one like that for my birthday, obviously much smaller—it's on a necklace.'

'Just like this? A crystal—with rainbows inside? They're incredibly rare and precious you know.'

'She's got some tiny ones on a bracelet too—are they valuable then?' Boyd asked. 'Have you got yours with you, Rag?'

Rag shook her head, 'I know mine's valuable cos its set in silver, and I keep my precious things safe at home.' She looked pointedly at Boyd's arm—he pulled his sleeve down over the glimpse of gold at his wrist, hiding the torc bracelet from sight.

Penry gave Rag his most glamorous smile, 'You must show me your treasures... one day.'

'Get out of here!' Mac interrupted, rolling her eyes. 'Now, you tell them properly what you told me—about your father and stuff.'

'Ah yes,' Penry thought quickly—it was obvious to him that though they were wards of The Liosalfar of the Keep, they had no idea how to tell alfar apart... and while they were helping him, he wasn't about to inform them. 'My father was given the stone, but unfortunately... I misplaced it...'

'You lost it according to what you told me!' said Mac.

'Yes,' said Penry sadly with an exaggerated sigh, 'and to make amends I went to get it back. To do that, I had to use a summoning charm—so somebody could invite me, and I could cross through the Veil and retrieve my father's stone.'

Rag was watching the handsome young alfar with rapt attention. 'You made your way through all on your own?'

Boyd cleared his throat, 'And so did we—remember?'

'Oh, yes,' said Rag, still fascinated by Penry, 'but those doors were there already.'

'The Liosalfar showed you the doors of his Keep?' said Penry.

'Sort of—later. The first one—I—I just found it.'

'A secret door?'

Rag shrugged, 'Not secret, just forgotten.'

'Anyway,' said Mac, 'back to the point. Glastonbury must be 120 miles away—we can't walk that far in two and half days.

'Well you could... but it would be very difficult,' said Boyd thoughtfully. 'Forty miles a day is not impossible, but it would be extremely tiring. You'd be totally exhausted at the end.'

'Walking!?' exclaimed Mac, 'No way! There has to be another way.'

'Do you have horses here?' Penry asked.

'Yes we do,' said Boyd, 'but you can't just hire some horses and ride away. You'd need a place to stable them overnight for a start, and if you didn't take them back after a couple of hours the stables would report them stolen, then you'd have the police after you.'

'Could we buy them then?'

'No, that would be too expensive—unless you have a lot of money?'

'Could we buy one horse...? There were wooden carts at that farm where I arrived. We could borrow one of them and the four of us could ride in the cart,' said Penry.

'Four?' said Boyd. 'We can help, but we aren't going with you.'

'We could maybe... phone Uncle Wulf and ask him...?' said Rag hopefully.

'Rag! No,' said Boyd.

'And we've only got my Mom's credit card, and no way are we buying horses on it. She's going to freak about the rail tickets as it is.'

Meanwhile at just about that moment... Mac's mother received her text—and a phone call from the organisers of the school trip saying Mackenzie was missing, and how the coach driver saw her with a suspicious-looking long-haired Goth kid in funny-looking clothes ... "who was staggering around the place like he might be on something."

At this point Mac's mother, as a senior diplomat, rang the American embassy's security section to report her daughter was missing—possibly even kidnapped—and could they put a trace on her daughter's phone? Shortly afterwards, when checking if there were other messages, she found a payment reference for two First Class train tickets to Bristol. Mac's mom was livid: 'I swear girl, when I get you home...' she muttered to herself as she cleared the screen on her phone.

She told the Secret Service they needed to get the local police to check the CCTV at stations around Stratford-up-on-Avon and Wilmcote—her daughter had bought two train tickets, so maybe not kidnapped, but she must have been coerced into running off, probably by this Goth boy she was with.

ʃ

CHAPTER NINE

In the park—Mac began to look around her. 'I must have left my coat on the bench at the station. My cell is in the pocket—I need to go back for it.'

'Are you sure you didn't drop your coat on the way?' said Boyd.

'No. I put it down as I went to grab Penry when he threw up... We have to go look.'

'Somebody might have handed it in as lost property,' said Rag. 'You could wait here for us Penry, if you don't feel well enough.'

Penry smiled at her winningly. 'Thank you Rag, but I feel much better. I will come too, after all... I must—I can perhaps wait outside the building if it becomes too much for me.'

Rag may have been about to say *you're so brave*, but her brother interrupted her.

'Yeah, better if we all stay together until we decide how to get you to Glastonbury.'

The short walk back to the station was uneventful—Mac walked across the bridge first. Penry took a deep breath and ran full pelt over the iron bridge at surprising speed, thus reducing his exposure time. 'Yes, I feel my feet are tingling,' he said when Rag asked him how he felt, 'but the sickness was much reduced.'

Outside the station in the car-park, he carefully avoided getting too near any of the vehicles—unfortunately he and the others were clearly seen by the CCTV cameras and showed up on the security screens of the newly alerted rail staff inside.

The four walked up the wide stairs to the platform and looked around.

'There it is, under that bench,' said Mac dashing forward to grab her coat off the floor. She gave it a quick shake to remove the dust, and her smartphone fell out of the pocket and hit the stone platform hard.

'Oh no!'

She quickly picked it up and saw the screen had cracked into long fractures.

'Ah Man! Will you look at that? No!'

'Sorry,' said Boyd. 'I'd offer to lend you one, but we don't have them.'

'No cell phones...?' said Mac.

Just then a member of staff in a hi-vis jacket approached them. 'Excuse me miss—is your name Mackenzie?' he said.

They turned to face him.

'Only your mum is very worried about you running off—so if you'd like to come with us, I'm sure we can soon get all this sorted out...'

Boyd noticed another man was approaching them slowly from the other side; he nudged his sister, 'We have to go,' he whispered. 'Now!'

He grabbed a nearby suitcase and ignoring the owner's shout, Boyd threw it at the legs of the man walking quickly towards them. The man stumbled over it and fell to the floor.

'Run, Mac!' he shouted, as Rag zig-zagged out of the way of the approaching hi-vis man, and Penry and Mac ran the other side of him. Penry reached the stairs first and hurtled down them. The man's outstretched arm snagged Mac's elbow as she reached the top of the stairway; this caused her to lose her grip on her damaged smartphone... which went clattering downwards, bits of glass screen flying off as it hit every step before she did.

Rag and Boyd were just behind her. Penry had kicked another wheelie suitcase over and the guard in the foyer lost a few vital seconds avoiding it. They ran full pelt through the open doors to see another member of staff trying to catch Penry as he dodged between the parked cars, yelping as he bounced off the metal in his haste. Rag grabbed Mac's arm to try and hold her back as she was dragged helplessly in Penry's direction

'Penry!' shouted Boyd, waving to attract his attention. 'Park! This way!' Rag pushed Mac ahead of her, 'Run as fast as you can!'

Penry avoided the security man and sprinted after them down the underpass.

'Over the bridge and right,' Boyd shouted, running behind the girls, 'down the river path.'

They raced down the path at the edge of the park towards a set of imposing old buildings; Penry was running alongside Boyd now.

'Keep going,' shouted Boyd. 'The path runs behind there. Then cross the main road and into the Gardens on the other side.'

The railway guards had given up the chase as the young-sters raced through the park; they turned back to the station to phone the regular police for re-enforcements.

Having crossed the busy road—Rag had to grab Penry's arm and haul him back from stepping in front of a car, then push him onwards to follow Mac through a gap in the traffic as the American girl wavered on the far edge of the road struggling to move forward. They ran through the large gates of the formal gardens. Penry gritted his teeth—even more cast-iron to avoid.

'Slow down,' hissed Boyd, 'don't attract attention, walk quickly towards the trees.'

'There is so much noise,' muttered Penry.

'Traffic? Noisy?' said Mac. 'You want to go to New York if you want to hear noisy—this is literally a walk in the park!'

They were through the formal flowerbeds and beyond the lake among the mature trees when Boyd slowed and put his hand up. He turned to look behind him. 'There's nobody following that I can see.'

Mac flopped down to sit on the grass. Rag joined her. 'What do we do now?' said Rag.

'If the rail staff knew about you Mac, then it's probably because your mother phoned the police and told them you'd run off. They are going to be looking for you,' said Boyd. 'We need to keep off the main streets until we can work out how to get you two to Glastonbury—and that might even mean having to walk there!'

'So what do we do now?' said Rag.

'Well...' said Boyd, 'we could go back to Auntie Carol's and use her phone to speak to Uncle Wulf.'

'I don't think that we need to bother him with these things,' said Penry hastily.

'Oh he will help us,' said Rag. 'I'm sure of that.'

'Yes, that's what concerns me,' muttered Penry.

'If I phone Mom from your aunt's place and tell her everything is fine—she can call the police off.'

'Yes—that would be a help,' said Boyd. 'We go to Auntie Carol's then?'

Rag and Mac nodded agreement.

'Ok, we can go out of the back of the park and walk through the side streets, it's not that far.'

Boyd walked away followed by the two girls... and reluctantly Penry had to follow them.

As soon as they exited the rear gates of the park on to the main road, a police car hurtled by—then screeched to a halt. A policeman jumped out of the passenger door and shouted at them to stop.

'Back! Back through the park,' shouted Boyd, already running. The others were with him as they ran through the bushes and shrubs.

'Round that way and head downhill to the riverbank,' panted Boyd, guiding them away from the main area of the gardens into the surrounding bushes.

At first they could hear thudding footsteps some distance behind them, but they petered away as the policeman chasing them ran straight along the path and back into the heavily planted borders full of tall shrubs. They were able to slow down and pick their way through the concealing undergrowth.

'Where do we go now?' said Mac. 'Because I'm really not liking this—being chased by the police.'

'We need to get you to a phone so you can speak to your mother,' said Boyd. 'The old boat house is over that way on the other side of the river, we could hide around there maybe, until the coast is clear. Penry—we have to cross another iron bridge, can you do that? It's more than twice as long as the first one.'

Penry nodded grimly, 'Yes. I can do that.'

They crept down the narrow, stone-walled walk that led to the end of the substantial, ornate cast-iron Victorian foot-bridge. Penry eyed up the distance, before speaking. 'Mac, if you start to run across, I will follow and overtake you, and hopefully you will catch up to me before I'm pulled back onto the bridge.'

'Ok,' said Boyd, 'on a count of three, Mac... one, two, thr...'

Mac shot off across the bridge at full speed. Penry chased after her and easily overtook her before the middle. At the far end he slowed and struggled to put one foot in front of the other, until Mac caught up with him and he launched himself onwards to explode off the end of the metal walk-way like a cork out of a bottle. He collapsed to the ground dry-retching and sweating.

'Oooooo... that wasn't good,' he groaned.

Rag arrived and quickly got her water-bottle out. 'Here,' she said, pushing it into his hands.

'Quickly,' said Boyd, 'Behind the boat-house, let's get out of sight.'

The place was deserted and nobody was in the nearby street. They jogged quietly behind the buildings, but found it was all locked up. They walked a little further on looking for a way in, squeezing between the tall hedge that screened the boating lake from the road, until they found a place to clamber over the tall, wooden fence.

On the other side they found they were on a treacher-ously narrow margin of long slippery grass at the very edge of a stretch of water. In front of them were a dozen wooden rowing boats moored together side by side in a line that lead to the planked landing stage at the open back of the boat-house.

'If we're careful, we can walk from boat to boat and get to the shed,' said Rag.

'You think?' said Mac.

'Yeah,' said Rag, 'piece of cake!' She stepped down into the first one, which wobbled alarmingly for several moments.

'Woah—careful!' said Boyd.

'It's ok,' she said as the boat stilled to a gentle bob. 'Mac, you and Penry probably need to go next so you don't get further than one boat apart. And Boyd can follow you and fish out whoever falls in.'

'That's not a comfort,' said Mac.

'You'll be fine—he's a water boy, swims like an otter.'

Rag stepped slowly over the gunwales into the next row boat, careful to make as little movement as possible.

'I will go next—then Boyd can help you if you need him,' said Penry.

'Do you know about boats?' said Mac looking apprehensive.

'I have sailed—I can manage.' He stepped down into the rowing boat, which barely moved as he adjusted his balance. 'Are you ready,' he said, 'I'm going on to the next one.'

Mac bit her lip, stepped down into the boat, which fish-tailed away. Boyd caught her flailing arm and steadied her. 'I'm with you,' he said and stepped in behind her.

He instantly got his balance and the craft steadied for him. 'Now, as Penry leaves that boat, let it still and we'll step in behind,' said Boyd, holding onto Mac's arm.

Rag was almost at the landing stage by now. When she stepped out, she crouched down and hung onto the gunwale with both hands to stop the final rowing boat rocking as the others approached. Thankfully, without incident, and much to Mac's relief, they all stepped onto the wooden platform without getting a ducking in the water.

Exhausted by their efforts, they sank down on to a heap of tarpaulins inside the shed. But after what seemed only a few moments, the door-handle rattled—somebody was outside. Boyd put his finger to his lips and beckoned them deeper into the shadows at the back of the boat-house, behind the racks of stacked kayaks. They scurried away to hide.

The door rattled again furiously, and this time the lock cracked apart from the surrounding wood. The door opened slowly. They could just about glimpse the dark shape of a tall, muscular man in a heavy hooded coat silhouetted in the open doorway.

Rag and Mac froze; Mac put both hands over her mouth to stop herself making a noise. The figure took a step forward and peered around the shadowy inside of the boat-house, before calling out loudly and clearly... 'Pentagaron...? Come out. Show yourself!'

Penry sagged against the wooden shelving, and then turned to Boyd and hissed, 'That's my gard, I have to answer him... and he may be able to help us.'

Penry stood upright and edged around from behind the stacked boats, the others followed him slowly. Rag emerged just in time to see the tall man push back his hood and show his face—it was the same liosalfar from earlier in the day outside their old home.

Rag whispered to Boyd, who was ahead of her, 'Aren't we supposed to stay away from him?'

ʃ

CHAPTER TEN

The tall alfar folded his arms across his chest and gazed sternly at Penry in silence. Penry wilted a little from his usual self-confident demeanour, before attempting to step up to the commanding role again.

'Greetings Galad. Where have you been?'

'Why, you little...' Galad snapped his lips shut and composed his annoyed snarl into a coldly neutral expression. 'Your Lord and father has not missed you as yet. It would be better we return before he does.'

'Ah', said Penry, 'that is where there could be a small problem...'

Just then there was the heavy thudding sound of running feet outside the door: 'Police, police, stay where you are!'

They heard the shouts from outside and froze, just as two uniformed policemen burst through the doorway.

That's all of them froze except Galad, who whirled around to face the charging police officers with a turn of speed that took both men by surprise. The first he felled with a direct punch to the jaw, the second stumbled into his colleague and Galad dispatched him with another couple of blows, leaving them both unconscious on the floor.

Rag and Boyd stood open-mouthed. Penry looked around at them smugly, openly taking credit for what his gard could do—while Mac reacted with horror, 'Jeez—they will *kill* you for that!'

'I doubt that,' said Galad.

But he hadn't time to continue before there were more shouts and running steps from outside. This time the pair of officers saw their colleagues on the floor and advanced much more warily. 'Officer down!' shouted one, 'Taser, taser, taser!' shouted the other.

'Get back,' said Galad quietly to the youngsters, slipping his coat off and quickly wrapping it around his arm.

The two policemen came through the doorway and took up threatening stances, batons raised, both shouting instructions.

'On the floor!'

'Down, down! Hands behind your head!'

'Down—NOW!

Mac whimpered and put her hands up; Rag and Boyd half sank to their knees. Penry stepped back deeper into the shadows.

Galad stood his ground, impervious to the commotion. He took a small step towards the officer with the taser—who yelled another warning and fired.

Galad sidestepped the flying wires with uncanny speed, and took the claws of the taser in the folds of his coat, which he dropped as they struck the thick leather. He yanked at the wires before the policeman could discharge it again, taking a blow to the body from the other man's baton as Galad surged towards them. The liosalfar was fast and lethal, his fists and feet were accurate and disabling, and the two policemen, who had tried to fight back, were swiftly dispatched into unconsciousness even though they managed to land a few blows.

Galad shook himself, gathered up his coat and kicked the taser into the river.

'We need to go, and go now, young master! Explanations can be made later.'

'All of us,' squeaked Rag.

'I think that would be wise,' said Galad. 'Don't you?'

He turned and began hauling a kayak off the stacking frame.

'We are best by river, than running through the streets.' He dropped the boat into the water and went back for another. 'Master Penry...'

'We two must stay together—Mac, get in this one.' Penry grabbed a paddle and held the open kayak as steady as he could, while Mac climbed in. 'Are you sure we have to do this?' she whimpered, hanging onto the sides of the boat.

'Yes,' said Penry, and pushed the kayak off as he jumped in behind her.

Galad's face was thunderous, but he didn't argue. In the distance they could hear police sirens. Boyd caught the end of the second kayak and guided it to the water. 'I can paddle. My sister comes with me.'

Galad nodded curtly and held the craft for the two to clamber into. He pushed them off from the landing stage. As Boyd settled down to dip with the paddle, Penry was already pulling away.

'Straight ahead, then to the left onto the river. Paddle hard and keep under the trees. I am behind you.' Galad spoke urgently in a commanding voice that brooked no argument.

He fetched a final canoe, threw a paddle into it and pushing it forward from the jetty with both hands, he leapt in. Galad grabbed the paddle and dug swiftly into the water, soon catching up with the other two as they turned from the boating lake into the river proper.

'Harder, paddle faster!'

Rag could see Penry grit his teeth and push the double-ended paddle into the water more urgently from side to side, pulling ahead of her and her brother. Boyd followed suit, digging deeply into the river as Galad came abreast of them; the liosalfar's alternating strokes were smooth and barely splashed.

'Not too deep,' he said to Boyd, 'too much and the water will slow you down.

Boyd nodded and corrected his paddling; the craft responded with a turn of speed that surprised both Boyd and Rag. They were moving quickly through the calm, green water that smelt of old leaves and silt; and as the course of the river twisted in wide loops and the overhanging willows grew more profusely, the noise of the sirens receded behind them.

Very soon the river broadened out into a blazing flow of shining ripples, and they were among fields basking green in the sunshine. The roads and houses were at an increasing distance away from the far bank of the river, which they were careful to avoid. Galad spotted a spit of sand extending off a bend into the water.

'Head for that bar, Penry. Beach your boat there,' he called.

Penry obediently followed his instructions and Boyd followed after. They were scrambling out of the boats onto the sandy shingle as Galad drove the tip of kayak onto the spit and jumped out into the shallow water to splash ashore. 'Up the bank, don't wait!' he called out, shooing the four ahead of him.

At the top of the muddy bank, he looked around him as he fumbled under his coat and produced an unusual knife with a pale, spiralling blade from the leather sheath at his belt.

'We need to get away from here completely. You will stand behind me—keep still, and as soon as I walk forward you must follow immediately, or you'll be left behind and trapped here. I cannot come back for you.'

He turned away from them, paused in concentration, then stretched up, reaching forward with the blade, above his head height, and brought it swiftly down through the air to the ground. Rainbows of colours briefly twinkled and flowed, seemingly along the edges of a tear that fluttered apart. Galad straightened up and stepped forward.

'Follow me!'

Penry nodded and took Mac's hand firmly, though she tried to pull away. Rag was at her side, 'It's ok. I think I know what this is. It'll feel weird for a moment, but you'll be fine,' she said.

Penry dragged Mac through quickly, followed by Rag, with Boyd a step behind them; already the tear in the Veil was sealing back together from the highest point downwards.

Galad had turned and was standing facing them from a couple of steps away, pointing his knife at the tear and deliberately bringing the point of the blade slowly downwards through the air. He was breathing heavily as if he'd just run a marathon. With the swirl and folding of silks in the wind, the rainbows vanished from the air as the Veil sealed itself.

Galad doubled over from the waist, his head down, the long, shaggy remains of his sheared white hair falling forward to hide his face.

On the other side of the Veil, the formerly swirling, rainbow-coloured air was now quietly invisible, laying still in the sunshine. A police helicopter clattered low overhead, but all the pilot could see was three abandoned boats on the edge of the river-bank and empty green fields.

ς

CHAPTER ELEVEN

Abruptly Galad collapsed to the ground on his hands and knees. Mac went to his side.

'Are you ok?'

Galad nodded, 'A moment—I will be fine.' He was making an effort to get his ragged breathing under control. 'Do you have any water?'

Mac fumbled in her bag and produced her flask. Galad saw it was made of metal and hesitated.

'Here—I have some.' Rag got her bottle out and went to offer it to Galad. Boyd put out a hand to stop her.

'What? It's only water,' she said. 'That can't hurt—anyway, we're duty bound to offer what hospitality we can, remember?'

She held out her leather and glass flask to Galad, who took it gratefully and drank.

Mac looked puzzled and a little offended. 'Metal flask,' Rag said to her quietly. Mac's lips formed an 'ooo' and she nodded slowly in understanding, 'So he's same as...' Rag nodded.

'Thank you,' Galad took a gulp of water. 'It is... it must be the air, over there, in towns... it makes me... breathless,' he mumbled.

Rag didn't entirely believe him, otherwise Penry would have been affected too... but she didn't say anything. Galad paused and sipped the water slowly and his uneven breathing calmed; after a few minutes he seemed to regain his strength and stood up.

Mac had been staring around her, 'What just happened? Where are we?!'

The river still sparkled in the sunlight as it flowed nearby, but the water looked much cleaner and clearer, and the banks were rockier, all trace of the town across the fields was gone... even the cultivated fields were gone. The greenness of the countryside around them was similar in appearance, but subtly different, wilder, more open.

'We have crossed over,' said Penry delightedly.

Mac looked puzzled, then astounded, 'You mean—we're in Fairyland?'

Galad gave a hollow laugh, 'No. The Fair Folk are not in this land, not anymore. Their strongholds are in the Summerlands of the South West.'

It seemed he had recovered his composure completely as he cradled the spiralling blade he still held in one hand. He brought it to his lips and blew gently along the length of the blade; he kissed the crosspiece of the golden hilt, and replaced the knife reverently in the sheath at his belt. Having completed his little ritual, he turned to Penry with a frown.

'Pentagaron—explain yourself. And you should introduce me to your new friends.'

For once Penry seemed at a loss to explain himself. Mac stepped forward and held out her hand, 'My name is Mackenzie—and you are?'

The tall man glanced at her outstretched hand, then ignored it and placed his right hand, the fist clenched, to his chest and gave a slight bow towards her.

'You may call me Galad.'

Penry recovered himself and interrupted Rag as she opened her mouth to speak. 'And this is Morag, and her brother, Boyd—they are the wards of the Liosalfar of the Northern Enclave,' he said, almost as a warning to Galad, or so it seemed to Boyd.

Galad looked at them with new interest, 'Wulfric Kennet-son...'

'Do you know him?' exclaimed Rag, 'Can you send him a message and tell him where we are?'

Galad paused, considering this with a frown. Boyd stepped forward, 'They will be looking for us. And if you know him, you know...'

'Yes—I know his power. You have nothing to fear from me. I have no quarrel with him or his kin.'

'Really?' Rag folded her arms and continued, 'Well Russ and Peat didn't seem to think so!'

'His broons were they...? Yes—though they don't have the look of their clan.'

'And what's that supposed to mean?' Rag snapped, narrowing her eyes at what she perceived as a slur.

Galad raised his hands, palms out, 'It means nothing to me,' he said.

Boyd jumped in, 'No, but they are under Uncle Wulf's protection'

'Uncle Wulf is it?' Galad gave a slightly twisted mocking smile that made Boyd colour with anger and clench his fists at his sides.

'No, young Boyd, I mean no disrespect, but anyone can see the alfar in those two.'

'So?' said Rag, bristling in defence of her friends. 'I know they look different to Gam and the others, so what?'

Boyd mumbled with a slight frown, '... they did tell me, their mother had been... took...?'

Galad nodded in understanding, 'Yes—that would be the way of it. And your Laird Wulfric took them back in?'

'Of course, why wouldn't he?' said Boyd. 'The Keep's now their home.'

Galad shrugged, it was not his concern, and turned to Penry. 'Well young master—what now? Explain yourself.'

'I came to find something that was lost, years ago. I knew where it was, roughly, but I read about an old charm that said I needed to have somebody freely invite me through the Veil to cross over. Mac used her blood on the stone and recited the summoning charm and it worked. Everything was fine... until I wanted to go back and I couldn't break the summoning bond. Neither could I get this—to open the veil.' He reluctantly took the Elfstone from his pocket as proof.

Galad looked at the luminous crystal axe, then at Penry. 'That's hardly a surprise. If you had read with more diligence you would know it takes Fair Folk spells to conjure a tear with that stone, it's not something you could do without their aid.'

'That is why we were travelling to the Great Tor, so I could use the stone there when the Veil thins at Midsummer, and separate us when I opened a portal.'

Galad snorted and shook his head. 'Are you not listening to me? That will not work.'

'But what about this binding thing—can we at least break that?' said Mac.

'Show me—stand before me, and then move apart...'

Mac and Penry tried to walk away from each other, but at barely twelve paces apart they both began to struggle to take a step.

'Enough,' said Galad shaking his head. 'You should not have meddled, Master Penry, this binding is not something I can break on my own. Even if I could, Miss Mac needs to return, as do the Laird's cubs.'

'But can't you... you know...' said Penry, pointing his index finger and twirling it in small circles.

'Use my blade? No. It can only be used sparingly—it saps a huge amount of my energy, too much...' He shook his head. 'I have used it twice already today, using it a third time so soon risks draining the life-force out of me. Even if I opened the Veil, you may not be able to cross if I haven't got the strength to hold it apart—and you certainly will not be able to cross if I'm dead.'

They all faced each other in silence for a moment.

'So... began Rag, ever curious, 'Is your blade another sort of special stone, then?'

Galad looked her in the eye, 'No, not really,' Then he walked away and began to look around them and take stock of where exactly they were.

Boyd nudged Rag hard in the ribs with his elbow. 'What?' she hissed in annoyance.

'His knife—it's a spiral—like a unicorn's horn?' Boyd spoke quietly. 'Remember what the Buggane said? You only get to steal a unicorn's power by using Dark Magic to kill it and eat its life force? They said he'd done something really terrible—I bet that's it, that's why he's an outcast.'

Rag's mouth formed a silent oooo... 'And Russ and Peat were so angry with him...' she whispered back.

Galad came back to join them. 'We shall keep to your plan, Penry—we must all travel to the Great Tor. Hopefully, the Queen of the High Court may be persuaded to use the stone to both cut a path and sever the binding so Miss Mac can return home. And I am sure the Laird will send his broons, they will find Morag and Boyd soon enough. He's already laid his mark on them to be your Gards.'

'What mark?' said Mac and Rag almost together.

'Show them,' commanded Penry.

Galad gave Penry a mutinous look, but slowly pulled up his sleeve to show his left forearm; a dark shadow of intricate knotting moved slowly under his skin.

'Eeeew!' said Mac, 'that is so Harry Potter!'

'Who?' said Galad, looking puzzled.

'Never mind...it's not important...' she mumbled.

'We must get to Droithglarma, but not the stone—I forbid it!' Penry broke in. 'The Queen cannot have the stone. It rightfully belongs to my father. When we get to the Tor, you must make the tear!'

Penry's stance made it clear his demands should be met without argument. 'The Veil will be stretched thin at dawn—you won't need a lot of force—and you are MY gard!'

Rag glimpsed the sinuous dark knot under Galad's skin writhe angrily before the alfar quickly dragged his sleeve down. His eyes blazed briefly with fury, as she'd seen them do when Russ and Peat insulted him, but he said nothing and looked away. Penry turned his back and walked off. After a few moments, Galad turned to face Boyd and his sister, his face now completely composed.

'It would be better we all travel together. However much you doubt it, you will be safer travelling with me than on your own. There are folk here who love neither mannish nor alfar. When we have safely released Mackenzie, I will see you are returned without harm to the North and into the care of Wulfric Kennetson.'

Boyd opened his mouth to speak, but thought better of it. Galad continued: 'You are not yet of age, I'm sure he will have some idea of where you are already.'

'How can he know, we haven't been able to send a message—he probably thinks we're on our way to Birmingham.'

Galad smiled sadly, pausing for the briefest moment before speaking.

'You are his wards. He will know.'

'How?' demanded Rag.

'Pentagaron's father laid his thrall on me as his son's gard. It means I can find him. Your uncle is far closer to you two; the effects of his gardship will be something natural to him, not imposed—and stronger, even at this distance.'

'But he couldn't find my father when he was lost,' said Rag.

'The thrall of finding only works with somebody who has not reached their maturity. You may be missing, but you are not truly lost—then he would sense... a hole, a lack of *you*. If you died, or even if your father had died, Wulfric Kennetson would feel the absence keenly—and know immediately.'

Mac has had enough of this chatter, and being treated like a bundle to be dropped off when they were ready.

'That's all very well,' she said with a scowl, 'but I am in Fairyland and I should be in Warwickshire. Mom and I are going to Paris in four days' time and I am NOT missing that trip!'

Galad huffed a little snort of amusement. 'Then Miss Mac, we should start. We will follow the river, and where it connects with the Great West River, we should be able to buy passage on a barge heading down to the sea. From there, at the port down the coast, we can strike inland. If we walk through the night from the sea, we should be able to cross the marshes and reach the Great Tor before dawn of the third day—and all will be safely resolved.'

Rag and Boyd looked at each other questioningly.

'Come, we should start,' said Galad, preparing to leave, 'we still have a day's walk ahead of us.'

He strode off down the riverbank, now followed closely by Penry... who invisibly pulled Mac along in his wake.

'They said to avoid him,' said Boyd, 'but what choice do we have?'

Rag shrugged her shoulders and looked at her brother. 'We'll probably get some sort of message from Uncle Wulf sometime soon. He'll come, or at least, send somebody for us.'

She walked down the riverbank after the others. Boyd sighed and followed her—after all, he thought, what else could they do?

ς

CHAPTER TWELVE

Rural meadowland and rough pasture bordered the river, interspersed with patches of woodland, some managed, some evidently untouched and wild, full of undergrowth and brambles. The only movement other than the tree-branches swaying was the occasional twitch of squirrels' tails and the hop of rabbits, which paused to watch them walk by from the safety of the thickets. Walking near the riverbank they avoided most of the more difficult areas of forest, but the trek seemed endless. Galad assured them they would reach the nearest market town by nightfall—the best place they could hope to get transport onwards to the Great West River.

It took six hours of walking and they were all exhausted by the time they arrived, except Galad who appeared to have regained his stamina. There was a small farmstead at the edge of the town, the first place they came to, and after pleading they could go no further, Galad agreed, they could rest here and he would go and make arrangements.

'You could find us an inn in the town, somewhere with food and a decent bed,' said Penry.

Galad shook his head, 'We don't want to draw unwanted attention,' he said, looking at Rag and Mac. 'We can stay the night here—I will speak to the farmer. Their clothes pick them out for comment,' he jerked his chin towards the youngsters, 'and we don't want to be overly noticed. I'll go and see about passage on a sea-bound barge when I've secured us board and lodgings.'

He disappeared into the farm building. The four collapsed near the stone horse trough in the cobbled yard and waited... and waited.

Eventually Rag said, 'Do you think he's left us?'

Penry shook his head, 'He can't do that. My father would have his skin. I bet he is feasting and drinking while he leaves us here to starve.'

'I don't think he's that bad,' said Mac.

'No... look,' said Boyd.

Two young women came out of the farmstead and walked towards them, one with a heaped tray under a cloth, the other with an armful of blankets. They both wore large aprons over the top of gathered skirts reaching almost to their ankles, and sturdy buckled shoes over finely knitted stockings

'Master says you're to sleep in the hay barn for the night,' said the one with the blankets. 'Come—Biddy has your supper, and if'en the Otherone does as he's bid—you'll get some hot stew later.'

'Where has... our friend gone?' said Boyd.

'The Otherone agreed to do a service for the Master...'

'What service? Why did he leave us?' said Penry standing up.

'La—you be Other too—and what the stars are the rest of yer?' she said and took a step backwards.

'We're just travelling through, we mean no harm' said Boyd rising to his feet carefully, empty hands held out. He glanced at his sister, and she nodded before standing slowly.

'Just passing. We're very tired...' said Rag.

'And we are very grateful for your generous hospitality, ma'am...' said Mac with a bright smile.

'Alright, I suppose... Come this way then,' said the young woman, and lead them towards the hay barn.

'Well said,' muttered Penry in Mac's ear.

Mac flashed him a scowl now the women's backs were turned. 'I know what that sort want to hear!' she hissed, 'don't mean I mean it!'

Inside the barn were mounds of stacked hay; the first woman dropped the blankets on one. 'You can nest here, snug like—Biddy put the tray atop the old manger.'

The other younger woman did so; her eyes were round with curiosity as she took in their clothing: their trainers, the girls' jeans and Mac's brightly printed cotton top; Boyd wore a dark pair of loose, many-pocketed trousers, like the broons, and a long-sleeved band tee-shirt with a large multi-coloured logo... She looked at them as if they were the most exotic creatures she'd ever seen... which they were.

'La... Elsie—did you ever?' she breathed.

Elsie sniffed in a superior manner to hint that she wasn't impressed by their odd clothes. 'Passing through, you say?'

Penry gave a gracious bow, 'Our thanks to you both. Yes, we are simply travellers, looking for a passage by barge to the coast. Once my gard has found us places, we shall be gone.'

'Gard is he?' said Elsie, 'Hope he's as handy at fighting as he looks to be, then.'

'Fighting?' said Boyd with a frown, 'why fighting?'

'Biddy, take the cloths off—there's your supper, good cheese, butter, and white bread, the Otherone paid for that already. There's a jug and beakers—you can fetch water from

112

the wellhead yourselves.' She turned to shoo Biddy out the door ahead of her.

'What about this fighting?' demanded Boyd.

Biddy turned at the door, 'Master's got trouble with a wodwose, and yon's agreed to sort 'im out.'

'Hush your mouth!' Elsie gave her a push, before half turning, 'Yer night's paid for. Don't fret—yer fella looks strong enough, he'll be back for you. The privy is aside the house and there's a candle and lanterns—don't set fire to the barn!'

And with that Elsie pushed Biddy out the door and they were gone.

'But, wait... what's a...' said Rag, going after them—but the two young women had bustled off into the farmhouse, closing the kitchen door behind them with a bang.

'So what do we do now?' said Mac.

Penry had walked over to the tray and was cutting a thick slice of cheese with the small wooden-handled knife set on the platter.

'We wait,' he said. 'We can eat, and sleep, and hope Galad doesn't take too long about seeing off their wodwose, and then we get some hot supper with luck.'

'But what's a wodwose?' said Rag.

'A wild thing of the woods, very tree-like—usually very strong, and generally bad-tempered—so I've heard,' said Penry.

'Aren't you bothered about Galad getting hurt?' said Mac.

Penry shrugged, 'He's paid to fight, and he's paid to keep me safe. He will do as much as is needed to get us on our way. Mmm... this cheese is very good—do you want some?'

The other three regarded him in silence.

'What? You don't think he's up to it?' Penry grinned, 'Believe me, he's fought worse.'

'How do you fight a ...wodwose?' said Mac.

'Here—let me cut you some cheese, and the bread is freshly baked...' Penry ignored Mac's question and handed her a thick slice of bread, '...there's butter too,' he said. 'Come on Morag, some cheese for you? There's no point starving while we wait.'

Rag accepted the proffered hunk of yellow cheese. 'Boyd?' she said. Her brother came over to the stacked tray. He picked up a piece of the sliced bread from the wooden platter.

'A wodwose is a sort of Wildman of the Woods, except he's more tree than human... ' Boyd said quietly.

'Oh you are jokin' me! Our guide has gone off to fight a frickin' tree!' yelped Mac, almost dropping her bread and cheese.

'Are they... are they very strong, then?' Rag asked Boyd the question, but Penry answered.

'Yes, their flesh is tough, like wood, they can bend and not break—but Galad was chosen as my gard because his strength and skills are well known. He will not let me... us, down.'

...And my father would send his warriors to hunt him down if he did, thought Penry... then he bit his lip and frowned. If Wulfric Kennetson knew where his wards were... then surely his father would know where he was? But that was a dangerous thought that he tried to push away—his father would rely on his appointed gard... He wouldn't come searching himself... would he? Penry shook the idea off—his father never had before, why should he now? And anyway— in three days he'd be back and he'd have the much missed Elfstone with him. Penry smiled to himself—that would make his esteemed father notice him at last! He patted his jacket and felt the comforting curve of the crystal in his inside pocket.

They were all asleep when Galad returned. The light from the horn lantern he was carrying was enough to wake Rag. She nudged Boyd who was sleeping beside her; Mac was the other side of him, she woke when the others stirred from their blankets.

'Wassup?' she yawned, then she saw by the dim light that Galad's face was bleeding, 'Wooooah!'

Boyd was the first to throw back his blanket.

'Have you water?' rasped Galad, his voice cracking with fatigue. He sat down heavily on a stack of hay, before putting the lantern on the floor carefully.

'Here...' Boyd stood and fetched a beaker and jug from the tray.

Galad accepted the beaker and drank it straight down, 'More,' he said. Boyd refilled the cup. Galad drank that down and wiped his mouth with his sleeve. 'Did you save any food for me?'

'I... I did,' said Rag. She held out a slightly squashed sandwich of buttered bread and cheese, wrapped in a small cloth the women had left on the tray. Galad nodded his thanks and took it, wolfing down the bread in great mouthfuls. Rag could see the skin of the alfar's hands was ripped as if he's been fighting his way through thorn trees. By this time Penry had woken up too

'Oh good—you're back.' His eyes focused on the blood stains across Galad's face that extended into his white hair, and the deep, parallel scratches across the arms of his leather coat. 'Put up a fight did he?'

Mac rolled her eyes.

'What? I was merely saying,' said Penry.

Mac pulled her backpack towards her and opened a side pocket, 'Antiseptic wipes, and cream—it's for bites and stuff,' she held them out. Penry simply stared at them. Boyd took the first-aid supplies off her.

'You need to clean those cuts—they look deep. And this will help heal them—it's sort of like a marigold salve,' he said. Galad gave a slight nod.

'I can do that,' said Boyd. 'I—we—have been practising with the animals at Uncle Wulf's Keep. I can clean them up.'

Galad smiled wryly. 'Do you mean me, or the animals?' he said.

Boyd coloured a little, 'No—I mean... I can do this. I know how.'

Galad nodded he could go ahead and handed Boyd the slip of cloth previously wrapped around the bread and carried on eating his sandwich.

Boyd wet the cloth and leaned forward to wipe it across the old blood on Galad's forehead. The alfar winced. Boyd could see splinters of black wood, like long thorns, embedded in his skin.

'Rag,' said Boyd, 'come and hold the lantern for me so I can see properly.'

His sister immediately got up and stood behind him, holding the lantern up so that Galad's face was in the light. She could see numerous deep scratches raking down his face and around one eye. They were irregular and deep, as if something had been intent on poking his eye out. There were more wounds around his throat that looked like a thorny rope had been tightened around his neck. Rag held the light as still as she could, but it was now late into the night and it was chilly. She shivered.

Galad caught hold of Boyd's wrist as the boy swabbed his neck. 'Fetch your sister a blanket, she's cold,' he said.

116

'I will get it,' said Penry before Mac could reach for it. He picked Rag's blanket up and went over to drape it around her shoulders. 'Do not worry,' he whispered in her ear, 'everything will be fine.' He gave her shoulders a comforting squeeze and stood back.

'Was there just the one?' Penry asked.

Galad eyed his charge up, 'Yes, young master, just the one.'

'Good. It wasn't any trouble then.'

'Penry,' said Boyd, 'why don't you go and fetch some more water from the well.'

'I have no light,' said Penry.

'Here, Mac,' said Rag, 'you hold this lantern for Boyd, and I'll light the other one.' She handed it over as the girl came across to them, then went to her own backpack.

'Mac,' said Boyd 'you wouldn't have some tweezers would you?'

The girl nodded and paused to search her make-up bag, before handing them over to Boyd. She held the lantern high while he used the tweezers to carefully pull out slivers of dark wood from the alfar's wounds. Galad winced occasionally but kept still under Boyd's hands.

Rag took out her father's strike-a-light and cleared a patch of stone-flagged floor so she could get a flame without setting the hay alight. The straw kindling she'd twisted into a little rope took light at the second strike and blazed brightly. She lit the candle and lodged it firmly in the horn lantern they'd been left by Elsie.

Galad raised an eyebrow and smiled. 'Impressive—quite the little salamander... Ow!' he yelped as Boyd applied the ointment to the deeper wounds on the cheek below his injured eye.

'Sorry,' said Boyd.

117

'No matter,' replied Galad, 'it will heal.'

'Penry—I still need that water... I need to bathe your hands,' said Boyd to Galad. The alfar stuffed the last of the bread in his mouth and held his hands out for Boyd's inspection. Most of the damage was superficial, but the long gouges in the skin looked sore and red even where they weren't bleeding.

Boyd dabbed at them with the antiseptic wipes. Galad hissed but didn't take his hands away.

'Did you—did you kill it? Boyd asked quietly.

Galad shook his head. 'I drove it off. It shouldn't come back while we are here—if it comes back later to claim its territory...' The alfar shrugged, 'Well, we won't be here. Penry—Boyd needs more water.'

'I know, I know. I said I was going...' said Penry huffily.

'I'll come with you,' Rag said to Penry. She held up the candle lantern and took Penry by the arm and they went outside.

The night sky was clear and full of stars and the air was cool and damp. In the east, the sky was already lightening with a pre-dawn glow.

'Why would there be more than one wodwose?' said Rag, as they walked the short distance to the well. Abruptly Penry stopped. 'Um... I don't think I can go any further.'

'What? Oh I see,' said Rag, '...the binding thingie.'

Penry shrugged, 'Can't help it. And the wodwose... they keep together in bands—like trees in a forest.'

'But we didn't see any forest around here when we arrived.'

'That might be the problem,' said Penry. 'The farmer is cutting down too many trees.'

He attempted one more step then stopped. 'You will have to wind the bucket up, I can't reach—but if you hand me the water, I'll carry it back. If your brother can finish cleaning him up we might still get a couple more hours sleep before morning.'

ς

CHAPTER THIRTEEN

It was the familiar clank of wooden buckets that woke Rag in the morning; then she turned over and instead of feather pillows she got a face full of coarse straw—which woke her up completely. She sat up and yawned and stretched her arms. Beside her, Boyd was still asleep, as was Mac and nearby, so was Penry. She looked across the floor of the barn to where the tall alfar was asleep on a pile of hay nearer the door. He suddenly sat bolt upright, a knife in his fist, held at chest height pointing outwards. He blinked, quickly looked around him, and slowly relaxed—then he saw Morag looking at him and dropped the hand holding the knife out of sight at his side. He nodded to her, and pushed the blanket off him. He'd taken his hooded coat, jerkin and weapons belt off, and slept in his shirt and trousers—and his boots, she noticed. He stood up out of the mound of straw and stretched the stiffness out of his back and arms, making the small sounds she'd heard her father make when he first got up; not quite gasps or groans, more the satisfaction antic-ipating movement...

Which made Rag think of her father... how was he? Had he missed them? There had been a little improvement since they'd got him back, but his mind was till foggy. His body seemed to be burning away his flesh from the inside, so that he looked thin and gaunt, and his eyes still had that haunted look—although now the blue-grey film had cleared so that he could see. Uncle Wulf said he would recover, but it all seemed very slow...

She watched as Galad went to the large door and pulled it open, allowing thin early morning sunlight to spill across the floor towards her. He walked outside. Rag squinted, and yawned again. Beside her, the new source of light was making Boyd stir from his blanket. He pushed it aside and half-sat up, propping himself up on his elbows, and looked around.

'Where's Galad?'

'He woke up a minute ago and went out—maybe he went for water, or you know—the privy?' Rag said.

Boyd nodded, 'Good idea. I need to wash this dust and straw off me.' He stood up.

'Why bother? It will brush off as the day goes on. Do you think we get breakfast?'

'Well if you get up and come outside with me you might find out,' replied Boyd, shaking out his blanket and folding it.

Morag groaned and flopped backwards onto the straw, pulling her blanket up over her chin. 'Do I have to?'

'There is no breakfast in bed here.' Galad had returned; his white hair was soaking wet, as was much of his shirt. He'd washed the remaining blood off his head with a bucket of water from the well.

He bent to his long pack, pulled out another rumpled shirt and shook it out, before pausing to strip the wet shirt over his head. With his back towards the youngsters, they could see multiple scars across his body; thin, pale lines faintly criss-crossed his back. As he turned and shucked into

121

the fresh shirt, they could see old scarring that curled the skin into shallow ridges over his ribs. There were more, long-healed cuts over his upper arms and shoulders, and smaller, puckered scars in the muscles of his chest and abdomen that might be from something piercing him, like arrows, or a lance... He shrugged the shirt down and tucked it into his trousers.

'Come on then, you laggards—the farmer and his wife owe me a good breakfast and I intend to take full advantage of that.'

He tossed his wet shirt over a rail to dry off a bit in the sun and strode out of the barn.

'That looks like an awful lot of fighting,' said Rag quietly.

'Remember what they said—he doesn't have to keep his scars—he chooses to,' said Boyd.

'Even so...' muttered Rag.

Boyd lent across to shake Mac's shoulder, 'Wake up—time for breakfast.'

An unexpected, but familiar voice came from the door-way.

'Breakfast?'

There was a long, lean silhouette leaning against the open door. 'That would be welcome,' said the newcomer, who stumbled inside and slumped down wearily on the stack of hay where Galad had slept.

'Muirdoch!' said Boyd.

'You're here! Why? I mean—why are you here?' said Rag.

The tall figure dressed in supple black leather leaned forward and rotated his arm at the shoulder with a drawn-out exhalation of discomfort.

A second, slightly shorter, muscular figure dressed in dark brown clothing appeared at the barn door and spoke: 'Why else? Did you not think Wulfric Kennetson would send for his own?'

The speaker walked in and looked around him without a hint of a smile. Rag and Boyd were immediately struck by his strong resemblance to Russ and Peat, although he looked a few years older and far more serious. He had their finely chiselled, handsome features and dark hair, but there was a haughty pride about him that was more like Muirdoch, or Wulfric. He was dressed like they'd seen Wulfric, in fighting gear: a thigh-length quilted leather jerkin patterned with bronze studs, and high boots. He held himself stiffly, head high, one hand resting on the pommel of the long knife hanging at his side from the baldric hung across his chest; his long dark brown hair was tied back in several plaits, but there was a narrow streak of pure white running through it that began at the hairline above his right eye.

'This is Vandyke—your new gard. He has travelled further afield than his two brothers, hence Wulf sent him to escort you home,' said Muirdoch, still rotating his aching shoulder. 'You spoke of breakfast?' he continued, 'I want bacon—not porridge.'

'Who... who...?' whispered Mac, still half asleep, but struggling up to squint at the outlines of the newcomers, who were silhouetted by the strengthening daylight behind them.

'Don't worry, they've come from our uncle, they're fine,' said Boyd, brushing the straw off his clothes.

'How did you get here?' said Rag, shaking out her unruly red hair and running her fingers through it to get rid of the fragments of hay.

Vandyke took a step back with a look of mild distaste at the sudden cloud of dust-motes and straw drifting in the sunbeams. He turned and walked outside again, standing with his back to them as he looked across the farmyard.

Rag frowned—*who did he think he was?*

'We flew—or rather, I flew, Van was on my back.' Muirdoch said, 'but I fear I will not be able to return immediately. We flew through the night, and I am... more tired than I should be.' He said regretfully.

'We are grateful. I'm surprised you could fly all this way at all, you've only just recovered,' said Boyd.

Mac tugged Rag's sleeve, 'He flies??' she mouthed.

Rag nodded, bending down to whisper, 'I'll tell you later, but he's our uncle's friend. He can be a bit grumpy sometimes, but he's ok.'

Muirdoch inclined his head, acknowledging Boyd's question and ignoring Rag's whispering. 'Your Uncle would have come himself, but circumstances precluded his absence. However, we are here—now, perhaps you can help us to breakfast? Van?'

The tall broon turned around slowly from surveying the farm-buildings. Boyd was fairly sure he saw a sneer on his face before the broon composed his features into studied neutrality.

'Lord?' said Van.

'This looks a poorish sort of place, but I dare say Boyd here can show you where we can obtain food. I don't suppose they have coffee, but small beer, bread and bacon will do...'

'It will do very well,' Galad had approached them silently across the farmyard. Van spun around at his voice and was already in a half crouch, hand on the hilt ready to pull his knife from its sheath.

'Peace, friend—I bring breakfast,' said Galad, still in just his half-open shirt, boots and trousers. He raised both his hands to show he had no weapons about him.

Boyd was close enough to see Van's eyes narrow in mistrust at the sight of Galad's shorn hair, but the broon stood slowly from his attacking stance, and gave the alfar a curt nod. Galad smiled back benignly, ignoring the weapon in Van's fist.

Galad remained just outside the barn's entrance, immediately behind him Biddy and Elsie, each carrying heaped trays of food, goggled at the sight of the newcomers—and the half-drawn knife.

Boyd found his voice first, and went over to Muirdoch. 'This is Galad. He helped us... when we had to escape. Ummm... the police were chasing us, but we hadn't done anything wrong.'

'They were helping me,' Penry came forward from the shadows were he'd been standing. 'He is my gard, and he is no threat to you. I guarantee it.'

'You do?' said Muirdoch, looking amused. He turned towards Galad, 'Then we accept your good intentions.'

Galad bowed with a sardonic smile. Van curled his lip in a sneer, but thrust his knife safely away.

Rag had come forward to stand beside her brother, she glared at Van, 'Just who does he think he is?' she murmured in Boyd's ear. He nudged his sister's ribs with his elbow. 'I'm only saying is all,' she whispered.

Galad ushered Biddy and Elsie forward with their well-laden trays—which they put down hastily without a word before scuttling back to the farmhouse.

'Shall we?' he said, 'Miss Mac, Morag... will you help yourselves?'

Rag's mouth watered at the sight of bacon slices, eggs, sausages, thick slices of bread, hunks of cheese, a big bowl of fried mushrooms... and glistening chunks of fried black pudding that she wasn't keen on, but she knew her brother liked. Muirdoch too, as it turned out, he helped himself to some immediately. Galad put several pieces of bacon on bread and handed it to Penry, who hadn't attempted to help himself. The svartalfar took the wooden platter with barely a nod of thanks before sitting down to eat ravenously. Galad ignored the discourtesy, but Muirdoch noticed it, and afterwards watched the alfar with curiosity as he ate.

Boyd made a platter of bacon, egg, sausage, mushrooms and bread and turned to hand it to Van. The broon hesitated slightly before accepting being served, something again that Muirdoch noted with amusement.

Rag saw her brother hand the plate over before he'd got anything for himself and thought Van's pause before taking it was a show of arrogance and that he was too proud to picnic on a barn floor. She scowled at him... who does he think he is, and how dare he be so disdainful?!

Van, of course, was simply not used to being served by his laird's kin. He mumbled his thanks to Boyd and sat down on some hay near the door.

Mac edged closer to Rag after they had made their selection from the platters. 'When you said, "he flew here" you didn't mean that literally...' said Mac quietly.

Rag nodded, unable to speak around her mouthful of bacon sandwich.

'Really? He can fly—so, he is like... a fairy?'

Rag shook her head furiously, and hurried to finish chewing. 'No, not that—he's a...well he's...' Rag stuttered to a halt, trying to think how to explain Muirdoch without frightening Mac. 'He's a noble creature, and although he can be dangerous, he's our friend—and he can shape-shift into a horse, and a huge black bird,' she said quickly and bit into her sandwich so she didn't have to reply immediately.

Mac's jaw dropped for a second, before she decided it must be a joke, 'Nah, you're kidding me—he can't do that!' she said, '...Can he?'

Rag nodded, mouth full, and shrugged as if to say *...yeah, that's normal for here.*

Mac picked at a crust. 'Okay... if you say so,' she said cautiously. 'What about the other one—warrior dude?'

Rag swallowed, 'We know his younger brothers, they work for my uncle, but I haven't met him before. They're really nice and good fun, but him—I think he's much too full of himself,' she said quietly.

'But he has barely spoken to you, and he hasn't spoken to me at all, or Penry.'

'Exactly,' said Rag, 'We're not good enough!'

They both looked over to where Boyd was trying to start a conversation with Van.

'So how long did it take you to, um, fly here?' said Boyd.

'About four or so hours.'

'How did you find us? Did Muirdoch know?'

Van was eating. He shook his head and briefly twitched his left sleeve up a little so Boyd could glimpse the twisting pattern under the skin on the inside of his forearm above the wrist. Boyd couldn't see the entire mark but he realised it was like Galad's, only Van's was silvery pale.

'Uncle Wulf did that to you?'

Van nodded.

'Can he undo it?'

Van swallowed and shot Boyd a stern look, 'Wulfric Kennetson is my laird. I am his liege-man and I serve him gladly. Whatever he asks of me I will do.' Then he put down his platter, got up and walked away. 'Muirdoch, lord—I am going to fetch water,' Vandyke said before disappearing out of the door.

Boyd turned to face Muirdoch, who merely nodded with a slight smile, as if to say—all is fine.

Penry came over to sit near Boyd, 'He's a surly one that broon—though he has something about his manner that's almost familiar.'

Boyd didn't reply, but he thought to himself—that's because he behaves like you. 'Still...' Penry continued, 'My gard will keep us safe. He's proved himself already, has he not?'

Boyd nodded, 'Yes, he was very brave to fight that wodwose alone.'

Penry snorted, 'That was his duty. When he has got us safely to the Great Tor, he knows my father will show his gratitude.'

'Yes,' said Boyd, 'but that's for helping you, he doesn't have to do anything for us.'

'But you are my friends,' Penry gave Boyd a generous smile, with just a tiny push of glamour. 'He will always do what he can to help my friends.' Penry got up and went to see if there was any bacon left on the trays.

Boyd blinked and smiled after him, unexpectedly suffused with warmth for Penry... something when he thought about it moments later, he'd never felt before. Boyd had always thought of himself as helping Mac, not Penry—she was the one who'd got caught up in this strange world without really knowing what was happening to her... He glanced across and saw Mac and his sister whispering together. He also saw Muirdoch stand up, stretch and move towards Galad.

'Walk with me a moment,' Boyd heard the Water-horse say to Galad, who looked up at the black clad figure, then got slowly to his feet. The two left the barn and turned to walk along the side of the building that faced away from the farmstead.

This piqued Boyd's curiosity and seeing no one was looking at him, he crept out after them to see if he could overhear what they were saying.

ᔕ

CHAPTER FOURTEEN

Muirdoch led the alfar outside and around the corner of the barn. The wooden barn was shielded by saplings and bushes and there was a dry-stone wall running at right-angles away from it towards a thicket of dense hedging half way down the barn's wall; Muirdoch made for the stone wall to lean against. Galad followed him; he'd put his jerkin and the cross-harness that held his knives back on, but not his leather coat. Galad sat down on an old staddle stone a couple of arms-length away from Muirdoch. They watched each other in silence for a few moments.

'I know what Penry is, but not who he is—or why his father can command you,' began Muirdoch.

Galad shrugged, 'I find myself—open to employment. When you are...' he twirled his hand to indicate taking his appearance into account, 'you cannot always be choosy.'

'But a svartalfar...'

'As I said,' Galad's voice hardened, 'I do not always get many choices.'

Muirdoch held up a hand in acknowledgement, and they sat for another moment or two in silence.

'Besides,' said Galad, 'your broon, he is half svart, as you well know.'

Muirdoch nodded.

'...and I would even hazard—by his looks, he could easily be one of the Svart Lord's bastards. He has that aspect—prideful... but in him there's damage as well. Does he know who his father is?'

'I believe he might do, or at least strongly suspects,' said Muirdoch, 'which may be why he and his half-brothers are so fiercely loyal to Wulfric as their laird.'

'Half-brothers?'

'Different fathers, but like his, Svart.'

'And the mother?'

'Safe—she escaped when her sons were very young, and scratched out a living in hiding on the mannish side.'

'Until Wulfric Kennetson found them.'

Muirdoch nodded. 'They owe their lives to him, and even if he chooses to forget it, they never will. Hence—they would willingly die for their laird, or anyone he regards as kin. Anyone.'

Galad nodded, 'I take your meaning—but those children are in no danger from me.'

'Then we understand each other.'

'We do.'

There was another pause—during which, out of sight, Boyd pressed himself closer to the barn wall, hiding among the scrubby bushes to get close enough to hear what they were saying.

'You may not know it, but I realise how difficult it can be to be on the outside... of acceptance,' said Muirdoch quietly.

Galad raised his head. 'What do you mean by that?'

'I see the form of that blade on your belt. I can guess what you did. You must have been sorely pressed to make such a choice...'

Galad sprang to his feet, his face twisted with anger. 'My choices were my own! I need no pity from strangers. Or your sympathy for "my mistakes", as you'd call them!'

Muirdoch stood up slowly and faced him, eye to eye, '*your mistakes*—is correct. You should never have done what you did. I don't care what drove you. But I do understand desperation.'

Muirdoch turned on his heel, speaking over his shoulder, '...and I would offer some understanding to you, but no matter!'

Muirdoch stalked back towards the barn, and Boyd barely got away ahead of him.

As Van returned with the buckets of water, he saw Boyd scuttle out through the bushes, and dart across the yard to the gate out to the road, followed some moments later by Muirdoch, who rounded the corner of the barn with a face like thunder. Van sighed, he liked Muirdoch, but *Each Uisge's* passionate temper was well known in the household—hopefully, this black mood would soon pass. As he reached the barn door, the shorn alfar, Galad, returned as well, after obviously having had words with Muirdoch by the look on his still wounded face.

The two paused and looked at each other, before Van stepped back to let the other pass. Galad shook his head and waved the broon through the doorway ahead of him.

Inside, the girls seemed to have made an attempt to clear up by piling empty platters back onto one tray and uneaten food on another. Now Mac was using a wide-toothed comb in an effort to put Rag's unruly red hair into place; though from Mac's determined face, and Morag's scrunched up eyes and gritted teeth... it wasn't going without a degree of pain.

Van ignored both of them and concentrated on Penry, who had brushed himself down and was seated in waiting, like a lord about to hold court. Galad went to Penry's side; he folded his arms and stood legs braced, feet apart.

Muirdoch took a bucket from Van, went down on one knee beside it and scooped water over his face and neck and washed his hands. When he'd done splashing, Boyd re-appeared, his face the picture of innocence; he sidled past Van and went to sit with Mac and his sister. Morag gratefully escaped Mac's administrations when the girl paused the combing to smile at her brother.

Muirdoch stood up wiped his wet hands down his thighs and faced the others. 'We need to decide what to do next,' he said, 'do you have any plans?'

'Yes. I have,' said Penry, 'we need to go to Droithglarma for the Midsummer dawn and greet it at the top of the Tor. It suits our needs that the Veil will be very thin at that time—Galad here, can cut through it. The charm of binding between myself and Mackenzie will be severed, and we can both go our separate ways.'

'What binding?' Muirdoch frowned.

'Nothing I did,' said Galad. 'He managed that all on his own—but I believe it can be undone.'

Muirdoch nodded, 'If you say so, it means nothing to us—but Boyd and Morag do not have to be there. I can take them back to the Keep... although I have not recovered all my strength and it will have to be one at a time—but Van is now their gard, and can look after the one I temporarily leave behind.'

'What—do they have to go?' yelped Mac, 'I don't want them to go—they're my friends ... they are my only thread to normal among all this weird shit!'

Boyd patted her arm, 'It's ok—we will help you.'

'And in my turn,' said Penry, I am honoured by their companionship.' He turned a beguiling smile towards Morag—the two of them staying with him was certainly a part of his plan!

Rag unexpectedly found herself warming to Penry... who continued to smile at her. 'Of course we must stay with... Mac,' she said, 'it's not fair that she's thrown into all of this. We must help her to get back to her mother.'

Van frowned, 'And how are we to do that?'

He could see that Penry smiling so sweetly was to push his own agenda, although Van didn't know what that was. All he could see was an arrogant svart princeling wanting his own way.

Galad cleared his throat to get their attention, 'I—we—plan to go downriver by barge to the Great West River, and then get passage down the coast to the fishing port at Bysgota. From there, we will have a 15-mile walk inland to the Tor, but hopefully we can rent a string of ponies and be there well before dawn.'

'Mmmmm,' Muirdoch furrowed his forehead in thought, 'it sounds simple enough... but simple things are never that simple. Morag, Boyd—if you are determined to join them, then Van must go with you.'

'What?' yelped Van, before quickly biting his lip to choke back any further outburst.

'We cannot allow the laird's wards to travel without defence...'

Galad opened his mouth to speak, but Muirdoch raised a hand and continued, 'Galad, has his own charge—you need turn your mind to yours.'

'As you say, lord,' mumbled Van, bowing his head, but he looked rebellious.

'We don't need him,' said Rag more angrily than she meant to, 'At least... if he has other things to do, I'm sure we can manage by ourselves... pretty much...' she finished lamely as all faces turned to her.

Muirdoch inclined his head slowly. 'Bravely said Morag, but you don't know this country and you are far from home. Vandyke...' he looked across at the broon, 'has a duty to perform, and he will do so to the best of his abilities.'

'Yes, lord, of course.'

'See? He almost sounded like he meant it.' Muirdoch gave a crooked grin as he looked towards Van—who met his eyes then looked down at the floor.

The Water-horse turned to Galad, 'You know the High Queen and the Summer Court will be at the zenith of their power?'

Galad nodded, but before he could answer, Penry cut in, 'It is not our intention to bother the High Queen with this small matter...'

'If you stand on top of her Keep, you cannot fail to 'bother' her!' said Muirdoch, 'Yet, if approached diplomatically, she could be of aid to you.'

'No! ...Lord.' Penry was emphatic, but he quickly smiled to take the sting out of his refusal, 'We can take care to quickly release Mac from this charm and she will be free to go her own way.'

'Damn straight. I never wanted to be here in the first place!' said Mac, 'Although ...I have found new friends,' she said looking straight at Boyd.

Galad caught Muirdoch's eye and they both hid a small smile...

'...as have I,' said Penry looking intently at Morag—who blushed.

Galad rolled his eyes.

'Shall we get on then?' said Muirdoch, 'By the sound of it we all have far to travel, and much to do to afford everyone's safety.'

He looked at Van, who lifted his head, his face the inscrutable visage of a loyal and dutiful liegeman. 'Aye, lord, I shall be watchful,' he said, and then coolly looked each of the others in the eye one at a time, as if daring them to disagree.

'Then we should get ready—I believe I have earnt these blankets,' said Galad, gingerly touching the deep gouges across his cheekbone, 'so fold them tight and put them in your packs.'

'But they smell of... barn,' said Mac.

'The smell won't trouble you when you're aboard a ship at night—the cold wind will,' replied Galad, who was stuffing a thick blanket in his leather pack with ease. Easily enough that Rag wondered if this alfar had a magical pack like the buggane's, one with more room on the inside than there looked from the outside.

'And we may as well collect what remains of breakfast. You may be hungry later, before we get passage on that barge,' said Galad.

Obediently, they stooped and collected the leftover food, wrapping up what they could in the breadcloths. Mac found a crumpled plastic bag in her back pack and offered to put Boyd's share in with hers.

'Tha...thank you,' stuttered Boyd, 'that's kind of you.'

Rag hid a grin, but Boyd noticed and scowled at her—which made her smirk even more.

'Vandyke—a brief word,' said Muirdoch, walking out into the yard; he strolled towards the well head. Van followed a few steps behind to where the Water-horse waited idly kicking at the brick surround, his black-shod foot raising tiny puffs of dust from the old mortar.

'You know you really will have to watch them like a hawk,' Muirdoch said while seeming to lounge casually by the well frame. He glanced over to the kitchen window of the farmhouse. He waved amiably, and the two curious female faces retreated hastily from peering through the glass.

'I know,' said Van with a sigh, 'and it's not that I resent doing it, but babysitting...' He shrugged.

'I dare say you'd rather get back to wrestling that wyvern you were called away from,' said Muirdoch.

'Oh he had got himself well dug in—I dare say he'll be there when I go back.'

'Listen,' Muirdoch put his hand on Van's shoulder. 'They are young. They can be impulsive, especially the wee girl— just treat them like they were your younger brothers.'

'Aye, but them I could give a clout round the ear when they got bothersome!'

Muirdoch laughed out loud, 'Much as you might be tempted... restrain yourself best you can.'

He clapped Van on the shoulder. 'But we have got other things to discuss... the Fair Folk are strange people, very secluded these days, and very factional. You must take care as you travel through their realms not to do anything to upset the balance of power between the three Queens and their Courts. The High Court will be at the peak of their power, but the Seelie and Unseelie Courts shouldn't be dismissed as weak, or ignored as in some way lesser to the High Court's fairs.

'I will see that both Morag and Boyd tread carefully,' said Van.

'And the mortal girl. This Galad will take care of the princeling—that is what he's being employed to do—that doesn't mean he will look out for anybody else... although I hope I'm mistaken in that. And while we are speaking of him—do not underestimate him. He may have fallen, but he is still a powerful one—and he could yet redeem himself. Even he may not be totally lost.'

'Aye lord, if you say so.'

'I do, Van. I think his heart and spirit may be twisted, but they're not completely darkened, not yet anyway...'

'Yes—well, "seeing is believing", as Gam always says.'

'We shall have to hope things don't come to pass that you have to find out.'

They walked back to the barn. The others had gathered their packs and now refilled their water bottles from the fresh bucket of water Van had previously taken inside.

'Are we ready to take our leave of this place?' said Galad. 'Then we can start—we've still got a good walk to where the farmer says we can get passage on a river barge going downstream today.'

ς

CHAPTER FIFTEEN

It was still early enough to have only a few people out and about in the fields that spread out from the river. Those that were, were generally on the well-trodden paths that crossed the hay meadows and pasture, or skirted the crop-fields and the many orchards ranked with fruit trees; apple, plum and pear, each fruiting with an as yet under-ripe crop.

'Good land,' muttered Galad to no one in particular, 'very old, and fertile from the river floods.'

'Which means they took it from someone, or something, else...' Van scanned the further hills beyond the river's floodplain, 'It's still well-wooded up there,' he said. Galad shrugged.

They walked for nearly an hour along the broad path by the river's gentle curves. Galad kept them going at such a fast pace that for the youngsters it precluded the ability for anything other than the briefest of conversations. Van dropped a few paces back to the rear to walk with Galad.

'Are you familiar with the Courts of the Fair Folk?' Van asked, 'I have only met a few solitary fairs in passing, I don't know a great deal about them.'

Galad nodded. 'They each have their favoured ranges and within those realms their power waxes and wanes with the cycle of the natural year. These days they are very secretive and mainly keep to themselves. They're self-sufficient and seldom feel the need to trade with outsiders.'

'Which would account for not seeing many when I've been abroad.'

'If they were there—they saw you, and chose whether or not you saw them,' said Galad.

Rag couldn't help overhearing, and now she wanted to know more, even if it meant walking with Van nearby.

'Can they make themselves invisible, then?' she asked.

Galad shook his head, 'Not vanish entirely, but they can make themselves extremely hard to see—so I suppose that is a sort of invisibility.'

'How do they do that?' she said

'By blending in.'

'Yes, but how do they do that?' persisted Rag.

'They have deva—from their Court, their place,' said Galad.

'Like alfar?' Rag said.

'No,' said Penry, 'not at all like alfar. Fairs are simple beings of wood and dell,' he said dismissively. 'Their small powers are drawn from the green forces of trees, water, rocks and earthworks.'

'Do not underestimate them Master Penry,' said Galad. 'They are quick to anger and in their own realms they have powers enough to do major damage to anyone and anything they take against.'

Rag looked momentarily anxious.

'Do not worry,' Penry said to Rag in a loud whisper, 'I will protect you.'

140

Van rolled his eyes and sucked his teeth, which annoyed Rag—how could he be so mean to Penry when he at least was trying to make her feel comfortable? She stalked forward to rejoin Mac, Penry followed her—it was easier for him to walk the nearer he was to Mac.

Boyd stopped and the others passed him as he crouched to tie his shoe.

'Halt!' called Galad, 'Wait for Boyd—and take a quick rest. Have a mouthful or two of water, but don't waste it. We can't get more that's reliable until we get to the loading dock.'

Rag, Mac and Penry sank gratefully to the grass verge. Van leaned against an old tree stump, while Galad walked a few steps to sit on an old cairn of boulders, the largest of which was carved with a waymark that let the bargees know how far they were up river. Boyd stood up and walked to where Galad sat.

'I'd like to know more about these Courts,' said Boyd.

Van turned his attention towards Galad and the boy.

Galad took a long drink, and then nodded as he wiped his mouth with the back of his hand.

'The Queens are like queen-bees in a hive, every one of their fairs looks to them. The High Court hold power from the Spring Equinox to the Autumn Equinox, their zenith being Mid-summer, hence they're also called the Summer Court. There are two others, The Seelie and The Unseelie Courts. The first gain strength after the Midwinter fortnight has passed until the Spring quarter ends, the UnSeelie's power runs from the Autumn Equal up until mid-Winter's Eve.

Van frowned, doing the computation in his head, 'That leaves the height of Midwinter and the longest nights...'

'That depth of the year's darkness belongs to the Unseelie Queen and her champion from the Shadow Court.'

'Who are they?' asked Boyd.

'Nobody you ever want to meet,' Galad said, getting to his feet again. 'Come—we need to get on,' he said, waving the others up before striding forward.

Boyd fell in beside Penry, who was walking behind Mac and Rag. Van brought up the rear, still keeping an eye on the old forest that now crowded closer to the river as the hills rose and the wide plain became a steep-sided valley.

'What do you know about the fairs and their realms, Penry?' said Boyd, 'You seem to know about the High Queen.'

Penry sniffed his disapproval, 'They are different to both of our kind, their bindings are only deva, green forces of wood and water, air and stone. You are familiar with your bindings?'

'Yes,' said Boyd, 'I'm told I'm water and Rag is fire.'

'Yes, I dare say, but you'll have something else as well, be it air or earth. Being alfar—we have something of each of them, and also...' Penry changed his mind, and changed the direction of his conversation, 'The High Court's centre of power is the Great Tor, and I suppose the surrounding land...'

'That immediately surrounding land is mainly water,' said Van from behind them.

'So you do know something about them,' said Boyd turning around.

'I know roughly where they are, not who they are,' said Van.

'And?' said Boyd.

'Well, if you don't need me—I'll talk to Mac and your sister,' said Penry quickening his pace to walk ahead of them.

Van said nothing. He joined Boyd and they walked in silence for a short while.

'I really would like to know more,' said Boyd quietly.

'I can tell you the little I know for certain.' said Van, 'The... Penry, is correct—The High Queen has her palace of glass under the Great Tor, and her powers stretch across the Droithmere, all the way north-east to the Hills of the Gorge, and in the other direction by way of the Perrot river, almost to the coast. The Seelie Court range through the wooded hills to the eastern side of the Great West river, and the Oaks and forest-land that run down from there to meet the Gorge—they like the Hawthorn woods that top isolated hills; people often call those 'Fair Hills' even those who know nothing about them...'

'You mean people like me?' said Boyd.

'People who live hereabouts—to them fairs are mostly tales and legends.'

'And alfar as well?'

'Not quite so much—but there are certainly people like the farmer's maids who know all of us simply as Others.'

Boyd chewed his lip as he thought about this for a few minutes.

'And the Unseelie?' he asked.

'I have never met an Unseelie fair, but I believe they take the Plain and the Downs to the south-east from here. They hold the darkness and cold of winter dear. They draw power from the barrow-mounds and standing stones—their Queen has her seat among the Giant's Dance, I'm told, or near it.'

'The Giant's Dance? That's what we call Stonehenge, isn't it?'

'Is it? Yes, I believe you're right.' Van was staring up at the rising hills and dense woodlands that had crowded much closer to the river along this last mile.

Along the path, Galad had stopped and was waiting for them to catch up.

'Ahead, the river snakes around several bends and through a narrow gorge,' he said. 'On the other side at the head of the gorge is the loading port—they can't get the big barges any further upstream. If we go up and over the top of the hill we can save considerable time from walking the route of the river path.

'The woods are thick up there,' said Van looking at the tangle-wooded slope rising above them.

Galad looked at him in silence for a moment. 'We will not be among them for long—the trees have been cut down on the far side.'

'That is what worries me,' muttered Van.

ς

CHAPTER SIXTEEN

They had clambered up the increasingly steep and narrow path for about half an hour. The trees seemed to be growing closer together now and the rough ground was filled with briars and tough bushes growing between them. It hadn't been a particularly warm day, there'd been a persistent wind blowing along the river, but among the trees they could feel themselves becoming hotter and stickier as they climbed. Rag had taken off her thick hoodie and tied it around her waist. There seemed to be more flies up here; if they brushed against a low branch, they disturbed swarms of tiny insects that buzzed around their heads and landed on their faces.

'Go away!' Rag grumbled, waving her hands to drive the annoying flies away from her face.

'Have you—noticed...' panted Mac, 'there—are no—birds—up here. You'd think there—would be—with all these—flies.'

'That's true,' said Penry, 'it is very quiet...'

Just then they all heard a loud crack, and a thorny tree with a scrawny trunk dropped across the barely-seen path behind them.

'Woah—that was lucky,' said Mac. 'We could—have been under that!'

What made her scream loudly was that the tangle of thorny branches climbed upright and lumbered towards them. It snaked out a twisted branch with many twiggy fingers and snatched at Van who was at the rear. He ducked under the grabbing branch, drew his blade and slashed at the stalking tree coming towards him.

'Wodwose!' he shouted, 'Run!'

Mac didn't need telling, she all but collided with Penry who was in front of her, and he leant forward and grabbed Rag by both arms from behind and pushed her forward until she almost crashed into Boyd.

Ahead of them, Galad drew the long knives from his harness, one in each hand. Two further cracks sounded ahead of them as loud as pistol shots. Two more wodwose staggered upright from the ground and faced them menacingly. They reached out to grab at the youngsters as their headlong rush led them towards the outstretched branch-like arms. Galad slashed at the undergrowth to clear a fresh route away from the attacking wodwose.

'Follow me!' he yelled, setting off away from the murderous tree-creatures.

A spiky branch grabbed at Rag and tore through the thin fabric of her light shirt. Her arm felt as if it had been shredded by thorns and she shrieked, as much with surprise as pain. The branch missed Penry, who ran passed her, grabbed her hand and pulled her after him by force. Ahead of them Galad was slashing to clear a path through the dense, greenness of tangled scrub.

'Rag...!' shouted Boyd, pausing to look for his sister.

'Just run!' shouted Van from behind him. The broon paused and tried to hold the path to let them get away.

The wodwose repeatedly thrashed its branches, using them like whips to drive the broon backwards. Every time it hit, the long, thorny fingers gouged slivers out of Van's leather coat, or ripped the exposed fabric of his sleeve. He turned to run and a tangle of finger-like twigs caught one of his plaits. Van yelled, spun around and with a single sweep of his knife cut off his own hair along with a few twiggy fingers. The wodwose roared with a loud crackle that sounded like rending timber, snatching the branch back.

The broon darted back and swiftly stooped to retrieve his lock of hair, then ran after Boyd, pushing the boy ahead of him.

'Go, right, right,' Van yelled steering the boy, a hand firmly gripping Boyd's back pack.

Another stupendous series of cracks and another two wodwose came crashing downhill through the undergrowth towards them.

'This way—away from the river. Or they'll have us over the cliff!' yelled Galad. He turned at a sharp angle and tried to head down the slope, sliding through dead leaves as the drop steepened.

'Follow him—this way,' shouted Penry launching after him. Mac had to follow much faster than she could manage, and with a scream fell over and tumbled down, taking Rag and Penry off their feet when she collided with them from behind. They crashed through the bushes—then all three screamed, because suddenly... there was no ground beneath them!

They fell through the air for what seemed like ages but was only a brief second, before landing heavily in a huge pile of leaf litter. They hadn't broken any bones, but the sudden abrupt landing drove the air from their lungs.

Boyd saw them fall. 'Rag!' he shouted and pulled free of Van's grip. He couldn't see them or hear them. 'Rag!'

Galad realised they'd fallen down somewhere; he changed direction catching hold of the boy and pushing Boyd ahead of him. The wodwose were gathering to form a line behind them and were advancing menacingly, branches out-stretched to form an impenetrable wall of thorny sinews. As they pushed through the bushes, Van scrambled through the undergrowth to join Galad and Boyd... and teetered over the edge of the natural hollow in the side of the hill. He all but somersaulted down the steep slope to end up in the heap of leaf litter Rag, Mac and Penry were just beginning to stagger up from.

Above them, Galad shouted 'Jump!' and took Boyd with him off the cliff edge. Van lunged out to grab Rag and hauled her aside as the big alfar and her brother landed heavily. Van fell backwards; he had his arms around Rag and she was on top of him. She was so stunned it took a moment for her to realise, then she instantly flailed her way free and hurriedly crawled off him, accidently kicking him between the legs on her way...

'Ooufff...' gasped Van, curling over on his side.

'Cave,' shouted Galad and lunged towards the large, dark hole at the back of the shallow cliff-face.

'No way,' shouted Mac, but Penry grabbed her hand, 'We must hide!' He dragged her after him, followed by Rag and Boyd. Van regained his breath, got up from his hands and knees and hastily followed them into the darkness.

Inside the mouth of the cave, the roof dropped lower and as their eyes became accustomed to the lack of light, they could see that several passageways led off the opening into the hill—passageways that looked too precisely chiselled to be natural. Van frowned as he rubbed a hand over the rock wall. 'It's a wyrm tunnel!' he exclaimed.

'That's a helluva worm!' said Mac.

'No... I don't think he means that sort of worm,' said Morag.

'No,' said Galad, 'this wyrm was altogether larger.'

'Was?' Penry asked, 'It has gone?'

'From here, anyway—I cannot smell it, and believe me, you can smell a wyrm, even the small one that made these tunnels.'

'Small...?!' exclaimed Mac.

Boyd touched her arm. 'Not earthworm... this wyrm is a sort of... little wingless dragon...'

'Oh you are shittin' me!'

Boyd shook his head. Galad had crept nearer the entrance to peer outside, a sudden shower of falling earth made him jump backwards. It was quickly followed by even more loose soil.

'The wodwose are trying to seal the entrance!' He pushed forward through the falling dirt only to recoil as a whip-like branch snaked across the gap. 'Van, join me!' he shouted.

The broon pushed Rag back to the rear wall and ran to the alfar's side, but a blow across the chest from another spiky branch knocked him backwards off his feet. He regained his footing, as Galad slashed at more writhing branches. Abruptly, more earth mixed with rock fell from overhead, pushed through by giant sinewy roots.

'Get back,' shouted Galad, still trying to make headway against the flailing branches. Van lurched to his feet and hacked at a branch groping through the opening. It recoiled from the blow, but in doing so grabbed hold of the earth at the side of the entrance and pulled more earth down, narrowing their means of escape.

More rocks and soil fell from the roof, 'Galad!' yelled Penry.

The alfar turned and saw the increasingly large pile of loose rubble inside the cave that had begun to separate them. He took a step back, while swinging his knives at a groping branch spiked with long thorns. 'Van—back,' he shouted, 'we must take to the tunnels. They won't be able to collapse the bedrock so easily.'

Van grunted as he hacked at strong, spiny twigs trying to grasp at him,

'Are you sure?'

'We cannot go forward, we must go back.'

'But what if we can't get out,' wailed Rag.

Galad was now at her side, edging her backwards from the rock-falls. 'Wyrms always make many entrances—we will find another.'

'But...'

'Morag—while you can see—make a fire,' said Galad.

'But... but...'

'There are old, dry roots here. Quick Penry, help me pull them down.' Boyd called out, grasping at a length of root hanging loosely against the cave wall. 'Hurry!'

Penry did as he was told and grabbed at the trailing roots. Mac joined him in scrabbling at the wall.

The entrance to the cave was partially filled at one side; at the other side was a long dead branch. 'We need that,' shouted Galad. He dived forward and took a hold of one end dragging it towards him. Van grabbed at the other end as the alfar pulled it inside the cave. Another heavy fall of earth cascaded over them, but they kept hauling the branch with them.

Inside the shelter of the solid rock tunnel Rag crouched striking her flint and metal to make sparks.

'I've got no kindling!' she shouted,

'Here, use this.' Mac dived into her jeans pocket and pulled out a wad of tissues. She dropped them on the ground and Rag's sparks made it catch light immediately. Galad saw the flame and quickly tore off a fistful of dead bark from the old branch. Fortunately it had been inside the cave entrance long enough to be completely dry—he dropped it by the flaming paper. Rag nudged it into place and the bark began to catch light.

'More, I need more.'

Van hacked at the branch, splitting it, and Galad pulled it apart into long pieces. The opening in the hill was rapidly filling with mounds of loose earth. Galad held a piece of branch to the flames and when it was alight thrust it hard at the probing roots above them. They hastily withdrew with a bubble and hiss of steam. He kept singeing them, and the living roots pulled back from causing further falls of rubble.

Boyd had a wreath of old roots that he dropped beside Rag. In the light of the flames he could see more to pull down, but the light from the original entrance was rapidly diminishing. With a final avalanche of loose soil—the cave was sealed shut.

All eyes turned to Morag who was carefully building up a small brightly flaming fire from the old roots and branch. Satisfied it wasn't going to fail, she sat back on her heels.

'Well—what now?' she said, trying hard to still the tremble in her voice.

'Are we—trapped? I mean—can we wait a while and dig our way out?' whispered Mac.

Galad shook his head, 'They will stay outside...'

'And we do not have the time to wait—remember?' said Penry.

'There will be other entrances to these tunnels, a wyrm never has only one,' said Van.

'Then how do we find them?' said Boyd, still tugging hard at a reluctant root, which suddenly gave way in a shower of dry earth.

'Now we have fire—well done little salamander—we need to make torches,' said Galad, 'then we can explore—carefully.'

'I don't like this,' whimpered Mac softly.

Boyd put his arm around her shoulder, 'I don't like it either,' he whispered in her ear, 'but at least we're all together.'

She smiled at him gratefully, but he could see she was very near to tears.

'Let us be busy,' said Galad with deliberate cheerfulness, he could see how shaken the youngsters were. He dropped his pack and pulled out a blanket, nicked the edge and began tearing it into strips.

'Penry, please help Boyd wind the roots into balls about the end of the remaining pieces of branch along with the blanket lengths. They are wool, they may stink as they burn, but they will keep smouldering and last longer as torches. Van...?'

'Aye, lord, I will check the nearest passageways.' He walked away, still with the drawn knife is in hand and was soon lost in the gloom.

'Won't he need a torch?' said Boyd.

Galad shook his head, 'Broons have good eyesight, they can see even in near darkness.'

Just then a tiny beam of bright light illuminated the tunnel. It was Mac, she had a little pencil light on her keyring.

'You had a light all the time?' said Penry.

'I forgot,' said Mac.

'That's good to know, Mac,' said Boyd, 'but maybe save the battery until we really need it...'

They all fell silent at that thought, and standing in the firelight continued to bind the four torches they were making out of blanket strips and old wood.

ʃ

CHAPTER SEVENTEEN

They seemed to have been stumbling through the darkness for hours, but Galad knew it wasn't that long. He was at the front with a lit torch, Van at the rear with another, and the three youngsters and Penry walked between them carrying the two spare torches. The tunnel was roundish and surprisingly smooth—Rag said so aloud and was abashed to hear Van reply: 'That is because the wyrm wears the rock smooth with its body brushing against the walls.'

She could see that Galad, walking ahead of her, had a clear head-span of space above him. She mentally calculated the body width and probable length of a wyrm—that Van said was a not a big one... and decided she really didn't want to meet a big one... Then she thought of the dragon she'd met back at her uncle's keep and against her better judgement had to ask him. 'So... do wyrms turn into dragons?'

There was a sound of muffled laughter from Galad, 'No little one, they are very distantly related, but noble, flying dragons do not come from earth-dwelling wyrms.'

Rag frowned at being called 'little one' but gave it a pass because Uncle Wulf often used those words as a term of affection, and Galad was another alfar like her uncle... sort of.

'Then what are they?' she continued.

'They are themselves. They are earth and water, whereas the great dragons are fire and air. And then... some of them are pure water, or ice...'

'But you have no need to fear them—they are few these days,' said Penry from behind her as they walked.

'I don't fear them. I met one at my uncle's, and he spoke to me. And Boyd has a dragon bracelet made of...' she went quiet, realising perhaps she shouldn't mention that.

'Does he? Here?' said Penry.

'What did the dragon say to you?' asked Galad.

Morag quickly realised she had a way out and answered Galad's question, ignoring Penry's. 'He was very polite and he said he saw me,' she replied.

'The dragon said he *saw* you?' mused Galad.

'Is that bad? said Rag.

'No. No, it is good... probably. It means he has taken you into his memory, not simply your appearance, but your... innermost being. He saw all of you, your past, your present, and at least some of your future.'

'They can see the future?'

'Not quite—he saw you—your future. Dragons live in a very different way, they move between worlds, time streams... even we alfar do not always understand where they go, not entirely. But if he *saw* you, that means something, both for you and him. ...And Penry—there are more than merely a few of them, they just don't come here that often.'

'Oh,' said Rag and went quiet while she thought about this new revelation.

Penry also went quiet and listened, but his thoughts were more about how this information about being seen by a dragon could be useful, and who to.

They had been walking for a long time and the first set of torches was just about burnt out when they suddenly came into a huge natural cavern of great tumbled rocks. Covering a large part of the floor of the cave was a dark pool of still water.

'Stay a moment,' Galad said and moved slowly towards the water. He knelt at the edge, appearing to listen—then he dipped a finger in the water and licked it. He cupped his hand and brought a palmful to his lips and carefully drank. Satisfied it was wholesome he called them forward.

'We can refill our water-bottles here, and light the new torches.'

His voice echoed around the cavern; its ceiling was so high it disappeared into the gloom above them.

'How can you be sure we'll have enough light to see us out of here?' said Penry.

'That water is rainwater—it came in, not up, that means there is a hole above us.'

'But it might just have percolated down through the rock,' said Boyd.

Galad shook his head, 'I would taste the stone, and I don't. I taste air.'

Boyd wanted to be optimistic and didn't query how the alfar could taste the difference. Van knelt and unscrewed his water flask to fill it; he drank some before putting the lid back on.

'Do you taste air?' Boyd said to the broon quietly.

Van gave a small smile, 'Taste it for yourself.'

Boyd felt that wasn't an answer but... He crouched down and cupped his hands in the water and drank. He held his second handful in his mouth and closed his eyes to really concentrate... and realised, he could taste a... softness was all he could describe it as, with a slightly *green* tang to it, like the smell of cut grass. He opened his eyes. Van was staring into his face; the broon nodded, 'There—you have it,' he said and stood up.

'I'm hungry,' said Rag.

'We can take a few minutes if you want to rest your legs and eat the breakfast bread.'

'Second breakfast!' exclaimed Boyd, which made Mac laugh.

'So which one are you then?' she said.

'I don't think I'm quite Frodo material,' said Boyd, 'maybe Merry.'

'Does that make me Pippin—or Sam?'

'Who are they?' asked Penry.

'Doesn't matter,' said Mac, 'it's just something from a movie.' She fished the packet of bread and cheese from her bag to share with Boyd.

Galad wedged his torch in a cleft. They ate in near silence, only broken by the slow drip of unseen water hitting the surface of the impenetrably dark pool.

'Are we finished?' asked Galad, 'Good. Morag, will you light the fresh torches?'

Galad walked around the cavern holding his new torch aloft, while Rag supervised lighting another one for Van. For a while they would have all four alight, although the old ones were nearly exhausted.

'Come—this way,' called Galad.

The tunnel he'd chosen had a very slight rise to it, barely appreciable at first but gradually they could feel the tension in their calf muscles from walking uphill. Then abruptly it vanished and they were sliding downwards on quite a slippery slope.

'No, no, nononoooo,' whispered Mac, who was becoming increasingly uncomfortable in the tunnels. The open cavern had been a relief, but now the rock walls felt oppressive, as if they were closing in. She gulped for air in increasingly short breaths. Boyd heard her and took her hand in his.

'Breath more slowly,' he said, 'deep breaths. You'll be ok'

She clung fiercely to his hand and tried to follow his instructions, but she was nearer to panic than she wanted to admit—something that Rag was beginning to feel as well.

Penry spoke up, 'Galad, are you sure this is the right path?'

Galad paused mid-step, said, 'Yes,' and continued walking.

From behind them Van spoke quietly, 'Boyd tell the young miss to take out her torch and shine it at the ceiling.'

'What? Ok... did you hear Mac—shine your torch on the ceiling.'

Mac fumbled in her pocket and brought out her key ring and switched the little torch on—and gasped.

The ceiling gleamed with huge veins of sparkling white quartz shot through with thick bands of gleaming silvery metal...

'See there?' said Van, 'The wyrm decided to go under this shard rather than over—that means the top of this outcrop of hard rock is very near to, or at, the surface. On the other side we will find a tunnel that rises.'

Although he might have had misgivings, Boyd was as anxious as the others for something hopeful. He squeezed Mac's hand, 'See—we will be out of here soon.'

It wasn't quite that straightforward, the passage did begin to rise—then it split into two passage-ways and the one Galad picked then split into another two—both eventually going downwards so he had them retrace their steps to where they could take the other way. Along that path, the floor eventually became slick with water, running down one side of the tunnel. Then turning a long bend they saw a tiny patch of light on the floor ahead of them.

'Sunlight,' gasped Van.

'Come. We're near,' said Galad and hurried forward. Above them was a tapering chimney of rock and high up at the very top was a small, bright, light hole filled by blue sky, but it was near vertical and very narrow.

They all stood beneath it and looked up.

'I... I don't think I can climb that,' Morag said in a very small voice.

'We are near—there will be another. Hopefully, a little easier, but if not... then climb we must,' said Galad.

Privately, Rag thought that even if they had to climb, Galad's shoulders would not fit through that gap!

The tunnel was still rising under their feet, but there was no new chimney. Rag was beginning to despair when Galad suddenly stopped; he held out his arm to hold them back and sniffed the air.

'Hold them Van,' he said and stepped forward quickly. He rounded a barely seen cleft in the tunnel wall and disappeared. Suddenly there was the sharp clatter of rocks slithering and falling—Galad cried out. The glow of his flaming torch disappeared—snuffed out in an instant as his wail still echoed through the tunnel.

The others froze. After a moment that seemed interminable, they heard the alfar's voice, slightly shaky—which was enough to give Van at least pause for thought.

'Come forward—slowly—and be very careful.'

Van came to the front, 'Wait. Let me go first, keep close behind me, but not too close...' he said and edged forward.

Just around the corner was a narrow slippery chasm filled with loose stones and debris that dropped almost vertically into the blackest darkness. On the other side of the vertical split in the rock, Galad was clinging onto the rough stones above a ledge. Above him to his right was a slope of scree... and a hole filled with bracken that turned the dim light shining through it to a soft dappled green.

'This must be the source of the rainwater,' said Galad, his voice firmer now, 'it falls through the gap and straight down...'

Rag shivered at the thought of how far 'straight down' was.

'The rocks are loose. I lost my footing and had to jump, which meant letting the torch go. Hold yours up so I can see the ledge more clearly.'

Van did so, keeping one arm spread out to keep the others from crowding forward. Galad edged from his narrow foothold to the wider ledge beneath the fall of scree. They saw him take a deep breath and exhale when he no longer had to cling to the jagged rock wall.

'What if he'd...' Rag whispered to Boyd.

'Don't! Just... Don't...' Boyd hissed back.

'I'm going to climb up and pull the ferns out to clear a path for more light,' said Galad.

He kicked into the scree with each footstep and made sure each handhold was secure before he climbed the short distance to the top—for a moment his body blocked the light, then he turned to snatch away the greenery and they could all clearly see the sky.

Van breathed a sigh of relief, 'We can all do this,' he said, 'we need to make a rope, the blankets will do. We tear one and plait the strips.'

'Will that hold us?' Mac sounded doubtful.

'It is only a safety measure, lass, that gap is easy enough to jump,' Van said with more confidence than he felt.

Meanwhile, Galad was tearing back the undergrowth until a larger hole was exposed, allowing more light in. He appeared at the top of the scree and called down. 'Van, take off your harness and belt and we'll link them together to make a safety line.'

'We're already seeing about plaiting a blanket into rope.'

'Good thought, but still give me your leather so I can tether myself,' called back Galad. 'There's a tree root out here that will hold.'

'Here, take this,' Van gave his torch to Boyd, but it flared wildly in the breeze from the outside and nearly set his hair alight.

'Throw it away, Boyd,' called Galad, 'you do not need it now.'

Boyd swallowed took a step forward and dropped the torch down into the blackness of the chasm—then wished he hadn't. The flaming torch kept dropping and dropping and getting smaller and smaller until it was a tiny spark when it vanished.

'Oh...' said Boyd out loud.

'Don't look. That is not the way you're going,' said Van. 'Here, help me tear the blanket. Penry—can you make a plait?'

'Not I', said Penry.

'I can,' said Mac.

'Good and tight?' said Van.

Mac nodded several times. At least she knew she could do that properly.

One at a time, with much trepidation, and the loop of plaited rope around their waist held by Van, they stood on the rim of loose stones and looked across at the arms of Galad reaching out to them after he'd tethered himself to the stout tree root...

They all successfully made the leap across that narrow, but terrifying chasm. The loose stones beneath their feet clattered and echoed as they fell into the blackness below... but they helped each other scramble up the scree and out into the light. Last to cross was Van, who paused and looked down. The black abyss below caught at his mind and wouldn't let go. Van froze, unable to move; he was mesmerised by the darkness.

'Come, leap and I will catch you,' said Galad.

'I can jump on my own!'

'I dare say, but a helping hand does not go amiss... tie that rope around your waist and throw me the end first.' replied Galad patiently.

'I...I...,' began Van, but he tied the rope around himself and tossed the other end to the alfar who wound it securely around his arm. The broon took a deep breath, but still hesitated.

'I will not fail you,' Galad said softly.

Van shouted aloud, a roaring battle-cry and launched himself over the terrifying gap. He was caught by Galad, who immediately boosted him up the slope and out into the light.

The sun was low in the sky now. It was clear they must have walked for miles and the day was all but over, and they were nowhere near the river and their passage south. But all of them took the first few moment of being outside to lie on their backs on the grass and drink in the darkening blue above them and the light... the glorious light.

ς

CHAPTER EIGHTEEN

Eventually Galad stood up and stared out at the landscape, turning on his heel in a slow circle to try and find something he knew as a waymark. Eventually he spotted a long straight line of trees snaking off into the distance. 'There! I think that must the Old Road.'

Van frowned, 'The Fosse Hurnt—if it is, we are far to the east of where we should be.'

Galad shrugged, 'If change plans we must—we can follow the road, and we should come to Markethtrave. It's a large enough town, there should be ponies for hire. Or we might find a carter to take us to Imolquay.'

'That must be 50 miles!' Van exclaimed.

'True, too far to walk from here, but if we can get a ride to there it is some 25 miles further on to the Great Tor—that we can walk in a day if we start early.'

'75 miles...' muttered Boyd.

'75 miles!' said Rag.

'Beyond Imolquay we may be able to contact the fairs of the High Court. If we can... and they agree to escort us down their hidden roads we will get there in time.'

'We have to get there at the right time,' said Penry.

'I cannot guarantee it... but in another day or two I will have recovered fully and be able to cut the Veil myself without coming to harm.'

'You are my gard to do as you must!' Penry said softly.

Galad looked at him without speaking.

'But does that mean I'm not going to get free. I miss my trip... and I can't go to Paris?' said Mac.

Galad shrugged his shoulders.

'I blame you for this!' Mac said, poking Penry in the chest hard, before flouncing off a few steps and standing with her back to the others, arms folded and fuming at yet more problems turning up.

Boyd went over and tried to decide should he put his arm around her. He waivered, then just put a hand on her shoulder. 'Don't worry, we can do this,' he said, trying to sound confident. 'We can get you home.'

They headed down the long slope of the hill towards the line of trees lining the Fosse Hurnt, which ran in a near straight line off towards the south-west—and straight towards the lowering rainclouds that were gathering in the western sky, now heading rapidly towards them on a stiffening breeze.

It wasn't long before the rain started. It poured from the sky, not so much in drops, but as stinging rods of cold water that soaked their clothes and hammered into their skin, stinging their faces and eyes so they could barely see. Galad's leather coat was the only thing that didn't seem to get soaked; the rain hung on its dark green surface in glistening droplets before falling clean away.

First Mac fell over, then Rag slid to the ground on the slick grass as they stumbled down the hillside.

'We can't carry on,' shouted Van into the wind, 'one of them will break a leg at this rate!'

Galad nodded; he had had the hood of his coat up, but it kept blowing back and long locks of white hair were plastered across his face by the wind and rain. The youngsters had on light summer clothes and hoodies and were drenched. Penry's dark hair was slick to his skull, glistening with rain; he was shivering as he reached to pull at Galad's sleeve. 'We need to find shelter.'

Galad nodded, 'Get your blankets out and hold them over you—go in pairs—Master Penry go with Miss Mac, and Boyd help shield your sister.'

'What about you two?' said Boyd, realising they only had two blankets left.

'We will manage,' said Van,' but we need to get out of this weather.'

'This way, said Galad shrugging his hood up again. He set off at an angle to their original path. 'We can shelter under those trees for a while and see if the rain eases a little and then make for Rosstrave, it's nearer.'

He trudged away, and the others followed in a bedraggled group, stumbling in the coarse grass, towards a spinney crowded with trees below a small hill. Once there, they pressed back against the tree trunks to take advantage of the drier ground, sheltered by the thick canopy of leaves overhead.

'These trees... they are 'good' trees—aren't they?' Mac said doubtfully, looking around her.

'Yes,' said Penry, 'these trees are just trees. Come and sit down, we may as well get off our feet for a short while.'

Mac sat down close to Penry, not that she wanted to, but at least his arm felt a tiny bit warmer against her side. She touched her bedraggled hair—it was soaked through. She heaved a sigh ...this was not going to be a good look when it dried.

Boyd shook some of the water off his blanket and sat down at her other side. 'Come on Rag, we may as well take a break.'

His sister sat beside him and he draped the blanket over their drawn up knees. 'It won't do much, but it'll give us some warmth.'

Rag's hair was as dark as tarnished copper now and clung to her head; she shivered and gave a nod, pulling the near-sodden blanket up to her chin.

Galad tossed his wet hair back from his face, but strands of it clung stubbornly and he had to claw them away with his fingers. Van leaned against a tree at his side and let his hair drip around his shoulders.

'If Rosstrave is nearer,' he said quietly, 'Why did we not go straight there?'

Galad wiped his face with his sleeve and sniffed. 'Rosstrave is a small place, and the people there look on strangers as targets to fleece of their money—and that's at best. If we are to hire ponies there it may well cost us dearly... that's if there's any to be had.'

Galad looked down at his wet muddy boots and sank to the ground, finding a prominent root to use as a stool. He pulled them off; revealing ornately patterned knitted socks that were damp and muddy where earth had fallen inside his boots. He flexed his toes and sighed with relief, before digging into his pack and producing another pair of similar woollen socks patterned by bands of complicated checks and zig-zags in several complimentary muted colours. He was unconcerned by his audience, but both Rag and Boyd, and Mac watched him intently. Eventually Mac said, 'I like your socks, where do you buy them?'

Galad grunted, having found a hole in the heel of the sock he'd just removed, then replied, 'I do not buy them. I knit them.'

'I've got some cardigans at home knitted like that, so has Boyd, at least he has jumpers and stuff—have you got socks as well Boyd?'

Boyd shook his head.

Galad wiped his pale grimy feet, drying them off the best he could. 'I dare say your uncle's broons would knit you some if you expressed a wish for them,' he said, replacing his old socks with fresh, dry ones.

'But you have to knit your own?' Mac asked, 'That's cool, a man knitting—my grandma is the only person I know that still knits.'

Galad gave a small snort of laughter, 'And you think it unmanly to knit?'

'Well... not as such...' said Mac embarrassed to appear sexist.

'Van—can you knit your own socks?' said Galad with an impish smile, 'And what about your brothers?'

Van looked down at the alfar's socks before looking at the youngsters, 'Aye, we can all knit—but not such a bonnie pair as those. Russ is the best amongst us.'

'Russ knits! Really?' said Rag.

Van looked stung, 'And why shouldn't he?' he said with a touch of irritation.

'Oh I didn't mean it like that,' said Rag quickly, 'I just meant... I... hadn't thought of them as... knitting.' Her voice faded to silence.

'She just means she hadn't thought,' muttered Boyd.

Galad stretched his feet out and wriggled his now dry toes before reaching to wipe some of the mud off his boots before putting them back on. He stood up and stamped his boots back into place. 'Here's a lesson for you young Boyd—always look after your feet...'

'...you won't get far without them!' Galad and Van said in unison.

Galad laughed, 'It sounds like we had the same lessons drilled into us,' he said, sitting down again.

'Aye, that may well be true,' Van agreed gruffly.

'What about you Penry?' Mac turned to him, 'Do you knit?'

'The household broons do that,' he said, 'my father has his sons learn different lessons, such as fencing and archery, games of skill and chance, like chess and backgammon... and how to make music.' He looked at Rag and smiled, 'I like to play for my friends.'

'My brother is good at backgammon, and chess,' said Rag leaning forward eagerly.

'Rag!—I am ok, but I'm still learning,' said Boyd.

'But you do not knit?' Galad said to Boyd, still amused.

'I—I could ask for lessons...' said Boyd, 'But those do look complicated.'

Galad laughed ruefully, 'It's taken me more years than I care to think about to learn the skill of knitting with five needles to make one of these,' he said stuffing the damp socks into his pack, 'But what else is there to do sitting at a campfire by yourself? And it will take me a good week of evenings' work to replace the holed one—so when I have the occasion for some quiet time I'll darn it.'

'We have been taught about sewing and darning,' said Rag.

'Sensible,' replied Galad, 'you need to be able to mend your own gear. Not all are blessed with a household to see to their needs, are they Master Penry?'

Penry sniffed, 'I don't see why you pick me out—I am fortunate that is all.'

Galad snorted, and stared out into the slackening rain, 'Fortunate!' he muttered under his breath. Though only Van heard him, and the bitterness there in that single word... let the broon understand something about the alfar he hadn't thought to find.

They waited for half an hour and the rain eased to a soft drizzle that landed in droplets and stayed on their hair and clothes like tiny glistening gems in the failing afternoon light. Galad chivvied them from under the trees and they started out, soon finding a cart track that guided them, but was now so filled with mud, they couldn't walk on it, though it pointed out their path towards the small market town. Galad warned them to wrap the damp blankets around them when they got there, to disguise their strange clothing, and to let him do the talking. Penry opened his mouth to disagree, but Mac gave him a fierce look that made him change his mind and keep quiet.

The rain had stopped by the time they could see red tile roofs some way ahead of them. Then they came upon another group of travellers standing at the side of the road with a considerable number of tethered ponies. A couple of the travellers were crouching as they sorted some packs and re-loaded them, while the others stripped the metal bits and bridles from the horses; quickly dropping them to the grass and replacing them with bit-less ones of knotted cord and leather. Muffled up in dark heavy cloaks, their faces were hidden... but they did have a number of unridden, unsaddled horses that might be available by the look of it.

Galad put his arm out, to call a halt; one of the travellers had spotted them and nudged his neighbour to turn around.

All these folk had very pale skin and sharp features; they were dressed in dark greys, blacks and purples...

'They're fairs,' muttered Galad, 'Unseelie by the look—stay back and let me speak with them. I hope I can buy some of those ponies. But if I shout—you run.'

He walked forward holding his hands out from his sides.

'Run where?' Rag whispered to Boyd.

'Anywhere away from here—but stay together!' said Van. He stood seemingly at ease, but Rag noticed his hand rested on the hilt of his knife.

As Galad approached them the Unseelie Fair Folk drifted to form a loose semi-circle facing the tall alfar. Beyond them, Rag could see a set of drunken standing stones, some leaning against each other; a couple fallen to the ground. The stones were at least as tall as Galad, but rough-hewn, or disfigured where long shards of blue-grey rock had cleaved away and fallen ages ago, and were now half buried in the earth. Galad was pointing at the ponies, and Rag saw the fairs exchange smiles with each other—smiles she wasn't sure could be trusted.

Mac, standing beside her, obviously thought the same, 'I don't think I like them,' she muttered, 'they look like they put make-up on to play Hallowe'en vampires and never took it off!'

With their hoods pushed back and in the still bright, evening light, Rag could see what Mac meant. The fairs deathly pale skin had dark purplish shadows around their eyes and shading their sharp cheekbones, and their lips were a dark shade of lavender. Their hair was very distinctive, either pure white with prominent black streaks, or the reverse; only a couple had all white or all black hair.

'The colour comes from having blue blood,' murmured Penry.

'What—like royalty?' said Mac.

Penry shook his head, 'No that's just a saying. Fairs literally have blue blood.'

Boyd touched his arm, 'Look—Galad wants us.' The alfar had turned towards them and raised one arm, hand up, but he only beckoned by twitching his fingers.

'He wants us to be cautious,' said Van. 'Let me go first, you stay behind... and walk slowly. Give yourself space to run down into the town.'

'What do we do there?' said Boyd,

'Hope that it's me running behind you!' muttered Van.

He walked forward head high, but kept one hand hovering around the hilt of his knife. The youngsters huddled together and walked a few paces behind him.

'See?' Galad said, 'we are just travellers caught in the storm.'

And they were a pretty bedraggled bunch with wet hair, mud and damp-stained clothing and shoes.

The fairs eyed them up dispassionately, before the one who seemed to be their leader spoke.

'And you would have us help you?'

'No! ...No, we seek to purchase some ponies—so we can make up for lost time. We would not abuse your hospitality by boldly asking for aid without payment.' Galad gave the watching fairs a big open smile, 'Would we?' He had turned to the youngsters and raised his eyebrows while nodding to show they should agree with him.

'Of course not... No, no... Happy to pay... Yep, absolutely...' They murmured in unison, only Van remained silent.

The leader noticed, 'And your broon agrees?' he said.

'Vandyke!' Galad said shooting him an urgent look.

Van set his jaw and kept his silence, but gave the slightest of bows.

'Then we can come to an agreement.' The leader said with a big smile—that to Rag's surprise revealed surprisingly sharp teeth.

Just then they heard a commotion of shouts and the thuds of many running feet coming down the road from the town.

The leader's head whipped around and he frowned and snapped his fingers at his companions. Immediately they began to gather their packs and grab the tethers of the ponies and trot towards the centre of the stone circle.

'You will honour us by accompanying us,' said the leader with a deep bow towards Galad.

'That's gracious, Ser, but why should that be?' Galad replied.

'We might discuss this, but let me invite you all first...' He swept his arm out indicating the stone circle—the air in the middle of which had begun to shimmer.

'And...? You offer this favour freely and without compunction?'

A long-shafted arrow whistled through the air and landed in the grass nearby—followed by another—and another...

'Yes, yes, Master Alfar—come now! Those townsfolk will not be choosy who they aim at!'

Van swiftly drew his knife. The blade flashed as it sliced an arrow from the air before it hit Boyd's shoulder.

'I think we must, lord,' he growled.

The first of the fairs and ponies were disappearing into the swirling vortex of air and vanishing through the shimmering pillars.

'Quickly now,' called Galad, 'hold onto each other and stay together!'

He grabbed hold of Penry by the arm and sprinted forward towards the unsettled air. Mac was dragged behind, and Boyd seized both her hand and Morag's and ran with her. Van was at their back as the last of the fairs and ponies ran through the diminishing ellipse of disturbed air—which abruptly stilled behind them as they vanished.

In the rough field the mob of angry townsfolk arrived, shouting and cursing the 'thieving fairs' who had 'stolen' their ponies. They came to a ragged halt as they saw the stone circle was empty. A few hacked at the remaining upright stones in fury, but their dull blades rang against the rock and they only succeeded in notching the weapons' edge.

Men who had brought ropes with them shouted instruction, along with vicious snarls and curses aimed at the departed fairs, and tossed loops about the stones—organising others to help them pull the standing stones down. They failed. They loosened one, but it lurched sideways against its neighbour and remained upright but at a slant. Their ropes broke and their fury gradually cooled to dull embers and dark mutterings, before they slouched back towards the town vowing, 'never to trust those damned fairs again!'

ʅ

CHAPTER NINETEEN

Boyd could feel his legs were running but he couldn't feel ground under his feet. His hand had a firm grip on Rag's hand and Mac's in his other, and he could feel a slight tugging on his back pack that he knew must be Van holding onto him. The dank air around them shivered in flashing waves that made his ears sing, seemingly under the changing pressure. Although the shadowy light flickered, there remained a near constant gleam around them, until suddenly they were out into bright evening air. He looked around; they were high on a flat-topped hill and appeared to have come out from under the immense arch formed by a huge dolmen of worked stone. The fairs were gathering their pony tethers and settling the nervous horses who showed the whites of their eyes in fear.

Boyd was aware of Van standing very close to his back; he felt the broon's warm breath on his neck as he whispered, 'Careful, Boyd. Keep your sister and the mortal girl close. These fairs are tricksters—we don't know yet if we are safe.'

Boyd nodded his head slowly and kept a firm grip on the girls' hands.

'I'm ok, Boyd, let go,' said his sister.

'Not yet,' he mumbled.

'Bo-yd!' She tried to tug her hand loose. Van put his hand on her arm. 'Stay with your brother—and keep behind me.' He stepped in front of them. Mac appeared to be in shock, 'Whaaaaaat...' was all she could manage.

Boyd pulled her hand to him, 'We're ok Mac, it was just...' well he wasn't sure what it was, 'It was just...'

'A vortex,' said Penry, pulling his sleeve free of Galad's grip. 'My father's... clansmen...' He thought it best not to say warriors, '...They have the means to be able to use them occasionally to move around.'

'What...!' began Mac, 'If you can do that, why are we walking to freaking Glastonbury??'

Penry held his hands palm up as if to deflect her anger. 'They can to some extent, with help... but I cannot. Galad will see us safely off with ponies to ride the rest of the way—I'm sure of it.' He smiled encouragingly, and Mac let her question pass.

Ahead of them, the fairs having settled their horses were preparing to camp.

Penry frowned, 'No, no... we need to go on. Galad tell them.'

'Master Penry—keep your mouth shut and your complaints to yourself!' hissed Galad, before he turned with a stiff smile to the approaching fair.

Boyd saw the satisfied grin on Van's face as he watched that exchange, before the broon quickly concealed it behind the neutral mask of a loyal retainer.

Galad began, 'Ser—you have fulfilled your generous offer of help. Now if we can discuss the price of the ponies...'

'Soon Master Alfar, soon... will you not refresh yourselves with us for a short while and eat?' Galad hesitated, 'I swear to you that you and yours will come to no harm from me as you eat and drink with us.' The fair spoke solemnly with one hand over his heart as he gave a small bow.

'Aye and what about the others?' muttered Van under his breath. Boyd thought he had been the only one to hear, but the fair's leader quickly turned his face to Van with a disdainful look, 'We are true to our word.' The fair paused,' Do you doubt us?'

It was said sweetly enough, but Boyd could hear the challenge behind the words. Van met the fair's eyes and acquiesced with a curt nod. Seemingly satisfied, the fair gave another of those alarming smiles showing his very white and pointed teeth.

'You are welcome then to our fireside.'

He moved away from them so smoothly... it was almost like he was on wheels! thought Boyd.

Rag tugged her hand free, but Mac still held on; Boyd gave her hand a small squeeze and released it. Penry walked forward, a step behind Galad; this pulled Mac forward as well. The fair leader stared at them, and pointed a long slim finger. 'You are bound to the mannish child, young master.'

'How do you know...'said Penry.

The Unseelie fair shrugged, 'I see the cord—we all can.'

The fairs nearest paused to glance up and nod, before resuming their tasks of building a fire and producing wrappers of food from their packs. Penry opened his mouth to speak, but closed it again when he saw Galad give him a warning look.

The sight of the bread and dried fruits reminded Boyd that they hadn't eaten since the few bits of left-over breakfast they'd had in the cavern. At his side, Rag's stomach rumbled softly—evidently she thought the same. He looked at her; she was eying the bread with hungry looks.

Galad had been surveying the hilltop and the pack of tethered ponies. He brought his attention back to the fairs, 'Ser—if we might use the old wood hereabouts we can build our own fire, rather than crowd you away from yours.'

The fair's face fell momentarily before he gracefully swept a hand towards the scrub and trees behind the dolmen with a smile. 'You may, Master Alfar. You are my guests.'

Galad bowed his head, and pulled at Penry's arm, 'Take Boyd and forage for some bits of wood, the driest you can find.'

'But...' began Penry.

'I would stay between you and the fairs—as your father would wish of me.' Galad spoke softly and Penry sullenly did as he was asked. And because Penry and Boyd walked away, Mac was compelled to follow, leaving Rag standing with Van in front of her. He turned to face her. 'Miss Morag—now would be as good a time as any to put your fire skills to use.'

He spoke quietly, with a hint of command in his voice that made Rag frown. She was about to open her mouth when Galad spoke, 'It is a better idea that we have our own hearth...'

Morag caught on to his thought. 'Rather than share theirs?' she said.

'That would be correct—let us just smile and nod, because it is not a good idea to be beholden to fairs—especially Unseelie, even if they are at the nadir of their power.'

Rag nodded, unslung her back pack and knelt down on the damp blanket she still had under one arm. She fished out her strike-a-light, and paused...

'I don't have any dry kindling.'

Van rummaged under his leather jerkin, where there was obviously a pocket; he pulled out his shorn off plait of hair.

'Here, lass—burn this.' He thrust it at her. She didn't offer to take it, so Galad reached for it and handed it over,

'It would be a good idea to burn this, before they,' he jerked his head towards the fairs, '...have an eye for it. Such a thing could give them a hold over him.'

Rag's lips formed an 'ooo' of understanding and she opened her tin. 'Won't it smell nasty?' she said, looking up at them as they stood over her.

Galad shrugged, 'It needs to burn and we need to have a fire to dry off our clothes and warm ourselves.'

Boyd came back with an armful of dried brush and twigs and Penry and Mac carried a small dead branch between them. Rag struck sparks and the plaited hair smouldered sufficiently for her to feed it small twigs and get the flames to burn. To her surprise, it didn't smell that bad—a bit resinous, not really like human hair, she thought ...but then, why should it?

Any further thoughts quickly drifted away because just then two fairs came over with some wraps of bread and strips of dried meat.

'Let me offer you silver for your generosity—so I might contribute to your expedition's costs,' said Galad swiftly pressing a coin into one's hand before they could refuse. They looked slightly crestfallen, but smiled and walked away.

Galad turned to the others ranging themselves around the small fire, 'We need to be careful. We do not want to give offence, but neither should we become beholden to them. A favour they give will always demand a favour returned—and that cost may be more than we want to spend!'

It was getting later in the evening and the summer sun-set was off to their right-hand side. Ahead of them to the south-west the land fell away, undulating down to the Great Plain that became misty blue in the distance.

The fairs began to drift over towards them to stand just outside the ring of firelight. The leader approached, 'May I sit with you while we discuss your wish to purchase our ponies?' he said courteously.'

'You are welcome, Ser.' said Galad, equally formally, 'We thank you for selling us food. As you can see, we were not planning on traveling this way.'

The fair nodded, and settled down gracefully, to sit with his legs crossed at the edge of the firelight; another two fairs sat down behind him. One of them passed him a wineskin, 'Will you allow me to offer you refreshment? Freely given,' he said.

Galad smiled graciously, 'I am their gard and I must keep a clear head.'

'And the broon?'

'He also has gardship duties to perform.'

The fair nodded and handed the wineskin back to his fellow.

'We do not see many of your kind crossing this way,' he began, 'what brings you?'

'We are going to Droith...' Penry broke off as Galad kicked his foot.

'To Droithglarma...' continued the fair, 'To the Great Tor?'

'We have a small task to fulfil there, said Galad, 'to break the bind between these two.'

The fair nodded sagely, 'Yes, as I said, we can see the silver cord running between them...'

'Really?' Rag blurted out, 'You can all see it?'

The fair turned to her with that unnerving smile, 'We can—joined heart and bone with a glamourie made from Stone. We see it as easily as we see glimpses of your flames and your brother's bright water.'

'How...?' she began before Boyd stared at her with a ferocious look, that brought her to silence.

The fair raised his arched eyebrows even higher, then smiled, 'We of the Fair Folk can always see the deva-light around everything, as much as we see rocks, trees, and sky. It means we can assess our friends from our foes...'

Van looked sceptical, and the fair turned to him, 'I see the sheen of your inherited purple... even if others cannot...'

He turned to face Penry with a smile. Penry looked confused and bowed his head to look at a loose thread on his jacket he suddenly found fascinating.

'So—what am I then?' said Mac.

The fair smoothly turned his attention to her, 'Why earth of course—with some air. As all mannish are. When we trade with the townsfolk we are almost overcome with their drab earth—we know them well enough to know they would cheat us if they could—so we must make our play first.'

He looked around at the other fairs for agreement. They all grinned, showing their teeth—like a pack of hyenas, Rag thought uncomfortably.

'Surely not everybody is out to... trick you,' said Penry.

'We do allow some to cross our realm freely. There's the Salt Woman, she trades with our Queen's permission—she and her crew may travel...'

'The Salt Woman? Melleth? We know her! Don't we Boyd? We met her in the north a few months ago.' Rag blurted this out, and earned a scowl from her brother.

'Indeed... She will be travelling south again soon. She'll take ship from the High Queen's port before the autumn storms prevent her leaving.'

'You and your brother know her?' said Galad with a frown.

'We—have met her—briefly,' said Boyd, 'I wouldn't say we know her...'

180

'But she told you all about...' began Rag.

'She was kind enough to make us tea,' said Boyd, self-consciously pulling his sleeve down, even though his drag-on-blessed gold bracelet was tucked well out of sight. He glared at Rag, who sullenly took the hint and shut up.

'She travels far,' the fair said mildly. 'Now her deva is somewhat more akin to yours, Alfar, and the princeling's, and...' he turned to face Van and gave a conspiratorial smirk that made the broon look away, and continued, 'Than to more ordinary... travellers.'

Mac scowled, she wasn't sure she wanted be dismissed as 'ordinary'... but then... everything here was so weird maybe ordinary was good?

Boyd could see her discomfort and he reached out surreptitiously to squeeze her hand. A movement not lost on Van.

'Well,' said Galad, 'this discourse has been fascinating, but shall we begin talking about buying the ponies and then we can be on our way?'

The fair nodded—and all of a sudden all four of the youngsters found themselves encircled with fine black ropes, thrown over their heads by fairs who had crept up behind them, almost invisible in the shadows cast by the flickering fire. The ropes were pulled tight. Galad leapt to his feet, his knives drawn, as did Van, but the fairs had long, dark, knapped-flint blades at each of the youngsters' throats.

Boyd tried to struggle away and the razor-sharp serrated knife was pressed hard enough to nick his skin... a thin, beaded line of blood glistened like tiny rubies at his throat, and rolled down his neck.

'Hold!' shouted Galad, flipping around the knives in his hands to point downwards. Van froze in the act of striking the fair's leader. The broon's teeth were bared in a fearsome grimace of anger and he did not relax his grip on his blade.

'Vandyke... Stand down,' said Galad calmly. Two fairs came to the alfar's side and went to take his knives, hissing as they brushed against the metal blades; they found some hide and wrapped them. One reached to take the spiral dagger at his side. Galad snarled, making the fair step back. 'Touch that and die,' the alfar spat out.

The leader waved a graceful hand and the fair stepped back.

'Know if you attempt to take a life, they will lose their lives—and it will be slow. Each time you misstep I will take a piece of them, an ear, a finger, a hand... Do we understand each other?'

Galad dropped his hands to his side. More waiting fairs disarmed Van, taking his already drawn knife from him... and a surprising number of smaller, concealed weapons.

'Galad! Do something!' shouted Penry.

The fair behind him cuffed him smartly across the side of his head.

'Young Master Alfar—your gard knows how to keep you alive. You should trust him to do that. But now—we must return to our Queen at the Henge of Clauhemine. There you can ask for her permission to cross our realm—she may even agree to break your charm of binding,' he turned to Galad with a smooth smile, '...a misstep on your part I dare say.'

'Oh no,' said Galad bitterly, 'he created that one all by himself!'

ς

CHAPTER TWENTY

The fairs bundled them onto the backs of the stolen ponies, and although the fairs had put plaited leather and looped rope bridles on the horses there were no saddles. Penry and Mac rode together. Rag and Boyd rode a pony each; all of them had a mounted fair at their side holding the ropes still around the youngsters' necks. Galad and Van also rode with an escort on each side of them. Because of the young ones inexperience in riding bareback with a bit-less bridle, their progress was delayed and it took them several hours to ride down to and across the plain. Even though on two occasions, the fairs were able to conjure the hidden road of a vortex to transport them all closer to the Unseelie Queen's court, their progress was slow.

'Our apologies,' said their leader mockingly, 'but we are only able to use those roads wide enough whereby we can travel with ponies.'

'Then why can't you let us travel the narrow roads without them?' snapped Penry, who was finding the long ride increasingly uncomfortable.

The fair riding beside him hissed at Penry, 'We do not know that you are worth leaving the ponies behind for, svart!'

'What did he just call you?' whispered Mac.

'No matter,' muttered Penry.

It was nearly four hours later that they entered the final circle of huge standing stones, and emerged into a great space of worked rock lit by floating globes of pale light.

'Behold Clauhemine!' said the fair's leader with an expansive flourish. 'Get them down,' he commanded the others; who caught the youngsters as they almost fell off the ponies. Even Galad and Van dismounted stiffly, having to stretch their aching legs and backs to relieve the cramps in their muscles from guiding their saddleless mounts. The fairs took the ponies away through a wide archway that seemed to lead outside again into a wooded glade, leaving the prisoners with a fair guard each, while others carried their back-packs for them.

Rag looked around her; they were in a huge seemingly round hall that was circled with massive stone pillars supporting... but when she looked up she wasn't sure if she saw an immensely high roof to a cavern or a starry night sky, or a distant ceiling painted with glittering stars... it was too far above and shadowy to tell. There was a strange sense of unreality, but she wasn't sure if it was just her who thought so... then she saw Boyd and Mac's faces and the looks of surprise and doubt and realised they were seeing the same strangeness.

Their guards pushed them forward towards the centre of the encircling stones, and then stood back. They found themselves among an inner circle of monoliths they somehow hadn't seen before—then suddenly, a retinue of fairs appeared out of the stones, as if the rocks were merely doorways...

These fairs were more lavishly dressed than the ones that had brought them here; their grey clothes weren't so much weathered rock as polished stone veined with silver. They wore dark jewels of glittering black, and had purple and jet embroidery on their sable trimmed, slate-grey clothing. Two warriors clad in leather plate armour, holding up glaives with wickedly sharp honed flint blades, entered side by side—they parted to reveal their queen.

The Unseelie Queen's pure white hair was elaborately plaited and held in place by tiny bone-white hairpins tipped with gold. Her long dark gown slithered along the floor behind her, shimmering with glittering embroidery, and her short cloak was made of white fox-fur. All the fairs' faces were the now familiar pale, pale lilac white, but her eyes were encircled with painted, glistening purple shadows that lifted to her temples with exquisite grace; the hollows of her cheeks and her lips were similarly shaded... at least Rag assumed it was make-up. The Queen was beautiful... mesmerising, in a hard, strange way.

Two of the guarding fairs kicked both Galad and Van hard behind their knees to force them to kneel. The others dragged at the ropes around the youngsters necks, hauling them down. The Queen laughed—a sound like tinkling ice floes on a winter river.

'No, no, let them rise—these are not prisoners, but my guests—are you not? Travellers seeking permission to cross this realm... Is that not correct?'

Galad rose to his feet stiffly and bowed, one hand to his chest, 'My Lady.'

Van shrugged off the hand of the fair holding him and gave a curt little bow.

'Ser Alfar, you may introduce your companions...' said the Queen.

'Majesty, this is Lord Penry, son of...'

'I recognise whose son he is,' said the Queen sharply, 'and who are these creatures?'

'They are the wards of the Liosalfar of the Northern Enclave...' said Galad, careful not to lie, but tacitly including Mac.

'All three—he gathers them busily these days... and that is his broon?'

'Yes, majesty—he is their gard.'

The Unseelie Queen nodded thoughtfully, and then smiled her brilliant but unnerving smile, 'Come—let me entertain you, and while you take your ease you may tell me your tale.' She snapped her fingers. Their original guards faded back into the shadows as the Queen's retinue arranged themselves into an honour guard that surrounded her reluctant visitors. She turned in a swirl of glittering blacks and greys and headed back through the doorway, through the upright stone that now opened into a long corridor of smoothed dark rock.

Galad led the way. Mac quietly reached out to hold Boyd's hand as they were marched away. Penry was directly behind her and held up his palm for Morag to take, as if he was escorting her to a formal ball. He smiled at her and winked, 'We will be fine,' he whispered as she took his hand.

Van followed behind them, his eyes missing nothing as the retinue of fairs closed in on either side.

Shortly afterwards they turned into another hall and walked through the encircling pillars to enter a suite of rooms that evidently belonged to the Queen. The retinue fell away as they walked in, and the carved doors were closed behind them. The room was a long oval and the stone floor was carpeted with rugs, both of embroidered and tufted wool and raw sheepskins. There were benches with woven cushions, on which were placed their back-packs, evidently brought here ahead of them. To the other side was a large table surrounded by high-backed chairs of carved, black bog-wood. The wide table held dishes of fruit, glaze-crusted breads, potted meats and fish, and a large haunch of steaming roasted meat on a great wooden platter surrounded by baked vegetables. On a sideboard was a display of cakes gleaming with sugar crystals; there were clear jellies moulded in fanciful shapes, and decorated biscuits—it all looked sumptuous. Van leant forward and whispered in Rag's ear, '...not a mouthful, not a crumb, whatever you are offered—refuse!'

Rag frowned, but nodded, taking her hand away from Penry.

'Your broon offers good advice,' murmured Penry. 'Not until we have made a deal can we accept the fairs' hospitality.'

He smiled, stepped forward and bowed to the Queen; she graciously acknowledged him with a nod. Two male servants entered from a small side-door holding long-necked silver jugs, another followed with a tray of crystal goblets.

'To begin, may I offer you freely and without reserve, water from my well to quench your thirst,' she said, 'this I do without desire to harm or hinder and with no expectation of reward.'

They all looked at Galad. He hesitated for a second, then smiled and bowed his head in agreement. 'We thank your majesty for her grace and favour, and accept without prejudice what is freely given.'

The Queen looked delighted and waved her servants forward to pour goblets of spring water.

'Take off your coats and sit with ease—See? I have even had my wardens return your weapons to your packs, so that we cannot be accused of stealing from you. Though, of course, we would wish you to leave them there, wrapped and secure, until you are released upon your way...' She smiled graciously with a wave of her hand indicating their property.

The youngsters were led to the benches and invited to sit while Galad stood with the Queen and slowly took off his coat. Van quietly stepped forward and took Galad's coat from him and laid it over their closed packs before stepping back. He stood by the wall, near the doorway they had entered from.

'What was that about,' Mac whispered to Boyd.

'You have to remember the old stories about fairies... fairfolk'

'I don't know any stories about fairies!' muttered Mac.

'What—none?'

'Not my thing. Nearest I came to fairies was Harry Potter, and the Lord of the Rings movies.'

'And Penry,' said Rag with a grin.

'I am not a fair!' said Penry quietly but vehemently.

Boyd ignored Penry and carried on, 'To accept food or drink as a gift of hospitality from a Fairy Queen puts you under her power. That's why there must always be the agreement beforehand that the offer is freely given without expectation of reward. Or you'll have to stay here for ever and ever.'

Rag patted Penry's arm, 'I'm only joking Penry, I know alfar are not the same thing.'

'That's ok then,' he said huffily and sipped his water. He suddenly smiled and took a gulp, 'This tastes wonderful!' he announced to the room.

The Queen turned towards him with a smile, 'I am pleased. This water rises from my own special spring.'

'Drink it,' he urged the others, 'I feel marvellous, all the aches and pains of riding have gone, just like that,' he clicked his fingers, and beamed at them.

Boyd drank cautiously as did Mac and Rag... but it was true; the water as soon as they swallowed it felt as refreshing as a long sleep, a good meal and a soothing shower. They felt so much better almost instantly; it was uncanny.

Rag sipped her water slowly; each drop seemed to wipe away her aches and pains. She turned to Boyd and spoke quietly, 'Do you think we could take some with us? For Dad? It might help him.'

'I don't know if we can—maybe we can ask before we leave.'

'What's that?' Mac asked.

'Our father... isn't well... This is helping us feel better, I wondered if it could help him.'

Penry didn't say anything; he was busy watching Galad and the Queen.

'You have not yet named yourself, Ser,' the Queen said to Galad.

'Majesty, you may call me Galad.'

'Ser Galad, I am happy to make your acquaintance,' she held out her hand and he stooped to kiss it, but barely brushed his lips through the air a fraction above her fingers. She gave a slight frown that had cleared from her face before he stood upright.

'You and you companions are my guests.'

'Not your prisoners?'

'No, no—Ser Alfar. My boundary wardens are always very careful and they have strict orders to bring all before me, save those I already know.'

'Like the Salt Woman?'

'Her, and others I have already met and with whom agreements have been made,' said the Queen vaguely. 'But you are simply travellers, are you not?'

189

'My gardship takes me to the Summer Queen's Court. We have a need to be at the Great Tor by dawn at Midsummer. We hope to request that she will sever the binding charm between the princeling and the mannish child.'

'Of course we can help you reach The Tor. I am sure our Sister-Queen will be pleased to accept our guests—and listen to your request. In the meantime... you are a champion for hire, are you not?'

Galad nodded his head slowly in acknowledgement.

'And are you willing to listen to my offer?'

'My Lady, my gardship is to Master Penry, his father...'

'His father is no friend to the Courts of the Fair Folk!'

'My Lady...'

'You know that already, Alfar. You know that the High Queen in her Midsummer heights has powers, even over his.'

'I accept her decision, be it to help or hinder, but the Veil must be split to allow the mortal girl to be unbound.'

'And only she will pass?' The Queen was curious.

'My Lady—the boy and girl are Wulfric Kennetson's wards, they come and go as he wills.'

She nodded, '...And yet—you too could sunder the Veil. You have a Unicorn Blade—for that you must once have had great need—to drink a life, eat a still beating heart—that is Dark Magic indeed.'

Galad stiffened; Rag could see him bristle like a scalded cat, his eyes blazing.

'Lady, what I did and why, are secrets that are mine to keep!'

'Peace, Champion,' she said soothingly, 'I do not question, merely enquire if the rumours I have heard about such blades are true.'

She patted his arm. He flinched before he could stop himself. Her lips continued to smile, but her eyes were cold as grey slate cliffs in winter.

Boyd also watched their exchange and he wasn't altogether happy, but didn't know what to do. He suddenly felt his hidden bracelet seem to slip and then tighten its grip on his forearm, almost like a squeeze of reassurance... but he pushed that thought away as too fanciful. He looked towards Van. The broon was standing with his back to a wall; he too was watching Galad and the Queen closely, but Boyd couldn't read Van's face.

The Unseelie Queen clapped her hands for her servants and spread her arm out towards the table, 'Come. Accept my bounty, freely given—as we have agreed.'

The fairs pulled out the tall chairs for them all to sit. The Queen at the head of the table, Galad to her right, Penry to her left, Mac alongside him, and Boyd and Rag opposite.

'You too Master Broon,' she said looking across to Van who was leaning against the door, 'take your place with us,' she pointed to the seat opposite Rag and beside Mac. 'You are also welcome at my table.'

Van hesitated but to refuse would be to insult the Queen, and in the heart of her realm that was too perilous a thing to do. He took his seat at the laden table, and an attendant fair poured more water into a crystal goblet for him.

ς

CHAPTER TWENTY-ONE

They were all hungry, and after some initial wariness helped themselves to the banquet laid out in front of them. Yet more food was brought up by the queen's household and placed on the sideboard, all sorts of spangled and gilded pastries, candied fruits and cakes. The Queen watched her 'guests' and nibbled at her food sparingly; her eyes seemed to miss nothing as in turn each of them felt the weight of her gaze upon them. As they finished the savouries on the table, she called for wine to be served to herself and Galad. She turned towards him to catch his attention, speaking quietly and only to him.

'Ser Galad, you are familiar are you not with the Three Courts?'

Galad sipped his wine cautiously, 'I am, Lady.'

'Then you know how the battles and skirmishes between us cause nothing but irritation all about the realms...' She barely acknowledged his nod of understanding, but continued to outline her plan.

'...therefore—to my way of thinking, if there was but one Queen to hold sway... there could be peace throughout all the lands.'

'If...'

The Queen waved her hand as if dispelling doubts and problems, 'No ifs... I could be that Queen—and you—could be my permanent and only champion. You could have power, prestige, your own Keep here... at Clauhemine... you could belong again.'

Galad became very still, the glass held at his lip. At his side Boyd seemed about to speak, but Galad kicked his foot to keep him quiet. So Boyd stared at his plate and listened intently as the Queen continued.

'I have watched them march across this plain on the other side of the Veil—the warriors with their horse-less carts of metal and their weapons—so fearsome, so deadly. The metal! All that metal! I could exert my glamourie over those mortals and they would become my army, my slaves to despatch where I please to fight for me. All I would need is for you to sunder the Veil and allow me to take command of them... We could even command them together, and with their deadly fire of metal shards... we can defeat my sisters, and bring all to acknowledge me as the one true High Queen... forever!' Her eyes were bright as she finished her speech. The alfar still hadn't moved—then he slowly put down his goblet.

Penry spoke up, oblivious of what was being said, 'Majesty, may we go and select sweets from your table?'

The Queen smiled in his direction without taking her eyes off Galad, and waved her hand. Penry and Mac got up and went over to the sideboard to select their next course of goodies. Galad waited until after they'd left the table before speaking.

'I could not use this blade for that purpose, majesty,' he said quietly.

'Then perhaps you could let me use it...'

Galad shook his head, 'A blade such as this has only one master.'

'No? Then you might show me how to make my own?'

'Never!!'

'Never...? Have a care Ser Alfar... if not for yourself, what of your companions? Do they not deserve long, happy lives... and to eventually leave here... Whole and ...unmarked?'

Galad hands gripped the arms of his chair, before he spoke more loudly, barely keeping his anger under control at her scarcely veiled threats.

'Have a care, lady! They are the beloved of the Northern Lord of the Liosalfar, and here also is the Svart Lord's youngest son...'

At hearing this Van's head whipped around to watch what was unfolding. His jaw dropped when the half-broon heard exactly who Penry really was... and who that meant Penry was to him.

'...If Wulfric Kennetson discovers his own have come to harm by your hand, there will be no place to hide—not underground or over it, nor in the waters, or the airs above!'

The Queen sucked her teeth in exasperation, raised both hands, and turned them in a swift gesture, curling her fingers to fists.

Instantly, the carved arms of the black bog-oak chairs twisted and writhed about Galad's arms holding them fast. More tendrils struck out from the chair-backs to hold Rag and Boyd about the chest, waist and neck, fixing them tightly in place, barely able to breathe, let alone shout out, no matter how hard they struggled. Van slapped his hands flat on the table top and tried to stand—the chair legs wound sinews of tough wood about his calves forcing him back to remain seated, while the table-top itself twisted up to make manacles that fixed his hands in place against the dark wooden surface. As Galad struggled, his legs were also bound fast by the black bog-oak chair, holding him tightly in place.

At the same time, the Queen shot a look over at Penry and Mac, pointed at them with a quick flourish, and they were paralysed where they stood.

The Queen smiled to herself in satisfaction, 'If you will not listen to reason—there are other ways.'

She snapped her fingers and an attendant picked up a carved ivory casket from a side-table and brought it to her; he opened the lid and placed it beside her. Inside where upright rows of spirit needles, long delicately thin steel spines, each one with a little sheath of pale bone encasing one end—so the fairs could hold them safely. The Unseelie Queen picked one out and held it up... thinner than a fine straw, but a finger-length long streak of agony for any fair.

'Pure metal and all the shocking pain that goes with it... I traded many nuggets of gold for these—at least the mannish travelling medico thought they were gold.'

The attendant at her side licked his lips and giggled.

'They tell me it makes the elan vital feel like liquid fire running through your veins, or lightning striking, teasing anguish through your muscles until they spasm in agony...'

She waved the attendant away and stood up. Taking a step nearer the tightly bound alfar, she pushed his sleeve up a fraction and plunged the tip of the needle into the exposed skin of his wrist, leaving it sticking upright in his flesh. Galad cried out, then bit his lip.

Rag and Boyd struggled to shout in protest, but the wooden sinews around their necks choked them into silence. The Queen selected more needles, and circled around him before she jabbed the point of one into Galad's neck. He squirmed and gritted his teeth. Frowning with dissatisfaction, she leant over and pushed another needle slowly into his wrist, then stepped back, straitening up to look Galad in the eye.

'Your times roaming the roads of the mannish and their towns have made the metal seem less harsh for you, Alfar,' she said, 'But we shall see...'

She quickly tore open his jerkin and shirt, exposing his bare chest. And equally swiftly, she stabbed a dozen needles into him leaving each one sitting upright, an inch deep in his muscles... from above his heart, in a line down to his belly. He snarled and writhed in pain, but refused to scream.

Boyd watched in stunned horror as the little bone bead-heads topping each flexible needle bobbed and swayed unevenly as Galad gasped with each ragged breath. Boyd shook his head furiously to try and free himself. He shouted as loud as he could, 'Stop! Stop!!' before the twisting carved bog-oak tightened around his throat and choked back his angry shouts.

Rag was crying and struggling in her seat; she tried to reach out, to shout out loud, but was held tightly by the stern, black bog-wood, unable to break free.

Van roared and raged, shouting blistering words in Gaelic, struggling in vain until the chair creaked with the effort of holding him in place, but the table-top warped further, man-acling his hands even more firmly so he couldn't pull himself free.

The Queen stood back and scowled. 'You are strong, Alfar. You manage your own pain, but can you manage theirs?'

She took a step, pulled back Boyd's sleeve and jabbed a needle into his forearm.

Galad shouted, 'No!'

'Ouch!' yelped Boyd.

She tried again; Boyd winced out loud, but nothing more. He felt his hidden bracelet tighten a little about his other arm, and a strange sort of warmth seemed to spread all through him.

Rag writhed in her chair in fury. 'Not my brother! No!' She shouted, outraged, trembling with anger... the wood of the table directly in front of her began to blister, then smoulder... and the sinews of wood from the chair binding her loosened fractionally with a shiver... and the tiniest trail of smoke.

Frustrated the Queen tried piercing Boyd's arm again, but still he didn't seem overly hurt by something a fair would find agonising. She stood back and collected more needles from her casket.

'So the young wards have no fear of steel—what about you, Broon? Are you immune?'

She strode around the table to face him and stabbed another long needle into the back of Van's hand, leaving it there. He flinched, grimacing with pain, but the wooden manacles held his hands fast. He only shouted out after the fourth one pierced his hand, right through to the table-top.

Mac and Penry couldn't move and could barely speak, but they saw and heard everything. They'd turned around to face the large table at the sound of raised voices and now watched in horror at what the Queen was doing. Penry was slightly behind Mac, he wasn't attempting to try and free himself, but Mac was struggling to reach out her hand. Her backpack was on a bench nearby, and in the top of it was her metal water-bottle...

'Noooo, Mac—don't—do—anything!' whispered Penry with an effort.

Mac was able to move her arm a fraction, but it was such a strain it left beads of sweat forming on her forehead. She concentrated really hard, trying to think of nothing but reaching... out... her... hand...

The Queen had her back to Mac; she leant forward over Van, jabbing more of the seemingly delicate, but lethal steel needles into the back of his hand and wrist. Finally Van screamed aloud as the painful shocks coursing through his fingers and up his arm became too much for him. The Unseelie crowed her success, all her focus on him as she pulled the neck of Van's shirt open and prepared a strike into his chest... Which meant her attention slipped a fraction and her power over Mac dropped away just enough for the girl to move and make a grab for the water bottle.

She broke free, ran across and whacked the Queen over the back of her head with the metal flask. It wasn't heavy enough to do damage, but the metal was enough to cause the fair excruciating pain. She dropped to her knees with a screech like fingernails on a blackboard.

Instantly the bind she held over Rag and Boyd was broken and they leapt free. The arms of the chair Rag was in almost shrivelled back, like a flame applied to green leaves... before they crumbled apart.

Boyd jumped up as his chair relaxed its hold and freed him. He pulled all the needles free from Galad's chest, but the alfar had been painfully injured and at first could only stagger to his feet, one arm leaning on Boyd's shoulder.

Rag dived towards Van as soon as she was freed and pulled the remaining needles from his hand as the table released its grip on his wrists. As the Queen staggered up, Rag plunged one into her arm. The Unseelie screamed and reeled away from the girl.

'Grab what you can to defend yourself,' shouted Van, picking up two of the fallen needles by the beaded ends in one fist and clumsily grabbing a silver jug from the table with his injured hand.

One of the Queen's attendants, summoned by the screaming, ran into the room. Mac whirled around and lashed out with the metal water bottle she still had a firm grip on. The fair wailed as it hit him on his out-stretched arm, and recoiled from her. Another two ran at Galad—Boyd threw a handful of needles at them. They didn't stick in the fairs, but the savage sting of the naked metal even hitting their skin made them wail and cringe back. Galad pushed himself upright and drew the Unicorn Blade. He lunged towards one attendant, slashing at him with the blade's point—blue liquid sprayed from the body and the fair fell to the ground; the other fair fled.

'Boyd, Morag—grab the packs, everything—leave nothing behind!' shouted Van, swinging the silver jug wildly like a club to fend off another fair.

'Call out my wardens!' shrieked the Queen, holding her wounded arm.

Mac bent to snatch up her backpack, and as another fair lunged at her, Van caught him across the head with the jug and stunned him so that the fair fell towards Rag's back as she reached for her ruck-sack. Penry pushed the fair off and swung his fist, so that in Rag's eyes, he was the one who saved her—although his punch barely connected. Penry grabbed her arm and Galad's coat and pack, as Boyd snatched up his own and Van's

'Together! Together! Come to me!' shouted Galad, 'Don't leave anything behind—we must run for our lives!'

ʃ

CHAPTER TWENTY–TWO

'This way,' yelled Van, running a few steps ahead of them, 'we came down here.'

The others rushed after him, Rag and Boyd still clutched a needle each in their hands

'Penry—quick! My pack—and don't dare drop that coat,' yelled Galad from behind them; freed from the metal needles he had quickly recovered. He caught the pack Penry tossed to him and fumbled to stuff the Unicorn Blade into it and draw one of his long knives at the same time as running...

In his haste, he failed to notice the spiral blade was not secured. It tumbled out and fell quietly to the floor and was left behind them in their rush to escape.

Van swung his jug wildly at an approaching fair. Boyd slashed at another, and although his needle barely scratched him, the fair shrieked in pain—but the fine steel caught in the fair's embroidered clothing, and was snatched from Boyd's grip.

'Run, Run!' Galad shouted. He spun around as he heard the thud of feet behind him and swung out blindly with his steel blade. Their pursuers fell back, but suddenly a flint-tipped arrow flew by his shoulder. 'Keep to the walls and shield yourselves!' Another arrow thudded into the dark leather pack across his back, but did nothing but hang there for a few moments before dropping away.

'This way—here!' shouted Van. They were nearing the open outer gate and beyond they could see greenery where the horses were kept tethered. Two fairs attempted to pull shut the open wooden gates.

'Room!' bellowed Galad, and rushed past the others. He slashed at one fair and blue spattered the wall and wood. The other fair cowered away and the alfar hit him across the side of the head with the flat of the blade, which knocked him out even before he could shriek and fall.

More arrows split the air, but failed to find a target though one lodged in the back of Galad's coat that Penry had flung around him and Mac. As they raced through, Galad paused to push the other wooden door shut behind them, and finding a long wooden spear left by one of the guards, thrust it through the latch, jamming it shut.

Van was at the horses, 'Boyd, my pack and get me a weapon!'

Boyd pushed the pack into Van's arms, 'Sling it around me—my hand's still paralysed by that witch's needles!'

Boyd slung Van's harness over his head and across the broon, and suddenly remembered his father's sailing knife—and the long, sharp steel spike it held. He fumbled one of Van's knives free of the hide wrappings for the broon, then thrust a hand into his trouser pocket and pulled the knife out.

'No—not yet,' said Van. 'Keep it for later, and then only if you find you must...'

Boyd hastily hung the blue lanyard about his neck and tucked the folded knife inside his sweat-shirt.

'We need to get the horses.'

Penry and Rag were already pulling the tethers free from where the nearest ponies were loosely tied to a rail—they selected four.

'Penry take Mac behind you, Boyd ride with your sister—quickly, mount!'

Galad boosted Boyd onto the pony and lifted Rag up, before quickly picking up his coat that Penry had dropped; he pulled the arrow loose and shrugged the leather on. He was already slinging his pack across his shoulder as he seized the reins of a pony for himself and mounted. Van cupped his hands together for Penry to mount, then pushed the pony towards a manger so Mac could clamber up behind the young svartalfar.

Behind them they could hear furious thuds as the Unseelie fairs hammered at the wooden doors. Van caught another pony's mane with his good hand and swung himself up onto its back.

'Quick before they have the gate open—drive the other ponies ahead of us, outwards through the trees.' Van waved his arms and shouted—the other animals, now freed, barged out of the loose pen and through the woodland.

They urged their ponies into the darkness, crouching down over their necks in case a low branch swept them off. Beyond the trees, the animals were skittish as they tried to follow the other beasts as they cantered across open ground and it was all Boyd and Penry could do to keep them under control. Rag clung onto her brother's waist and held on to the pony's back with her thighs. Mac closed her eyes, held onto Penry and bit her lip to stop herself shrieking, but Penry was a good rider and kept the pony reined back—that is until one of the loose animals careering from side to side ahead of him stumbled on some rocks and threw an iron horse-shoe that hit the young svart on the head.

Penry slumped forward over the pony's neck and let the reins fall loose. Mac wailed as their mount suddenly lurched sideways. Galad urged his own pony forward and grabbed for the loose straps.

'Hold him. Keep your seat. I have the pony's head'

Mac wailed again.

'You can hold on. You have him!' Galad spoke loudly enough for her to hear, trying not to raise his voice to spook her mount even more. 'Keep your grip and I'll get you down.'

They were well clear of the trees now and out under a brightly moonlit sky. The freed ponies kicked up their heels and galloped off. It was all they could do to turn their own ponies' heads using the rope bridles and stop them from following.

'Van—take the rear. Penry's injured we must halt,' Galad pulled Penry's pony up to a walk, then a stop, leaping off his mount to catch Mac and Penry as they slid sideways. Penry was unconscious when he hit the ground. Boyd pulled their mount up and stood with its head turned to face the distant glade behind them.

'I can't see anything,' he said.

'No,' agreed Van, 'not yet anyway.'

'Maybe they'll let us go,' said Rag, 'how's Penry? What happened?'

'Something flew off the ground towards us,' gasped Mac, shakily.

Galad was examining Penry's bleeding head, 'I think it was a loose shoe—unfortunately the locals here use iron—and it hit him hard.'

'But he'll be ok, won't he?' murmured Mac.

Penry's eyes flickered, but barely opened. He suddenly twitched violently, as if he was having a seizure. Galad held the princeling's head still as his body convulsed. Mac and Rag looked on horrified.

'Oh that does not look good,' whispered Rag.

'Don't say that!' wailed Mac.

Van turned his pony and walked it back. 'We need to go,' he said, 'can you ride with him, lord?'

Galad shook his head, 'No, Mac has the least experience; she should ride in front of me. Morag—can you hold him steady? Boyd and Van may yet need to be our defence and should ride behind us.'

Boyd's shoulders straightened, 'I can do that,' he said.

'Lord...'

'No Van—he can lead Miss Mac and his sister away if I have to stay behind.'

'Lord...'

'You are their gard. You will also gard Penry for me, if... things go awry.'

Van kept quiet and just nodded.

'Good. We understand each other. Help me get Penry on the pony, and Rag, you think you can ride well enough to keep him there? At a canter?'

'Yes, I can ride fast. As long as we don't have to jump any hedges—I haven't had jumping lessons yet.'

Boyd helped her slide down off the pony.

Galad gave a rueful smile, 'we will endeavour to keep away from any obstacles.'

With Van's help Galad re-arranged their mounts, finally reaching forward to catch Mac as Van boosted her up to sit in front of him. Penry was slumped forward over the pony's neck with Rag behind him holding him in place with one arm and hanging onto the reins with the other.

Galad had wound the plaited blanket rope tightly around Penry to keep him tied to the horse. 'Hold onto the rope and Penry, and let me lead the pony,' said Galad, 'he will follow my mount.'

Rag gave up the reins reluctantly, but realised it was better to be led by Galad than try and steer one-handed and keep hold of Penry—and he and Mac had to be kept relatively close or one pulled at the other and they might both fall off.

They headed west across open heath as fast as they could with the pre-dawn light at their backs.

ς

CHAPTER TWENTY–THREE

It was not that hard when the ground was relatively flat, but as they came to the river valley that bounded the Unseelie realm the land became more uneven, then marshy and swamp-like among the many rivulets and tributary streams, which slowed them to a walk. Finally on firmer ground again they managed a little better speed as they headed up towards the Great Ridge—but they were now desperately tired. It was all Rag could do to keep her eyes open and keep her and Penry balanced.

Galad slowed to a halt, 'How are you, Morag?'

She nodded, just about blinking back to wakefulness.

'And Penry?'

Penry groaned and gave a shiver. 'He comes to... then goes again,' said Rag.

'Keep going. We head across the Downs, and soon I hope we'll meet...'

Just then, seemingly from out of the ground rose three figures dressed in dull greens and light browns—more fairs, thought Rag sleepily, going by their sharply defined features, but these were brown skinned and brown haired with only a hint of dark violet to the rose-colour of their lips.

The three held curved bows already nocked with razor sharp, flint-tipped arrows, fletched with grey feathers.

'Hold, strangers. Who gives you leave here?'

Boyd's hand went to the folded knife hanging from his lanyard, but Van held out his hand palm down—'no'.

'I speak for them,' said Galad.

'And why does an alfar ride with mannish folk?'

'We were taken hostage by the Unseelie and as we made our escape my ward was hurt,' Galad pointed to Penry, 'He needs help, and we need passage to the Great Tor to seek it.'

'Aid from the High Queen?'

Galad nodded, 'If she will.'

The three fairs clustered together and whispered, before the leader spoke.

'We watch the border here, but we seek no troubles fleeing from the Unseelie.'

'Neither do we. We accidently stumbled upon them, and their border wardens took us to Clauhemine by force. The Queen wanted something of ours and tried to take it against our will. Show them your hand, Van.'

Van held out his hand—still with raw red punctures in the back of it.

The fair sucked his teeth, hissing at the sight of metal-made wounds.

'You must have a thing she wants badly.'

Galad nodded.

'And what would that be?'

'A rarity.'

'Not enough, Alfar. Show us this rarity and we will decide how much help you need.'

Galad hesitated. 'Show them,' said Rag, 'we need their help, Penry does anyway.'

'Rag, you can't say...' began Boyd.

'She means no harm, Boyd. Let me go into my pack...'

The fairs raised their bows again.

'First put the brown girl down and dismount before you do!' The fair said sternly, 'we don't know what tricks you have there.'

'No tricks, ser...'

He helped Mac lift her leg over the pony's head and slide down to the ground.

'Here,' said Boyd holding out his hand and Mac ran over to him, standing against the solid warmth of his pony's flank.

Galad slid to the ground, crouched on one knee and pulled his pack around slowly, lifted the flap and felt inside... He frowned, searched, pulled out the contents: shirt, socks, pouches, knitting needles, rolls of spare leather...

'It's gone!' He jumped to his feet, 'It's gone!!'

'What...?' said Boyd.

'The Unicorn...?' said Van.

'In the rush—I thought it was safe—I thought I had pushed it deep...'

'Are you sure?' frowned the broon.

'Vandyke, what kind of idiot question is that? If it was here it would be in my hand!!'

Van bit his lip. Boyd and Rag looked shocked.

Galad closed his eyes and took a deep breath, 'My apologies—to all. Van, I spoke in the heat of the moment, it was not my intention...'

Van shook his head, 'Lord,' was all he said, but his face was as stone.

Galad's chin dropped to his chest—he stood quite still, arms hanging loose at his side, looking like a broken man.

Penry groaned and stirred, which made Rag's pony shy nervously. Galad swiftly took the few steps to grab the dropped reins, and one of the fairs loosed an arrow at his back. The bow was not fully drawn so its force was less than half. The others gasped. The arrow's wickedly sharp pale flint point struck deep enough into the leather stretched across Galad's shoulders to hold for a second or two, then it simply fell to the ground. The fairs looked startled and raised their bows pulling them fully. Even Van looked surprised. Galad raised his arms; the reins loosely grasped in one fist, and turned around very slowly, keeping his hands well away from his knives.

'I—we—mean you no harm. We merely seek to cross your border. If you can direct us to the High Court's wardens we will take our leave, with no hurt taken or given.'

The fairs looked at each other; their leader spoke, 'No hurt was intended... or taken by you it seems.'

Galad slowly dropped his hands. Boyd saw Van's hand unobtrusively move away from the knife hilt at his belt to rest on his thigh.

The fair continued, 'We will direct you—and seek no reward for our favour—but... what is it you've lost that is so precious?'

'A Unicorn Blade,' said Mac.

The fairs stepped away from the alfar and hissed. Boyd tugged Mac's hand and shook his head.

'What?' she said.

The fairs had moved back and taken a moment to huddle together, but soon broke apart to face them.

One took a step forward. 'We want nothing of this. We will guide you to the top of the Great Ridge and call for the High Court's fairs to meet you. And we will refuse the Unseelie passage should they follow, but we will not fight them openly. This is not our battle.'

He raised his chin and stared at first Galad, then Van, then Boyd... and finding no opposition declared aloud, 'Good, we have it so.'

'Our thanks to you,' said Van.

'Do not thank us too soon—you must tell The High Queen your tale and let her decide. You are lucky—had this been winter, you would not have escaped the Unseelie Court. As it is her powers are diminished, she will not openly challenge the Summer High Queen on Midsummer Eve...'

'It's Midsummer's Eve?' gasped Mac, 'and Midsummer's day tomorrow! And we still have to get to Glastonbury—how far is that?'

Boyd squeezed her hand, and whispered. 'We can still do this.'

'What about Penry?' said Rag, 'He's hurt, he needs help.'

'The High Queen can help him—he has been hurt with iron has he not? The waters of the Carreg Well at the foot of the Tor will help heal him,' said the fair, 'And I dare say she will slip that bind between him and the maid.'

'How come you can all see it and we can't?' demanded Mac.

The fair shrugged, 'Your eyes don't see everything. Come, this way—it is not more than a few miles now to the dividing ridge. Beyond that we will strike a bargain for our aid.'

Galad helped Mac up onto the pony behind Boyd, 'Ride side by side with your sister,' he said and handed Boyd the reins.

'But...what about...' said Rag.

Galad raised a hand to stop any argument, and turned his back on the youngsters so he could approach Van, still mounted on his pony. He patted the pony's neck.

'Van—you must take them on. This fair will take you to the High Queen. Plead your case and see she helps Penry—I believe she will, if only to spite the Unseelie Queen. Penry has an Elfstone concealed inside his jacket—give it to the Summer Queen, which will be her payment for helping you. And I would make sure you do that before he wakes up!'

'And what about you?' Van said.

'I cannot leave it there—the Blade. I can't let her have it—and she will have found it by now.'

'She'll kill you!'

'If she ever learns a way to use that blade she'll kill all of us.'

'Then get help...'

Galad gave a grim chuckle, 'There is nobody who will help me. So... I must do what I can alone.'

'Surely...'

'No, Vandyke—get them to the High Court at Droithglarma. The Queen will send messages to Wulfric Kennetson to come and find you if need be—and I dare say Penry's father will deign to turn up and collect him—over my dead body certainly won't bother him!'

Van looked over at the youngsters waiting for him; they were drooping with exhaustion.

'They need you—you are the Gard now—to all of them,' said Galad.

'What shall I tell Penry?'

Galad laughed out loud, 'That little shit won't even ask!'

...Which made Van smile.

'Now go, there're still some miles, but you have a full day, dawn's only just breaking. I shall stay here and persuade the Seelie to take me back to the Henge—if there's a line of trees and a watercourse nearby I dare say they can guide me back to the Winterbourne, that's near enough—the Unseelie will find me.'

'What if the Unseelie loose their arrows first and ask questions later?'

'My coat will give me some protection.'

'I saw.'

'Yes... dragon skin, near-impervious to arrows.

'You killed a dragon!'

'No!! I'm not that powerful! ...It was a... gift—one I will always be grateful for, though it was...' His voice trailed away.

'Though... what...?' prompted Van, now curious.

'No matter. Ride well. I hope we may meet again, but don't hold me to a promise I might not come to keep.'

Galad hit the pony's rump hard and it shot forward a few strides. Before Van could pull the pony's head around, Galad had walked away from them, back towards the waiting Seelie wardens.

Van turned his mount's head towards the youngsters; beyond them stood the curious, fair marchwarden watching the interchange intently and now anxious to lead them away.

'Go ahead,' said Van, 'he'll lead and I will follow you.'

'What about Galad?' said Boyd.

'He has something to do—he will come to us later.'

ʔ

CHAPTER TWENTY–FOUR

The Seelie marchwarden led them at a walking pace along winding paths that zig-zagged gently through the increasingly dense woodland, up to the top of the ridge. Now at a walk, the rhythm of the horses' gait was enough to rock them to sleep and all three struggled to do nothing more than doze for fear of falling off. Penry was still half unconscious and barely stirred, but lay over the pony's neck, his arms and legs hanging down loosely.

After a while their guide stopped as the crossed through the open space of a small glade.

'You do not need the ponies now, let them go,' he said.

Boyd shook himself awake, 'Waaaah... we can't be there yet,' he yawned.

The fair shook his head, 'No, not yet. I will take you by our secret ways, but first you must wear a blindfold.'

'Why?' said Rag, 'How can we be sure you won't get us lost somewhere and leave us?'

The fair looked at her in silence. Van got off his pony and stretched his stiff back and arms

'I'm just saying... how do we know that?' she grumbled.

'Ask your broon—we do not lie,' said the Seelie fair.

Van was helping Mac dismount; the girl's legs almost gave way beneath her and she slumped to the grass. Boyd slid off the pony after her

'Can't we grab a little sleep? I can't keep going—and I'm thirsty,' said Mac.

The fair watched them for a moment. He looked up at the sky, turning to see where the sun was still low down towards the east, partially hidden behind wispy early morning clouds, before speaking. 'Broon—will you have them sleep?'

Van was holding the pony while Rag half slid, half fell to the grass and sat down. He looked at them, and nodded. 'We all need to rest—but only for a short while,' he said.

The fair had already taken something small from the pouch at his belt. He stood over Mac, 'Look to the heavens,' he said.

'What?' But she looked upwards, and so quickly she didn't have time to flinch, he dropped some liquid in her eyes.

'Oooo...' was all she had time to say before she sank back to the grass. Already the fair had moved to stand over Rag, then Boyd, with surprising speed, letting a drop fall into their eyes before they could flinch away or protest. They both sank instantly into sleep. The fair turned to Van with a questioning look.

'No—not me. Help me lay the other one down with them.'

Between them they took Penry from the pony and laid him down on the grass with barely a murmur from the princeling. But just as Van was about to stand up the fair flicked a drop of the potion from his fingers and blew it into Van's face. The broon gasped and sank back to his knees; he shook his head but the droplets were already in his eyes. He blinked once and saw the fair smiling, showing those very sharp teeth... then he too fell asleep and crumpled onto his side.

The Seelie fair nodded his satisfaction. He squeezed a drop onto Penry's eyelids, and then took a tiny pot of salve from his pouch and turning around, dabbed several touches of ointment onto Van's injured hand. Satisfied, he took the ponies' reins and tethered each of them loosely so they could graze at the edge of the glade. The fair returned to the sleepers, scraped a rough circle in the earth of the shortest patch of grass and pushed a stick into the centre, marking the faint shadow it cast with a stone. Then he sat down to keep lookout and wait for time to pass. After the shadow had processed across the first hour, he went to the tall oak at the centre of the glade and pressed himself tightly against the rough bark... and vanished.

Some while later a small troupe of Seelie fairs arrived, walking silently through the surrounding woods. They entered the glade and put down waterskins and some woven baskets holding bread and potted fruits. As they did, the first Seelie emerged from the oak and sat down with them. Shortly afterwards, he looked at the shadow, gauging the time that had passed before nodding to the others and standing up again. He bent over each of the sleepers and pressed a single flower petal between their lips.

Boyd coughed and spluttered and came awake. Mac licked her lips and frowned as her eyelids fluttered. Rag came awake with a cry and shot upright, 'What was that? What did you do?'

Van was also awake near instantly, struggling up and angry, 'I said not me!' he snarled.

The fair held out his empty hands with a faint smile, 'You also needed to sleep—and your hand?' he pointed at the broon's hand.

Van flexed his fingers, the cramping pain had gone. The broon looked down to examine the back of his hand and sniffed; he could smell beeswax, arnica, valerian, and something bitter... He grunted in surprise before looking up, 'I thank you for your service...' he hesitated.

'Which was freely given,' said the fair hastily.

Van nodded, 'Then I thank you again.'

One of the Seelie fairs, a female, though they all dressed alike in soft boots, leggings and thigh length tunics in shades of light green, dull yellows and pale ochres; she unpacked a basket of loaves and laid them on a woven cloth, along with pots of nut-butter, fruit preserves, and dried apples.

The youngsters eyed them hungrily, but Boyd held Mac's hand back when she reached for some bread.

'What do we do, Van?' Boyd asked.

Van was hungry himself, but he nodded towards Boyd, and held his hand up to make the others pause before he turned to their guide.

'We appreciate your generosity, but what have we to do? We have nothing to trade,' he said.

The first fair looked at the others in the troupe and they all seemed to agree as they nodded for him to make the deal.

'You have the ponies—which you no longer need. We will accept them in return for our hospitality—we offer you food, water, and safe passage to the hills nearest to Stourhead where we can have the Marchwardens of the High Court meet you to continue your journey.'

'All this for the ponies—nothing else from us?' asked Van, wanting to make sure what he was agreeing to.

'Yes—like for like. Ponies make good eating,' nodded the fair.

'Eating!' burst out Rag.

All the fairs turned to look at her.

'You're going to eat them?'

The fairs regarded her in silence. Boyd nudged her with his elbow, and frowned, giving a shake of his head.

'But...' she began again before another elbow from Boyd made her close her mouth and give him a sullen scowl.

'We accept your trade,' said Van, 'may we help ourselves to your generosity?'

All the fairs smiled widely; their lips were a crimson-ish mauve ...and they also have those unnervingly sharp teeth, thought Rag. They unpacked the other baskets, laying out the food and passing around water-skins to their visitors.

As Boyd leaned forward to claim some bread he spoke very quietly to Van, 'Will they really eat them?'

Van smiled over Boyd's shoulder at the watching fairs before replying equally quietly, 'What did you think the roast meat was on the Unseelie Queen's table?'

Boyd stopped chewing his mouthful of bread, 'Seriously?' he mumbled.

Van nodded.

'What did he say?' whispered Rag to her brother when he sat back.

'He said, we've already eaten roast leg of pony at the Unseelie Court.'

'No!' gasped Rag, 'We didn't!'

'Apparently—we did.'

Rag put down her bread and flavoured butter, 'What am I eating?' she hissed at Van.

He shrugged, and slowly swallowed his mouthful before replying, 'Nothing made of animals; this is wheat bread, hazel-nut butter, honeyed fruit—though they might find some smoked fish or baked quail's eggs for you if you ask them nicely,' he said.

There was a twinkle in his eye that Morag did not appreciate—was he mocking her? She scowled, but picked up her bread again.

The edge taken off her hunger, Mac looked around her, 'Er... people—what about the time?' said Mac, 'Don't we need to get on?'

'You may finish your food, Brown Girl—we understand your need to come before the High Queen, but we have time.'

'What do you mean—Brown Girl!' snapped Mac.

'Quietly...' said Van, 'they don't mean it as an insult. They mean you look more like them than the rest of us...'

'Oh...I guess,' said Mac, '...are you sure about that?'

Mac looked around and realised the nearest fairs were genuinely smiling at her; one female reached out to very lightly touch and stroke her hair. Mac flinched slightly, but managed to smile back, before whispering to Boyd out of the corner of her mouth, 'Can we go soon?'

'Soon as we've eaten—and we need to try and give Penry some water at least,' he replied.

Mac nodded and quickly finished off her breakfast.

ᔕ

CHAPTER TWENTY–FIVE

Galad bargained with the remaining Seelie fairs, offering two narrow strips of his precious dragon-skin leather as his fee for them to guide him back to the Grovewood, south of Clauhemine, and from there he could follow the Winterbourne north towards the Giant's Dance, and the hidden Unseelie Queen's Court.

He didn't have long to wait before her wardens stormed out of the barrow-mounds to surround him. He only defended himself from their attack, fending away their sharpened wooden spears as he bellowed his challenge to their Queen. Their leaders halted the onslaught to question why he would be so foolish to question her power at the heart of her own Court.

'My reasons are my own, but your Queen will have your hides as a war-banner if you fail to take my challenge to her.'

'First give up your knives, alfar.'

'You would dishonour me before your Queen if you take me before her unweaponed—I give challenge to her and her champion, and you'd have me crawl in on my belly like a snake?' Galad sneered, drawing himself up to his full height.

'Adders have a sharp tooth, alfar!'

'Try to take my knives and you'll feel mine!' retorted the alfar, easily a head, and more, taller than his captors, and actively looming over them.

The wardens clustered together, while others held their threatening stance and kept their sharpened wooden lances at Galad's throat. They came to a decision. Their spokesperson approached Galad.

'You must swear that your intentions here are only for honourable battle with the champion of our Queen's choosing...'

'I do...'

'...And for that we grant permission, in that this is your only reason to enter our realm unhindered, bearing arms.'

'I swear...' Galad placed his hand on his heart and bowed his head.

'Place your hands on the stone and swear your oath.'

Galad did as he was asked; placing both his hands flat on the tall dolmen stone beside them.

'I swear on my honour...' one of the waiting fairs sniggered at this. Galad's head whipped around to give a ferocious glare and the offending fair shrank back before Galad continued, '...On my honour—I come here solely to fight the Queen's Champion for the unhindered return to me of the Unicorn Blade, a blade more precious to me than my life...'

The first Unseelie fair grunted, 'As it may well be, Alfar— the Queen will summon her Wynter Knyght to despatch her challenger—all feel his dark presence and despair!'

Galad acknowledged this slowly with a single nod, 'So be it,' he said, 'lead me on.'

The fairs clustered around him, but kept a safe distance, as they lead him beneath dolmen and through the barrow-stones. He felt that weird change of pressure beneath his feet, the air about him flexed and the darkness flickered around him before the fairs led him out, not into the rooms of the court but out among the stone pillars of the Giant's Dance. He walked forward alone under the palest ice-blue sky, as his guards fell back to hold a well-drilled line behind him. Suddenly the air above the tall stones clouded over into a thunder-grey roof, and distant trumpets blared deep booming notes to announce Her arrival.

The Unseelie Queen and her attendants made their entrance through the stones, each fair glittering with dark gems, crystals and jet embroidery, both in their white-streaked hair and on their clothes of greys, sombre black, and purple, but none more lavish than the encrustations on the queen's robes. In one white-gloved hand she held the Unicorn Blade across her chest.

Galad almost started forward before he controlled himself to stillness, but not before the guards behind him had hastily raised their spears in readiness. The Queen waved her hand in a curt dismissal, and they stood down.

'So Alfar—you come to challenge me? In the heart of my own Court? Even in high summer many would say that was more than rash...'

Her attendants smiled at each other and nodded their agreement.

'Lady,' began Galad, 'I lost something here I value highly, and to regain it I gladly risk my life, for not to do so would risk my honour...'

'Some would say by your shorn locks that that prize has long past...'

Her court laughed appreciatively at her small joke.

'Lady, I challenge you for the return of my blade. I will fight the champion of your choosing, and if I win I claim the

Unicorn Blade to take away with me freely as my prize. If I lose, you may do with me what you will...'

'If you lose you will be dead! And slowly—by my will!' hissed the Queen.

'Then you agree?'

'I do, Alfar,' the Queen's tone of voice dripped venom and ice. 'When my champion has finished with you, I will have your red life blood dripping down over my stones to feed the worms of the earth!'

'Lady,' replied Galad, his head held high and proud.

'We understand each other, Alfar?

Galad nodded.

'Then I name my champion—the Wynter Knyght of the Shadow Court! He will come to join us here as night falls after the sun has set.'

'Lady—that is more than half a day yet. Do I have your word that I may take a sleep undisturbed until then?'

'Sleep all you wish, rested you will be a more worthwhile opponent, but you must remain here. We can find you a pillow and blanket—or do you prefer to simply wrap yourself in your dragon skin?'

'I will receive what bounty your majesty freely chooses to offer me...'

'Your debts are all about to be forfeit, Alfar. I can afford to be generous with my terms!' And with that the Queen turned on her heel and swept out, disappearing beyond the circle of stones with her retinue close behind.

Alone now, Galad slumped down to sit on a long horizontal stone with a great sigh. He knew he had wagered everything on this battle, but he also knew it was the only way.

Shortly afterwards some attendants brought him fresh bread and cold meat, water, and bedding, which they left by the inner circle of stones. When he'd sat down he realised how weary he was; he ate some food and drank deeply, before he made a makeshift bed on the ground. It felt too dangerous to lie outstretched on the stones themselves. The whole of Clauhemine was still shrouded in thick mists, but suffused by the brightening sunlight outside of the stones; the heavy enclosing clouds had lightened to pale greys. It wasn't long before he sank into a heavy, dreamless sleep— closely watched from the shadows among the stone pillars by sharp eyes, with sharp, black feathered arrows and flint-tipped spears in their hands.

ʕ

CHAPTER TWENTY–SIX

The Seelie fairs were preparing to take their visitors onwards as they'd agreed. But first Rag, Boyd and Mac had to agree to be blindfolded, which they weren't thrilled about...

'Why do we have to be if he doesn't?' exclaimed Rag.

'I will be blindfolded too if that makes a difference,' said Van.

'Mmmmm!' murmured Rag, 'I still don't see why!'

The fair at her side stood holding a length of cloth in silence.

'Oh alright, put it on,' said Rag, and the fair quickly wrapped the blindfold around her eyes. 'Boyd—where are you,' she said holding her hand out. Van took her hand in his and guided her a few steps towards her brother, who was having his eyes bound.

'Wait. You're not...' began Rag as she felt his touch, but before she had time to pull away Van had transferred her hand to her brother's arm.

'Boyd, B-Boyd...' said Mac.

'Don't worry—I'm here,' he said holding his hand out. Van put their hands together, and they each gripped the other tightly.

'Master Broon?' said one of the Seelie Fair Folk. Van nodded, 'I said that I would, so...go ahead.'

The fair blindfolded the broon, speaking quietly for his benefit, 'We do you no disservice, but the mannish folk should not see...'

'I understand, but I agreed to this.'

'As you wish.'

Then each of them was turned so that they stood beside and held hands or linked arms with the person next to them. 'Place Penry next to me,' said Van, 'I'll support him. Boyd can you take his other arm around your shoulder?'

'Yes, I've got him,' Boyd said after a short pause.

'We should have arranged this first,' grumbled Van.

'Peace—nothing will fail.' They heard one of the fairs say.

Rag found herself being turned and having her hand taken from her brother's arm and put into Mac's hand, 'You ok, Rag?' whispered Mac.

Rag nodded, and then realised Mac couldn't see her and whispered back, 'Fine.'

But she was disconcerted to feel her arm being hooked through somebody else's arm. She went to pull free, but her arm was firmly put back in place.

'No,' said a fair's voice in her ear, 'you must hold the circle tight as we travel.'

Reluctantly, Rag held on after realising it was Van's arm she was holding. She frowned beneath her blindfold, but there was nothing she could do—obviously he and Boyd had Penry between them, Boyd had Mac's hand, she had Mac's other hand... which left the circle closed by her holding Van's arm! Hopefully not for long... she thought. She was surprised somehow, how strong and sturdy his arm felt against hers...

Suddenly they felt like they lifted off the ground and she gasped and held on to the broon tightly. He held her arm closely against his side and she could feel his body—which felt both firm and warm... She smelt salt, and supple leather, and a rich greenness like fresh-cut meadow grass... very like his brother Russ's bear-hug. She almost went to pull away, then realised they seemed to be moving very fast. She could feel the air moving swiftly around them and her hair blowing all across her face... she thought some of that might be Van's hair too. And quite perversely the thought crossed her mind that she wished it was his brother, Russ, who was holding her arm clenched tightly to his side.

They seemed to be moving fast, in huge bounces that made them rise and fall within their bubble. Mac squeaked occasionally when they felt like they were falling, but Rag was determined she wasn't going to give Van the satisfaction of seeing, or hearing, that she was afraid, so she bit her lip and held tight to Mac's hand—just as Van's arm held protectively tightly to hers.

'How are we moving,' whispered Boyd.

'I'm not altogether sure,' replied Van, 'but they use the deva of the trees. Whether we are travelling tree to tree, or through the currents of the air some of the time... Just hold on to each other—they will not let us fall.'

Which was not altogether reassuring, thought Rag, but she clung to Van's arm all the same. Eventually it occurred to her that this felt like a really big roller-coaster ride, and if she thought of it as such... she could almost enjoy it. 'Think roller-coaster,' she whispered in Mac's ear.

'Oh... oh... I get it, yes, ok—only a roller-coaster, only a roller-coaster,' the girl whispered to herself.

They took quite a steep drop and Mac squeaked again, before shouting out, 'Damn, great, huge roller-coaster!' ... Which made Boyd laugh out loud.

As abruptly as they began, they started to slow and gently sink until they felt their feet on solid ground. Rag's knees buckled abruptly and Van had to tighten his grip on her arm to stop her stumbling to the ground... which made her cross with herself for allowing that to happen.

They felt their blindfolds being unbound and they all blinked in the sunlight. They were standing under a grove of Hawthorn trees on the top of a rounded hill.

'Below you is the Bruw river; our kin will lead you onwards from here,' said one of the Seelie.

Just then half a dozen new fair folk appeared. These were obviously High Court fairs of the Summerlands. Their hair was all shades of gold from ripening wheat to pale butter-cups. They had pale skin the golden colour of sun-kissed sandy beaches or newly cut wood, and their lips were rosy with just a touch of blueness under the dark pink. They were dressed in a similar style to the Seelie, but in many shades of blues, and darker, richer greens and browns that were embroidered and trimmed with tiny golden beads and glass buttons.

'We greet you, travellers.' Their leader, a female, said with a small bow. 'We are told you request a meeting with the High Queen and sanctuary from the Unseelie Court?'

By this time they had all untangled themselves to stand upright; although Rag felt that her cheeks might still be pink with embarrassment from being held so close to Van's body. Van and Boyd supported Penry between them. The svartalfar was still drowsily lapsing into and out of semi-consciousness.

'We seek her aid—as you can see one of us is injured...'

227

The High fair frowned slightly, 'You know our Queen has no love for the Svartalfar...'

'But we can offer her a prize for her help—both in his healing, and the unbinding of these two,' said Van.

The High fair nodded, 'We will take you to Great Tor of Droithglarma, and the decision will be hers when she has heard your tale.'

'And will we be there by dawn tomorrow?' Mac burst out anxiously.

The High fair smiled, showing white teeth, 'We should be there before sunset this day.'

'Oh good—we're in plenty of time then.'

Boyd squeezed her hand, because somehow—they were still holding on to each other.

'Time? Yes, but first I think we should visit the Carreg Well near the foot of the Tor—by the Queen's goodwill the water from Hen Carreg heals many hurts; it will help heal the young svart of the metal sickness.'

'It heals?' said Morag, 'Really? So maybe we could take some away with us...' she turned to her brother, '...maybe this spring water would help Dad.'

The High fair shrugged, 'For that great a favour you will have to ask the High Queen herself.'

'Yes,' murmured Rag to herself, 'I most certainly will.'

⟅

CHAPTER TWENTY–SEVEN

The High Court Fair Folk led them down to the narrow stream that was the source of the River Bruw; this time Boyd was intrigued to know how they would travel. If the Unseelie used earth and the Seelie seemingly favoured air... then the High Court surely used water as their secret mode of transport. He wasn't disappointed.

The fairs halted at the bank and consulted together, before their leader turned to them.

'We will ask the river to allow your passage through its waters,' she said, and waded out knee-deep into the stream. She stood still in the middle of the flow.

'How's that going to work?' Rag whispered to Boyd, 'It's barely deep enough to paddle in, let alone swim.'

Boyd shrugged.

'Do you think they have little boats and we float downstream?' asked Mac. 'I don't really swim that well—and Penry can't like this.'

Van shook his head, 'They move with the water as the Seelie move mainly with the air.'

'Oh, not more roller-coasters!' said Mac.

The fair had finished communing with the flowing water and stepped up onto the bank. Seemingly, she must have heard their questions, 'We don't move on or through, but *with* the water—you will see. The Bruw says she will take us to the Droithmere, but then we must make our own way to Hen Carreg. Come—each of you must pass through with one of us.'

'What about Penry? He can't be on his own,' said Rag.

'I suppose I can take him,' said the largest of the male fairs, 'if you must have the Svartling with you.'

'We do,' said Van, 'as you must see, he and this mannish girl are bound.'

'We see,' said the leader, 'we can keep them close enough together to pass without hindrance. Each of you must have our arms around you—do you allow that?'

'How—around us?' said Mac.

'Like this,' said the leader, stepping behind Boyd, putting her arms around him and loosely holding her hands together over his chest. 'Our deva enfolds you. It is tiring but we can keep you safely.'

Rag, Boyd and Mac looked at each other, Van looked at the fairs, 'We can make reparations to your Queen for our passage,' he said.

'We accept that,' nodded the fair.

'How long are we going to be swimming for?' said Rag.

'Not swimming in, flowing with...' said another fair patiently, coming to stand close behind the girl.

The taller male fair stepped down into the water, 'Bring the Svart to me and let me feel how he balances.'

Van and Boyd stepped down and transferred Penry into the fair's waiting arms. He took hold under Penry's armpits, leaning the young svartalfar's body against his chest; he didn't seem at all bothered by his weight. Penry murmured and stirred, but the fair shushed him to stillness.

'I can hold him,' said the fair, 'let the little brown one come next.'

Van and Boyd were still standing in the water.

'Er... what about our clothes? Should we take them off?' said Boyd.

'No way!' Mac blurted out, 'We get wet, they get wet!'

The lead fair laughed, 'Do not fret. As I said, we will keep you.'

Another male fair had stepped down into the water to stand behind Van. 'With your permission, Master Broon?' he said, his arms open. Van hesitated a moment before nodding and turning his back so the fair could put his arms around him. The fair leaned backwards, slowly at first, then he dropped flat into the water with barely a splash, and took Van with him and they vanished.

Rag stared at the ripples—the water wasn't deep enough for them both to have gone under the surface... she should be able to see something...

The lead fair motioned another two fairs forward. A female came up behind Mac, pushed her gently to the water's edge and extended her arms around her.

'I will go first, then you follow at my side,' said the fair holding Penry; he lay back into the river and they both disappeared under the water.

'Wait, wait!' yelped Mac, 'do I have to hold my breath?'

'No child,' said the fair behind her, 'you will be safe.' She tightened her arms around the girl as Mac suddenly tried to squirm away and they too slid backwards into the water—which effectively silenced the cry from Mac.

'Do you trust me?' said the fair's leader to Rag.

Rag opened her mouth to speak, but paused and looked towards her brother.

'We can do this, Rag' he said. Rag nodded

'Let her go before me,' he said, 'so I can see she's alright.'

'As you wish...'

The fair nodded. Another male came forward and took Rag by the hand leading her into the water.

'Close your eyes if you wish, you will not need to hold your breath. The deva around me will hold you too and we will breathe together...' he said, all the while slowly turning her to put his arms around her, then they sank backwards into the water.

Boyd watched Rag's slightly panicked face vanish under the rippling surface.

'Your guarantee she will be alright!'

The fair put a hand to her chest and bowed her head, 'I give you my pledge, no harm shall come to any of them from the waters of the Bruw. Now—shall we join them?'

Yes—No. Tell me first—how have they gone? This water's too shallow.'

She stepped into the water, nodding to the remaining fair—who simply stepped down into the water, crouched and shot forward as if taking a shallow dive into deep water.

'We travel through the water... perhaps 'inside' would be a better term...'

'How...' began Boyd as she encircled him with her arms from behind. Then he felt himself levered backwards against her... and they were in the water. More essentially 'in' the water than he could ever have imagined.

'We become part of the stream, entangled with it and we flow together,' he heard the fair whisper in his ear. At least he thought he heard a whisper but it was almost like the hippogriff speaking to him inside his head.

'Watch,' whispered the voice.

Boyd could feel her body behind him, but he felt himself slowly turn to his side as she rolled over, and instead of a flashing blur of sky above his head and flickering branches that moved impossibly quickly, he glimpsed browns and greens, that rapidly drew back. Then as the water deepened, there were swirls of tiny bubbles surrounding them, so many that it seemed almost a mist, but one in which he could see every droplet of moisture. They swirled and turned, presumably as the water turned and bent along the river-bed.

After the initial tension from the shock of the new environment, Boyd began to enjoy the sensation of movement. He wasn't wet, he didn't feel cold, he could breathe comfortably... and yet he was underwater and apparently moving very, very fast...

It barely seemed any time at all, perhaps half an hour but he couldn't be sure how time passed underwater and if it was different from ordinary time... He frowned and tried to consider that when suddenly they launched upwards and as his head broke through the surface of the water it was like walking through a waterfall—all of a sudden the entire weight of the river seemed to break over his head, but only for a second and then he was out and taking a huge gasp of damp air as they somehow leapt out of the water to the river-bank. They stood still and the fair slowly released her arms from around him. Immediately he felt gravity take over and the lightness of the water drained out of him leaving him firmly grounded again on his own two feet. For a few moments he blinked and swayed, feeling regretful that his time in the water had come to an end... before he felt he could straighten his knees and take the world under his feet again. It almost felt strange now, not to be weightless... He looked around for the others.

Van looked deep in thought and was staring out over the gleaming plain of water that lay beyond the vivid green of the sedge banks and reeds, glittering under the afternoon sun. Penry lay on the ground. Mac sat beside him and shivered—whether from cold or fear he didn't know; she just looked shell-shocked. He walked towards her; Rag sat near her. His sister was coughing and retching as if she'd taken in a lungful of water not air. He went to her.

'What's wrong?' he said

Rag coughed, but shook her head, waving her hand that she wasn't ready to speak yet. Boyd looked up; the fair who had transported his sister stood nearby, but didn't seem concerned.

'What did you do to her?!'

'I? Nothing. Her Fire seems at odds with the water—she tried to struggle free.'

'What...' began Boyd angrily, but Rag tugged at his trouser leg and shook her head. He sat down beside her, pushing his sleeves up out of the way; it was warm in the sun and the air was humid. He barely noticed the sudden warmth of the dragon-torc about his arm, or the fact it was glistening brightly in the sunlight. He patted his sister softly on the back.

She stopped coughing after a moment and drew in great ragged breaths that soon calmed.

'Ooooo... I don't want to do that again,' she said.

'Was it bad? I quite liked it.'

Rag shook her head, 'I could breathe, but it felt like I shouldn't be able to breathe. And then I started to feel claustrophobic, that I really shouldn't be there... and one part of me was telling my brain it was ok, and the other part of my brain was saying breathing underwater was so wrong!' She shook her head, 'It wasn't his fault,' she said, 'As we cleared the water I think I breathed in too soon... I'm ok. Honestly.'

Boyd was mollified, but felt a bit sad that his sister hadn't enjoyed the ride as much as he had. He went over to sit beside Mac. She took his hand without a word. It was only then Boyd noticed his bracelet gleaming brightly.

The fair's leader came forward to stand over them. 'Although we can carry you across the Droithmere to Hen Carreg, the currents here are slow and thin. It is better you take to your own two feet but, since you can't walk over water, I have sent ahead to ask the Swans if they will aid your crossing.'

'Swans?' said Van.

'The Swanfolk of Alavon—see, they're coming.'

Around the nearest reed beds through the flat calm of the glimmering water came a pale boat, long and low, but more than wide enough for two people to sit side by side. It had a high prow rising elegantly out of the water, carved into the graceful shape of a swan's neck and head. Behind it, moving equally swiftly, was a second boat. Each craft held four people dipping strongly with leaf-shaped paddles of pale wood, and there was another person standing in each stern holding a long oar to helm the boats through the water. All of them were dressed in shades of white and palest greys. When they got close enough Boyd could see they were more Mannish looking than fair; all of them were light-haired, worn long and loose, or dreadlocked into curls. All of them were tall, slender, pale-skinned with grey-blue eyes... and serenely beautiful.

As the lead boat nosed into the bank, the helmswoman walked forward through the paddlers, surefooted enough that the boat scarcely wobbled. She tossed her white-blonde hair back from her face and jumped down from the prow to the grass; she was barefoot.

'Well met, sojourners—whom do you seek?' she said.

THE ELFSTONE

Boyd noted with amusement that the usually composed and aloof Van was standing staring with his mouth open.

ʕ

CHAPTER TWENTY–EIGHT

Clauhemine—the clouds surrounding the huge stones had faded to rosy greys as outside the sun set and the daylight receded before the slowly oncoming dusk that heralded the gloom of night.

Galad woke up and looked around—nothing seemed to have altered. His gear lay untouched, though he'd used his long pack as a pillow to prevent it being searched. The was a flicker of movement beyond the outer stones and two attendant fairs appeared—one carrying a large tray of food, the other a silver hand-basin and jug of hot water, judging from the rising steam.

They approached slowly and openly to prove there was no threat. They placed the basin and tray of food on the large horizontal stone, and gave a little dip of the head that wasn't quite a bow.

'Our Queen, bade us see you refreshed before her champion comes,' said one.

'You want to see the pig washed and combed before you make the bacon?' Galad muttered sardonically.

They grinned at him, but there was no friendliness in their dark violet eyes. They drifted back into the growing shadows and vanished.

Galad got up and examined the tray: piled with freshly baked bread, nut-butters, ewe's milk cheese, potted smoked fish, and fresh fruit—his first thought was *...they certainly don't stint when it comes to fattening the calf!*

He ate a little bread before stripping off to wash thoroughly. The hot water and soft cloths provided felt good against his skin, even as he rubbed the wash-cloth over the familiar ridges and scars that criss-crossed his body. He knew them all, every point of damage—and everyone and everything that had inflicted it. He could sometimes forget they were there when they remained unseen under his clothing, but then... he felt a duty to keep a reminder of those beings he'd killed.

He shaved quickly using the small knife from his pack, and his larger blade as a mirror. Satisfied, he dried himself, ate some more as he re-dressed, putting the cast-off shirt back on as his other was still smeared with thick, dark sap from his fight with the wodwose.

He found his wide-toothed comb and arranged his ragged plume of remaining longer hair in a tight plait, warrior-style. He stretched, flexed and made himself ready in body and mind; he was in no hurry, let them wait for him...

The rosiness had disappeared from the surrounding cloud, and points of light began to sprinkle across the night sky now visible overhead. He looked up—the stars would watch him survive... or die, equally unimpassioned and distant. He became aware of the Unseelie Court's return.

The attendants appeared silently and stripped away the remaining food, bedding and wash-basin, vanishing swiftly. There were shuffling, shifting movements in the deepening shadows as the Fair Folk assembled, just the stray glimmer of eye or gemstone told him they were there, until the higher status fairs of the Court began to come forward to take their places, and witness what they hoped would be his ending.

The light from the sky was augmented by a steady cold glow from floating lamps like small moons that drifted in to hover above each pillar. Their light was allowed to fall in a circle in the centre of the stones, as the walls and rim remained sealed by mists and darkness. The stark contrast of light and shadow almost made a sporting stadium of the ringed stones. Galad waited quietly, knives held loosely at the ready.

There was a long, low resounding rumble, deep enough for Galad to feel the vibrations rise through his feet, up his legs to his stomach.

The Queen arrived and took her place... and at her side was a tall patch of darkness that held no light. The emptiness moved forward into the central circle and with each step it resolved itself into a mannish shape.

It appeared to be clothed as a warrior in scaled armour of shifting shadows that, as he solidified into being, became edged and tipped with ice. Each of his ponderous footsteps made the green grass beneath his booted feet wither and blacken as if blasted by frost. The Wynter Knyght stood full square, his feet apart and faced Galad.

There were several yards of open ground between them, but Galad could feel the intense cold that rippled off the Knyght into the Midsummer air.

The Queen spoke into the near silent atmosphere of expectation that filled the Giant's Dance.

'My winter champion awaits you Galad of the Alfar—you still challenge me?'

'I do,' said Galad, 'And as my victory prize I claim the Unicorn Blade of my making.'

'It shall be so.'

'You swear that before your Court?'

The Queen hissed her disapproval, and a low murmur ran through the waiting Fair Folk.

'You dare to challenge me, and then doubt my word! But... we shall see it done—I so swear!'

The rolling murmur quietened, the air of expectation thickened until it was almost tangible.

Galad licked his lips and rolled his head to flex the tension out of his neck and shoulders.

'I am ready!' he announced.

The Queen nodded and a single brass trumpet blared out a long note.

The Knyght raised his hand, fingers outstretched, and Galad felt a cold breeze waft against his scalp. He also felt the harsh tug of the shears that had once cut his hair, and a burning sense of shame flushed through him... as it had done once before. He shook his head to clear the memory.

The Knyght circled slowly, watching Galad carefully; he raised his other hand, suddenly holding a sword of shadow and swung it at the alfar. Galad sidestepped, but the tip of the shadow touched his thigh. Instantly, within the deep scar in the muscle, left there by a wound from a dragon's tooth, seared the agony of the original strike. Galad staggered and the Knyght whirled about to strike him across his shoulder before he could fend away the blow. The mere touch from the shadow sword seemed to plunge into the old wound caused by a steel arrowhead, shafting through the alfar's flesh anew making him gasp. Before he could move, the shadow-blade flat-sided him, striking a light, glancing blow, sliding down across his back. Galad felt again the wicked fire in his flesh as when he'd been captured by southern corsairs, tied down and whipped. The searing pain ran through every fine line that still marked his back in narrow pale ridges. It made him cry out before he could choke the sound back. It made him reel away... pain and nightmare memories flowed through him.

The Knyght stood his ground and watched the alfar intently, like a cat toying with a mouse.

Galad glanced down at his thigh—no sign of staining seeped through his clothes. He realised where the Wynter Knyght's power lay—no blood was drawn, but every old wound could be laid bare as if it was repeated afresh! Along with each nightmare, every despairing thought and memory...

He gathered his strength and trod the circle warily, keeping out of reach of the long shadow blade. Limping from the wound that throbbed deep in his thigh, his back stinging ferociously as if newly made scars were being rubbed with raw salt—he tried hard to fight down the fear inside that threatened to rise and choke him.

'You take unfair advantage of me, Ser—your long blade to my knives,' he called out.

The Knyght nodded and the shadow in his hand shrank down to match Galad's, he beckoned the alfar forward with his other hand. Galad instantly lunged towards his opponent, slashing at the shadow's out-stretched arm. His white blade flickered in the cold moon-glow and struck home—a small patch of darkness fell to the grass, withering away as it sank into the earth.

There was roar as of rising, winter gales, and the air between them near-froze. Galad felt his eyelashes crinkle and whiten as ice formed on them. He scrubbed his face with his fist, exposing his ribs. The Knyght swung his shortened blade and Galad screamed as he felt once again the genuine fire that had curled the flesh of his side. He retreated, panting, holding his elbow clamped to his side, convincing himself—there is no fire here, there is no fire here! But the pain remained inside his body... like the red aftershock of brilliant sunlight sears the insides of eyelids on a too bright day.

The Queen leaned forward eagerly, her eyes glinting, her teeth bared in a hideous smile; she snarled quietly. The Court shifted in anticipation of victory.

Years of battling settled into the alfar's mind and body, and he let that take over; he feinted and spun to thrust and slash almost from muscle-memory alone. He danced away the best he could as the shadow probed at his old scars, sometimes avoiding the Knyght's blade, sometimes not... each touch was a painful blow. He used his skill to avoid the penetrating thrusts that might end him when another near-lethal trauma from his past might be triggered anew.

They fought, and Galad tried to nip and snag like a hornet buzzing around a buffalo. He struck away small patches of darkness that shrivelled to the ground. He could barely think of them as flesh because the Knyght was wholly of shadows made into substance. Each time the alfar struck at their champion, the Court groaned, and each time the Knyght made Galad cry out, they hissed with pleasure. They fought on. Galad's limbs were weary. Even if he didn't bleed this time, his flesh screamed with old pains and foul memories awoken, so much so that the sweat of his exertions beaded his forehead. He shook his head to clear his eyes and he saw the Knyght relax his stance—the Shadow was becoming over-confident, thought Galad...

He backed off, wiping his forehead with the back of his hand. The alfar was alert and watching, knowing in this moment of seeming inattention the Knyght would be tempted to strike...

He did—and Galad was ready for him.

The Knyght lunged below Galad's belly with his shad-ow-blade. In his tender flesh the alfar felt again the swift slash of the obsidian knife that had sliced him... but as he screamed, more in rage than in pain, Galad leapt in the air to strike with both of his white knives, criss-crossing them to slash deeply through the cruel shadow's throat.

The Knyght's head fell to the earth.

Galad fell to the ground. He curled up around the agony of that final nightmare wound... trying to force his thoughts away from it, even as the fleeting memory drifted across his mind that he hadn't curled up around himself at the time...

To his side... the Knyght's remains, an empty shape of darkness sank into the ground, bruising and blackening the grass, leaving the earth frosted with ice crystals.

Around him, he heard a sharp intake of collective breath as the fairs became disbelieving witnesses to their champi-on's defeat.

Galad rolled over onto his knees and struggled to stand. The Queen was the first to her feet. She reached for the Unicorn Blade and flung it at Galad with all her might—then stormed away.

He dropped his two knives and caught the blade flat between both palms, a mere fraction before it pierced his chest and his heart. He sank back to the ground again on his knees. Around the pillars, the fairs were vanishing away beyond the stones. The surrounding mists fluttered into shreds that dissolved into nothing, and Galad was left alone under the stars of a clear, summer night sky.

He sank down, every sinew and muscle screaming with pain he could do nothing about. He struggled hard to hold onto his sanity and beat back the suffocating despair and nightmare desperation as old memories threatened to over-whelm him. He clutched the Unicorn blade to his chest as the revived agonies flowed through his mind and body and tried very hard not to pass out... he wasn't out of danger yet...

ς

CHAPTER TWENTY-NINE

Boyd waited for a few moments, but as Van seemed to still be dumbstruck, he stepped forward, and remembering what he'd seen Galad and Van do, he placed his right hand on his chest and bowed his head.

'Well met,' said Boyd, 'We need to get to the Carreg Well because our friend here is hurt, and we're told the waters will help him recover.'

The Swan-woman nodded, 'May I?' she said, and walked over to Penry. She put her hand on his forehead, Penry shivered at her touch as she parted his hair to look at his scalp-wound; she frowned, and placed her fingers at his neck to take his pulse before speaking,

'His heart is still strong. I think his head needs washing to remove the remaining traces of iron—I can feel it in his hair, and a draught from the healing spring will help.'

'So that's all we needed to do? Wash his hair?' said Rag.

The Swan-woman turned to her, 'The water from Hen Carreg will cleanse him more quickly than any spring or river could. And what about the rest of you?'

Van had recovered his voice, 'This girl needs the help of the High Queen to free the bind between her and the young svartalfar. They are here because of friendship...' he gestured towards Boyd and Rag.

'And yourself, Master Broon, you pick strange travelling companions.'

'Lady, I am charged with their gard.'

'Who would that be by?'

'My liege-lord, Wulfric Kennetson... and by the appointed gard of the Svart Lord of the North for his son.'

'And where is he—a poor gard if he leaves his duty to another.'

'He had another task... something of importance, and the more I think about it the more I believe I should return and help him.'

'You—want to go back there?' Boyd was shocked.

Van bit his lip, 'He did us a service and I disparaged him. But he knew he was going into great danger and he went anyway—and now you are all so near to the Well and safety... I should go back to him. Even if it's only to find out what has happened to him.'

'You think it is that bad?' Boyd said slowly. Van shrugged and shook his head.

'Do you think he's dead?' said Rag, 'Do you think she's killed him?'

'Which 'she' is that?' asked the Swan-woman.

'The Unseelie Queen.'

The Swan-woman hissed through her teeth, 'So you are running from her—thank your stars she is at her weakest, or you'd never have got away from her Court.'

Van had made his mind up, 'Nevertheless—I need to go back.'

'I don't know... is that such a good idea?' said Mac, having recovered enough to start paying attention to what was going on around her.

'He helped us, fought for us. He led us through the wyrm tunnels; he got us free from the Court. It does me no honour to leave him behind,' said Van, 'Perhaps the fairs can...' But then they looked around and saw the Summer fairs had gone—without a sound or a whisper they had left them with the swanfolk.

'Oh...' said Van, 'It seems they have left us in your hands.'

The Swan-woman smiled and gave a small snort of laughter, 'I dare say she and her cohort have things to do.'

'Yes, but...' began Rag, 'We would have said thank you... and... and... we don't know what they want in payment.'

'If they've left without asking, the payment will be something they know you can afford to give.'

'Yeah... but I'd like to know what,' said Rag

'And... um... what about us?' Boyd asked, 'what can we do? For you? And—what should we call you?'

The Swan-woman smiled at them and pointed at his arm—where he'd pushed his sleeve up the heavy dragon-made bracelet gleamed as it clung to his forearm. He self-consciously pulled his sleeve down to cover it.

'That's a rare thing,' she said.

'He cannot give that!' declared Van.

'We would not ask it.' said the Swan-woman.

'Good,' muttered Van, 'We can agree a suitable payment...' he said gruffly.

'But could we not simply do one good turn for another?' she said sweetly with a bright smile that brought him to silence...

Van swallowed, 'Lady—what would that be?'

'Nothing harsh, Master Broon... I think your ward may be able to give us some help in finding something lost—and I should name myself before I ask more. You may call me Finnola.'

'Van—and this is Boyd... Morag... Mackenzie, and that is Penry.'

Finnola nodded and smiled at each of them in turn, then said, 'Why don't we take a moment—we have refreshments to offer you—it is our pleasure with no obligations expected from you,' she added quickly when Van opened his mouth.

'Thank you—but how far is it to Carreg Well?'

'We have plenty of time; Hen Carreg is only a mile across the water.'

A Swan-man walked towards them carrying a large wicker basket over his arm; he had been helming the other boat.

'This is my brother Fintan...' said Finnola.

Fintan was even taller than his sister, with broad shoulders and a muscular chest; another swan-man walked behind him carrying a fine rope net with several glass bottles in, dripping wet from having been hung off the boat to keep cool in the water. He was equally tall and just as muscular, but his fair hair was dreadlocked, while Fintan's pale hair was loose and fell below his shoulders.

'...and this is our cousin, Gwynfor.'

Gwynfor nodded in greeting, put the corked bottles down at her side and withdrew a few paces back towards the boats and sat down on the grass. The rowers were taking their own refreshment as they waited in the boats.

'We have apple-cakes, saffron cake, or farl and cheese,' said Fintan putting down the basket in front of Finnola, 'can we offer you some cider?' He picked a stack of horn beakers out of the basket and handed them round. Finnola uncorked a glass bottle of pale golden liquid and poured it for each of them.

Van frowned a little, but Finnola interrupted his thought. 'This is soft cider,' she said, '...no alcohol, just pressed juice.'

'Tastes lovely,' said Rag, 'can I have some cheese, please?'

'Rag...' said Boyd, with a slight shake of his head.

'Your caution serves you well, Master Boyd, but we offer all this freely,' said Finnola, '... and when we've eaten, we can take you to Hen Carreg, and on the way we might discuss the favour you may be able to bring us.'

They ate and drank, enjoying the food in the late afternoon sunshine, but Van was aware of the passing time, and increasingly anxious about what might be happening to Galad. He stood up and paced down to the water's edge. The three paddlers remaining—there had been two men and two women in each craft—watched him mildly, smiled and nodded but made no attempt to speak to him. Gwynfor, the fourth paddler, stood up and came towards him; the swan-man raised an eyebrow questioningly. Van bit his lip shook his head and turned from the water towards the youngsters sitting on the grass. He spoke aloud to Finnola and Fintan.

'I need to go back to Clauhemine.'

'But...' said Boyd.

Van raised a hand to silence any argument, 'I must go—that's where Galad went. We... I owe it to him. Whatever happens, he does not deserve to face it alone.'

'Bravely spoken, Master Broon—but do you know what you are walking into?' asked Fintan.

'I cannot leave without knowing his fate—my laird will want to know what happened... and if there's a hope of aiding him... It's the honourable thing which I must do.'

'And you'll do that alone?'

'Yes—the Carreg Well is near. In his jacket pocket Penry has a valuable stone—Boyd you must gift that to the High Queen as a prize for helping you. When she has that, she will agree to keep you safe until I return, or...'

'Or what...?' said Boyd.

'Or she can send word to the laird and he will send for you, or come himself.'

'What about you?'

'I dare say I'll be back, but it's best to make all plans for all times.'

'I don't like this.'

'Boyd—you ran off with your sister to help your new friends—this is helping them.'

'So you're going to run off and leave us here?' said Rag. 'Your brothers wouldn't do that!'

'I am not my brothers.' Van looked hurt momentarily, before he composed his face into stony neutrality.

Boyd gave his sister a sharp nudge, and she scowled at him.

Mac had been watching quietly, taking everything in as usual, 'I think Van should go,' she said.

'Really?' said Rag.

'Galad helped us, all of us—and I don't understand half of this, but you can't leave a brother... If Van can help him, he should go.'

'What about getting to the Well, and Penry, and the Queen cutting the binding?'

Mac gave a big sigh, 'We were going to do all that anyway, and we wouldn't have got this far without Galad—and Van. If you're sure we can strike a deal with this Queen, then we're ok. So, Van should go and look for Galad—I don't want to see anybody hurt, but we have to look after one another.'

'I guess...' said Rag, 'I didn't mean I wanted to leave Galad—what's he doing back there anyway?'

'He lost the Unicorn Blade. He had to go back to find it.'

'A unicorn blade?' gasped Finnola, 'he took a unicorn's horn?'

Van's voice was carefully emotionless, 'Yes. And I do believe he has suffered for it ever since.'

'Still...' said Fintan, 'But if you want to seek him. I will fly you there.'

'Fintan...' said Finnola.

'Fly...' said Boyd.

'Outstanding...' said Mac.

Penry groaned and rolled over. Rag was the nearest to him she put her hand on his forehead, 'He does feel a bit hot,' she said.

There was a moment of silence when they simply looked at each other.

'I will owe you a debt,' said Van with a deep bow towards Fintan.

'You will owe *me* a debt if my brother is killed!' said Finnola sharply.

Fintan grinned at his sister. 'They have to catch me first—and no one ever has. I think I know what you want to ask our dragon-boy—and if he succeeds, what I do is less than half that debt.'

'What are you going to ask him?' frowned Van, 'I will not have him endangered—on my honour or not, I won't leave him to come to harm!'

'Peace, Broon—no hurt is intended. We believe he can help us find something lost long ago. A dragon-made neck ring was thrown into the Glassmere an age past, and search as we might we've never found it—but like often calls to like.

We think that with his bracelet, Boyd will be able to point us to its resting place,' explained Finnola.

'How can he do that?' said Rag, 'There're miles of water out there and we only have a short time before sunset then there won't be enough light.'

'We will fly him over the mere, circle it and let him look down. If it is there—I'm sure he'll feel its pull.

'And you will agree to this, Boyd?' asked Van, 'you can say, no.'

'Fly—on the back of a swan...'

'Our cousin Gwynfor will be honoured. He will keep you safe, never fear,' said Fintan, 'and you will do us a great service if you find this jewel. It is a lost heirloom of our family.'

'Yeah—yes, I can do that,' said Boyd.

'Good man,' said Fintan.

'Fly... Oh shit!' said Rag. 'Boyd—don't you dare fall off!'

ʖ

CHAPTER THIRTY

Having made the decisions to go in separate directions, there seemed no point in wasting time. Fintan and Finnola walked a short way apart and spoke quietly together. Mac and Rag quickly gathered up the remaining food and the beakers and filled up the basket. Rag found a bottle of water in the net and propped Penry up to give him some to drink. She managed to get him to take a few swallows, then experimentally tilted his head back over her arm and poured some water through his hair.

'Let me help,' said Mac, 'you hold him, I'll pour.'

They let the clean water rinse through his hair. It was difficult to know if it had helped, but he did frown and feebly shake his head.

'Maybe we just need more water,' said Mac.

'Maybe,' agreed Rag.

Boyd was standing with Van.

'Remember what I said, Boyd—do nothing you are uncomfortable with. The debt is not yours to pay. If you can point to where this torc lies, all well and good. And for the High Queen's aid—Galad told me that Penry has an Elfstone, a crystal axe-head—it's hidden inside his jacket—see she receives it.'

'What exactly is it about this Elfstone,' said Boyd.

'It's a rare thing, as rare as Galad's blade. They say those crystals are formed from frozen light—it will let the Queen cut through the Veil to allow Miss Mac through to the other side. I suspect it must be a thing of Fair Folk glamourie, and if so, only they can use it. It's just a good thing the Unseelie Queen knew nothing about it or she wouldn't have needed Galad or his blade, she'd have simply taken Penry and the stone along with him.'

'And then all her ambitions would come true...?'

Van nodded, 'The fairs keep very much to themselves in this part of the country, but there are plenty of Mannish villages and towns from here to the coast—her ambitions would do away with all of them, and without the balance of power between the three Courts—it would be like letting winter rule the whole year through.'

'Always winter and never Christmas...' murmured Boyd.

'What's that...?' said Van

'Oh—nothing, just something from an old book,' said Boyd. He looked at something over Van's shoulder. 'Wow...!' was all he said.

A truly enormous white swan stood on the banks next to the boats, a pale leather collar hung loosely at the base of its neck. The paddlers dipped their heads to him and the swan acknowledged them in return. The swan turned his head; his shining blue eyes stared at Van.

Van heard Fintan's voice inside his head, 'Come—mount. Keep your knees tight to my sides, don't hinder my wings, and hold onto the collar—don't pull so that you choke me!'

Van blinked, glanced at Boyd, who had heard nothing; the broon said aloud, 'Yes—I'm coming.'

'What?' said Boyd.

Van smiled, 'That's Fintan—he has given me my orders. Look after them, Boyd—you must be the gard now.'

'Until you come back...'

'Until I come back.'

Van took Boyd's forearm and clasped it firmly, wrist to wrist—then he walked quickly to where the huge swan was now waiting in the mere, and climbed on its back. One of the nearby paddlers handed Van a tightly wrapped bundle of clothing.

'Don't drop that,' said Fintan, 'I would rather not be naked when we consult with the Seelie marchwardens as to how you're going to proceed.'

'Your clothes?'

'Well I can't fly restricted by a shirt and trews!'

Van could hear Fintan's amusement, and he coloured a little at the thought the swan-man was otherwise 'naked'.

'You can trust me,' the broon mumbled gruffly.

The swan paddled out into clear water then began to flap its huge wings—he is nearly as big as Muirdoch when he is in bird form, thought Boyd as he watched them. The swan-man gained speed, splashing the water with each strike of his lunging webbed feet, then he was up and clear of the glittering wavelets. The bird and figure on his back rapidly gained air beneath them and went east with the lowering sun at their backs.

'We should get your friends into the boats and take them to Hen Carreg,' said Finnola from behind him. Boyd turned to her.

'They will be all right, won't they?'

'I believe they will,' said the swan-woman. She touched his sleeve lightly above where the bracelet curled around above his wrist, 'You'll have your turn soon, but first—Hen Carreg. Then we shall see.'

They walked back to Mac and Rag, and Finnola got Gwynfor to carry Penry to the boats. The swan-man picked up the young svartalfar in his arms as if he were a sleeping child.

'Are you sure about this?' Rag whispered to her brother.

Boyd nodded, 'Can't be that hard can it? Just fly over the water and look.'

Finnola helped Rag and Boyd into her boat, and Gwynfor took Penry and Mac with him as he took the helm of the second craft. The paddlers watched them with mild curiosity, but weren't overly concerned with these strangers. If either Rag or Boyd caught their eye they would smile, but didn't speak. Boyd took the place on the bench that Gwynfor had given up and took up a paddle.

They crafts moved swiftly across the water, the paddlers dipping in unison with short strokes. Boyd soon found himself matching their rhythm, while Finnola helmed from her vantage point standing in the stern.

In the middle of the mere were tiny islets of goat willow and alders, between multiple interconnecting channels kept clear of reeds, but heavily garnished with underwater greenery and waterlily leaves, and winding enough to require a skilled navigator. The largest channels evidently had enough depth to allow the paddlers to dip deeply and gather speed, and with the shallow draft of the crafts they flew across the surface of the glimmering water, now flecked with gold by the lowering Sun. The boats were hardly rocked by the gathering wavelets from a growing early evening breeze.

Rag barely spoke, she just watched the water and waves ripple by, and stared back at the wading birds who watched them warily from the surrounding reed-beds. The pace of the paddlers altered as they neared the shore becoming slower, using shallower strokes as the water under the craft decreased.

Boyd could see the rising piles of two low wooden jetties built out into the mere, long enough to accommodate several boats on each side though only one empty craft was there at present. Finnola's craft went to one side of the jetty and Gwynfor's to the other. As they drew up a familiar figure came forward to wait for them.

Finnola called out, 'Boyd—throw her the rope at your feet.'

He did so and the High Court fair that had helped bring them there caught it and tied it to the jetty. Finnola hopped off the stern of the boat, another white rope in her hand, and tied up, just as Gwynfor's craft was approaching. Boyd now saw that more fairs had been sitting on benches backed by a wooden palisade; they came forward to help moor the boats.

The nearer paddler rose to her feet and offered a steadying hand to Rag and then Boyd as they stepped out onto the jetty to where the fairs were waiting. Boyd recognised them as the ones who had bought them to the edge of Droithmere in the first place. The female fair who had seemed to be their leader spoke.

'Welcome again—I bring greetings from the High Queen. She will allow the svart to bathe in the spring and drink from Hen Carreg.'

Boyd gave the small bow of greeting that now seemed a familiar and normal gesture. 'We extend our thanks—and we can offer a gift for her generosity.'

'Is that so?' the fair smiled.

'Yes, Van, our gard, says it will be of value to her.'

'But he is not here to give it himself?'

'He... he had to go back. He's gone to the Court at the Henge—Penry's gard lost something he needed to get back... and Van has gone to find him.'

The fair drew breath through her teeth, 'He went to challenge the Unseelie Queen in her own Court—it must be valuable indeed.'

'Well, yes,' said Boyd, 'but Van went to find him to help him get back to us.'

'The broon is loyal to his own then.'

'Penry's gard is an alfar.'

'Another svart,' she said with a sneer.

Rag was standing beside Boyd now, 'No... I don't think Galad is. I think he's more like our uncle. Uncle Wulf is a liosalfar.'

'Uncle is it? The renowned Wulfric Kennetson... so the Keeper of the Northern Enclave has more cubs around his feet.'

'It's not like that. We're his wards and he's our guardian until—until Dad gets better!'

Rag was becoming angry—Boyd could always tell... his sister's hair started to bristle a little with static, and if you touched her you might get a flash of electric shock; he'd learned years ago to keep at arm's length when she was crabby. He could see that now and struggled to think about how to diffuse the situation—apart from jabbing her in the ribs with his elbow.

'Erm... please give our greetings to the High Queen...'

Finnola arrived in time to interrupt him, 'Surely...'

But the fair raised her hand to stop the swan-woman and continued, 'We understand you have an injury among you— we can deal with that to begin with... then I believe you have business with the Swanfolk, boy.'

Boyd nodded.

'The little Fire-child can accompany us and help the Mannish girl and the svartling.'

'But...' said Rag.

'You want our help don't you?' said the fair who had already turned to wave two other male fairs forward to take Penry from Gwynfor's arms, 'They can help him walk and you can help him bathe his head and drink.' And with that she walked away.

'Now, she really is a bossy boots!' said Rag crossly, 'She's almost as bossy as Van!'

'Let it go Rag—she wants you to help Penry. Let's get on with this and when everything is sorted, we'll meet the Queen, get her to cut the Veil and let Mac go home—and then we can all go home.'

'Ok—if you say so,' muttered Rag, 'But what are you going to do?'

'Boyd is coming with me,' Finnola said. 'The sun is near to setting but we still have time enough for a pass around the mere. ...It seems your friend wants you.'

They looked across to the group of fairs, two with Penry's arms across their shoulders; Mac was beckoning frantically, evidently worried about being left alone. Rag didn't speak to her brother, just gave him a friendly fist-bump to his arm before walking over to Mac. The two of them followed the fairs along the path, and another pair of fair wardens holding tall spears tipped with long, obsidian blades fell in behind them. Sunlight glittering off those wickedly sharp, black glass spear-heads was the last glimpse Boyd had of them.

ʃ

CHAPTER THIRTY–ONE

Gwynfor stood by the palisade; the swanfolk paddling the boats had come ashore and walked off in the opposite direction to the fairs, leaving Boyd and the two swans alone on the planks leading to the jetties.

Boyd looked from one over to the other, 'What now?' he asked.

'Come towards the shore and look out across the mere— does any direction draw you? Look hard,' instructed Finnola, leading him towards the end of the jetty.

Boyd stared out across the sun-gilded water and the banks of tall waving rushes, the alder trees growing slantwise at the water's edge, the low clouds drifting together, turning pink at the edges...

'I...I...' said Boyd, half turning back to Finnola, but seeing another enormous white swan a few paces behind them. The swan walked by them slowly, then slid from the end of the jetty and paddled around, to rock gently on the waves against the far side of the moored craft.

'Time to fly, young man,' said Finnola.

'Is that...?'

'Yes,' said a voice in Boyd's head, 'She will help you mount—leave your shoes in the boat and your pack; we can collect them later.'

Finnola had already stepped down into the middle of the boat, Boyd accepted her help to hand him aboard. He sat down on one of the paddler's benches and took off his trainers, and after a moment's hesitation, his socks as well. He left his pack there and then Finnola helped him sit on the gunnel and ease himself over Gwynfor's back. Boyd's legs dangled in the water as he sat astride the swan, and he shivered a little from the shock of the cold on his bare feet.

'Hold the collar and lean forward,' said the voice, '...then lift your knees up and hold tight—as if you were riding a race-horse.'

Boyd altered his position and nodded, his jaw clamped tightly shut. All of a sudden his stomach felt fluttery with apprehension and he thought, if he opened his mouth to speak now, the only word that would come out would be—No!

Gwynfor paddled away from the jetty, lifted his wings when they were clear and flapping harder and harder...

Boyd held the leather collar between both hands and closed his eyes. He could hear the splash of the water, feel the powerful drafts through the air as the great wings flapped. Under him he could feel the warmth of Gwynfor's back, feel the soft downy feathers against his bare feet, feel the raw power of Gwynfor's wing muscles shifting rhythmically... and then suddenly, they were gliding.

Boyd squinted, one eye open; the wind wiped his hair away from his face, and then as they circled, his hair was swept forward. They were high, very high... As he looked down, he saw another white swan rising to join them. *Is that...* he thought.

'Yes. Finnola joins us,' said Gwynfor's voice in his head.

Soon the two swans were flying almost wing-tip to wing-tip; they banked gently and dropped in height.

'Feel through your bracelet, Boyd. Like should call to like...' Boyd heard Finnola's voice. 'We will circle the mere—if anything calls to you. Concentrate your thoughts.'

It was difficult to look down from this height at the water rushing by far beneath him, and the wind dragged too much hair across his eyes to see clearly. They had completed one circle of the waters and begun another turn in their spiral. Boyd squeezed his eyes to slits and tried to feel his arm and the weight of the torc... and did it feel any different... did it feel...? Experimentally he took one hand from the leather collar and held out his arm and the bracelet, willing it to make a connection with whatever was down there. Suddenly, without warning he felt the bracelet warm briefly.

'Turn back,' he shouted against the wind.

'Where?' came Gwynfor's voice in his head.

'Back, back, circle again,' shouted Boyd.

The swans circled around and dropped in height. Boyd felt the faint warmth again and a slight tug.

'Again, again, circle this way.' Boyd stretched his arm out—he could definitely feel a glow like warm sunlight on his skin, but it came from inside his flesh. 'It's below us—somewhere nearby...' he thought.

The swans glided up and down the water, turning when Boyd said they'd gone too far, returning until he could feel a constant glow.

'Down below us—somewhere here.' He gasped, the bracelet shivered and shifted slightly on his wrist.

First Gwynfor landed, then Finnola; Boyd relaxed his legs to trail in the cold water, as Gwynfor paddled in a decreasing circle. Boyd lent forward so he could dangle his arm in the water; the bracelet still felt warm as his hand grew chilled.

The swans spiralled at Boyd's instruction, and at throwing distance from a large group of Alders on the bank... Boyd knew it was down there. The water was much deeper here, and murky enough so he couldn't see a thing, but he could feel deep inside his body that something was down there... something that made his bracelet shift and ripple—although when he looked at his forearm the gold looked solid and inert.

'It's here,' gasped Boyd, 'right here. You need to dive down to get it.' The swans were paddling gently to hold themselves in place on the water.

'No...' said Finnola's voice, 'you must go and fetch it.'

'Me?' said Boyd out loud, 'I can't do that!'

'You must,' Gwynfor's thought entered Boyd's head

'I can't.'

'You owe us a debt, Boyd—you agreed,' Finnola's thought came to him.

'Would you dishonour us by reneging?' Gwynfor's thought rumbled.

'Let me...' thought Finnola—and the swan circled so she could look into Boyd's face. 'Boyd—we have done as we agreed. Even now your friend has been bathed and has drunk at the well. He will be recovering. Your sister and the girl are safe... and my brother carries your gard towards dangers for both of them. It is time for you to do your part...'

'I... don't know... how do I find it? I can't see.' Boyd spoke aloud in reply to the thoughts in his head.

'Let your bracelet show you—dragon-born to dragon-born... it will not fail you...'

Boyd could still feel the pulse of the torc around his forearm. He looked down into the dark water and swallowed hard... *it's only water*, he thought, *I can swim well, I like water... it is only water...*

'Yes,' came Finnola's soothing thought, 'Only water. Take a breath, and dive...'

'Take a breath and dive...' repeated Boyd aloud. Then a thought struck him—flying back he'd be wet and cold—he should take his top off—and his trousers would weigh him down, best take those off as well...

'Leave your shirt across my back,' thought Finnola, 'before you get into the water.'

Boyd stripped it off over his head. The breeze felt chilly against his bare back—and the fleeting thought came to him—*was this my idea or hers?* The steel sailing knife lay against his chest; it had been warmed by his skin, but exposed, the metal immediately began to chill. He considered if he'd need it, but decided he wanted both hands free so he left it hanging from the lanyard around his neck. He loosed the button at his waist and the zip before he slipped off Gwynfor's back and into the mere, treading water while he stripped the sodden, heavy fabric from his legs. As he thought about what to do with them Finnola bent her neck and took hold of the waistband in her beak.

'Oh—ok,' thought Boyd. He held onto Gwynfor's shoulder with one hand and prepared himself with several deep breaths—then pushed himself away and down under the water to test the depth.

His feet couldn't feel the bottom. A flutter of fear went through him and he hastily kicked for the surface.

He broke through into the air with a gasp, flailing his arms to find some support. Gwynfor glided swiftly to his side. Boyd flung one arm over the swan's back, panting with the sudden inexplicable fear.

'Calm... breathe deep... settle your mind...' The thoughts pushed through his fears of the unknown. The swan had turned his head to look into Boyd's upturned face. 'We are here.'

Boyd nodded, he let go of the swan's back and trod water, shaking his arms out under the surface to get the blood flowing. His body began to feel used to the chill and he prepared himself to dive down. He took several deep breaths before holding the air in his lungs and pushing himself up to duck-dive into the depths with a flash of pale thighs and long-toed feet.

He opened his eyes. The deep water was full of tiny green particles of algae that swirled about him like soup. He kicked his legs hard to push himself lower, ploughed with his arms to take himself down to the lake-bed. It was dim down there, thick with mud that clung to the edges of the rocks and water-weeds. He squinted around, it was like trying to see through dense fog—then he realised he would need the bracelet to find whatever was down here. He extended his arm and tried to turn in the water slowly, feeling the folded knife hanging around his neck drift across his bare chest. When he felt the faint ripple in the bracelet on his out-stretched arm, he noted where from, before he had to push to the surface to take another breath—idly noticing that the swans' feet were paddling quite hard to stay in place.

His head broke the water and he gasped for air, 'I know... I know... give me a moment. Go again.'

He took several deep breaths to push air into his lungs, popped up in the water to get some power to push down and swam with his arm forward, letting his torc seek its cousin. He had to push down hard; his bracelet headed for the deepest area by an outcrop of underlying rocks. He knew it was lodged there—he wafted his hands to clear away the surface mud from them—which clouded up into the water obscuring his sight even more. He tried not to give into fear of what might be in these depths, lurking in the crevices, and pulled himself downwards, feeling his way down the rocks with both hands.

His knife banged against the jagged stones and for one second he thought it had caught there and would trap him... There was a crack in the piled boulders and... and... and...

His fingers reached into the murk and curled around something smoothly ridged, rounded... while his other hand brushed against something hard, angled deep into the rocks. This other 'something' felt long and rigid and was stuck fast. His own bracelet throbbed, and the neck torc seemed to shiver under his hand in answer. The mud swirled up around him as his feet kicked against the sediment at the bottom of the mere and he pushed for the surface, lungs burning under the strain.

His head broke the water and he took a breath a fraction too soon that left him coughing and spluttering. Water streamed down his face, curtaining his hair across his features like thick wet weeds. He scrubbed it away with the back of the hand holding the neck torc.

Both swans hissed loudly—which startled Boyd, then thoughts of jubilation came into his head—they were joyful to an extent Boyd found hard to comprehend.

'We can leave now—our pride is restored!' Finnola's thought came to him. 'Hold it tight and I will help you mount again.'

Awkwardly, Boyd held on to Gwynfor's neck and upper wing and dragged himself up onto the swan's wide back. Finnola helped by giving his thigh and hip a couple of good nudges with her beak, levering him into place. Gwynfor dipped to take hold of Boyd's trousers that she'd dropped, and swung them around for Boyd to catch.

'Tie them around my neck,' he thought, 'and put your shirt back on. Lean down as much as you can into my feathers, you will feel warmer.'

Boyd did as he was told. He retrieved his top from Finnola's back and took care to change the neck torc from hand to hand before he pushed his arms into the sleeves. All the while, because the sun had dropped down now, the evening breeze felt chilly on his bare skin. He pulled his legs out of the water as much as he could and held tight to the swan's back with his knees.

'Ready?' came Gwynfor's thought.

Boyd nodded his head; his teeth were beginning to chatter even though he thought he shouldn't be feeling this chilled...

The swans paddled out towards a straight stretch of uninterrupted water and began to flap their great wings to achieve the lift that would enable them to soar.

This time Boyd held onto Gwynfor's collar with one hand and nestled as low between the swan's wings as he could. Holding the torc necklace beneath his chest, his cheek pressed flat against the feathers, his bare feet tucked into the down of Gwynfor's flanks. He could feel his father's sailing knife, safely tucked back under his shirt, and knowing it was there felt comforting.

The two swans rose into the darkening air and headed back to the far-side of the mere and Hen Carreg. Flying low over the quiet mere, beneath them their passing reflections rippled white and clear across the glassy waters, as the gathering night skies darkened from blue-green to violet blue.

ᔓ

CHAPTER THIRTY-TWO

The huge swan flying over the rippling leafy woods above the Great Ridge cast a wavering shadow below him—no pale refection here, only a deepening shadow. It was the Seelie fairs looking up who saw a white shape silhouetted against the gathering gloaming; a shape that circled lower and lower, seeking a stretch of open ground to land on. The fairs around their hearth cooking their supper looked from one to the other—before gathering their weapons and retreating into the trees.

Van and Fintan, now dressed again in his loose pale grey shirt and long trousers, approached the camp-fire cautiously. Nobody came out to meet them. Van stared hungrily at the meat on the skillet over the fire. Fintan wrinkled his nose at the smell; he turned around slowly, holding his arms out to show he had no weapons. 'We do not bring hostilities to your supper,' he said loudly.

Nothing. No sounds. Only the spit of fat sizzling in the flames.

'If they've left it... it seems a shame to let it burn.' Van lifted a piece of searing meat from the skillet with the end of his knife and blew on it before gingerly taking a bite. He was on his second mouthful when he heard a rustle nearby.

'A shame when a thief takes a poor fair's supper in front of him!' said a voice.

'No thief, the meal was abandoned—and I was the one who provided it for you in the first place,' said Van continuing to eat, 'Will you have some, Fintan? It's well-cooked.'

Fintan shook his head, coughed, and stepped away from standing in the drifting cooking smoke. 'We don't eat meat, only fish... and snails and frogs... but they don't really count as meat...'

Van nodded and finished eating his pony steak, and was considering another piece when the Seelie fairs all appeared from the surrounding trees.

'Ah... good to see you back,' said Van, '...the supper is yours.' He gave a small bow.

'Yes—ours,' grumbled the Fair Folk's leader.

'Then can we sit with you and discuss a further bargain?' Fintan asked with a smile.

Curious as to what they wanted the remaining fairs came forward.

'Please—continue your meal,' said Fintan.

They waited until the fairs were seated again before they accepted the leader's slightly grudging invitation to join them and sit by the fire.

'You are welcome to sit down with us and we can offer you refreshments—without obligations on either side,' he said.

Van and Fintan sat down. Fintan refused the meat, but accepted some bread and a generous portion of nut-butter; Van took both meat and bread, he was hungry. They all ate in silence... and slowly the atmosphere of tension relaxed— enough for one of the fair to ask,

'So you have returned, Master Broon, and with a Swan-man beside you.'

'Rather he returns beside me.' said Fintan gently, 'At the behest of the High Queen, he seeks to return to the Unseelie Court in search of his friend.' Fintan gazed around him smiling pleasantly, 'And you know how the High Court of the Summerlands values its friendship with the Swanfolk of Alavon...?' He left the question open for them to think over.

Eventually their leader spoke, 'We acknowledge this, but what has that to do with the Seelie?'

Fintan looked at Van, who gave a discreet nod of acceptance, before continuing. 'We go as a matter of comradeship and honour to seek a friend who returned to the Unseelie Queen. We need your permission to cross your borders—and if you will agree, some escort—at least until the perimeter of Clauhemine is reached.'

This brought out a gabble of agreement and disagreement among the fairs. Until the leader banged his spear on the ground, and the others fell to low mutterings.

'For the sake of friendship with the Swanfolk—we could escort you to the path of the Winterbourne—and what have you to offer in exchange?'

Van opened his mouth, but Fintan raised a hand a stop him.

'For the sake of an escort to Clauhemine itself, and your bows as our protection... we can offer you...' He put his hand inside his shirt and tugged. A slight grimace of pain passed over his features and he produced a small white feather and held it up. The fire light was bright, but the white feather gleamed brighter...

'A gesture from the breast of the Swanfolk—a pass and pledge of safety, and guarantee of aid in need across the realms we safeguard.'

The fairs glanced at each other hungrily, their leader spoke. 'One feather... between all of us... is a scant bargain.'

'One feather to each of you who comes with us, and aid in perpetuity to the holder... until that feather is returned to us.'

Fintan held up the white feather and let them all have a good look and think about what the protection of a swan might mean...

Van looked down at the fire and wondered what he was going to have to do to pay off this debt... and how long it was going to take to do it!

The fairs withdrew from the fireside to stand and confer among themselves. There seemed to be a few points of argument that were rapidly solved—their leader came back, Fintan stood to greet him, towering over the fair, who wasn't short of stature himself.

'We must leave two here to perform our duty of wardenship, it does not seem right that they must forego a share of the prize.'

'We will agree,' said Fintan, 'a feather as token of our pledge to everyone who goes with us, and also for the two who remain behind.'

'Only one feather...' ventured one of the fairs.

'Only one,' said Fintan in a firm tone that brooked no argument.

They gathered in a huddle again briefly before returning to Fintan.

'We accept your offer.'

'Excellent.' said Fintan, 'Give me a moment. The swan-man walked to the edge of the firelight and stood with his back to them before pulling the front of his shirt up. He made several tugging motions, paused for a moment before continuing. Eventually he dropped his shirt and returned with a large handful of small intensely white feathers, solemnly handing them out to each waiting fair. He slumped to the ground beside Van and seized a water-skin, taking a long drink before he wiped his mouth with the back of his hand. Van noticed his normally pale cheeks were reddened. Fintan absentmindedly rubbed at his chest through his shirt, as he reached for the remainder of his bread.

'Does it hurt?' Van said quietly.

Fintan shook his head, 'More of an itch, and a little sore—like re-growth pain after moulting. Now had it been a wing feather that's a different matter—and as for tail feathers—don't ask!'

Fintan smiled ruefully and Van decided he would never ask. But the thought remained... 'Are you comfortable with offering them your protection in perpetuity?' He said.

Fintan spoke softly in reply, 'As long as they have the feather... but I think most, if not all, can eventually be reclaimed by my brothers and sisters—one way or another. That's if they don't get careless and let them blow away.'

Fintan gave Van a wink and a grin that made Van think the feathers might have a single time of use by each of the fairs, but not much more than that.

The fairs were gathering themselves together and making ready to leave.

Van and Fintan stood up and dusted themselves free of leaves and dust. Van looked thoughtfully at the swan-man, 'So—what will I owe you?' he said eventually.

Fintan smiled that easy, charming smile, 'I believe your young ward has already paid your dues.'

'Boyd? Is he safe? And his sister?'

Fintan grinned again, 'Both safe, both hale and hearty. Our sister's joy is unconfined... so I know he has returned to us what was lost.'

At that moment the fairs gathered and declared they were ready, so Van couldn't ask more.

Fintan nodded, 'Good. I'm going to go down among the trees and change. Follow me in a few moments and pick up my clothes. I suggest you tie them around your waist, then you can drop them for me after we land.'

'You're going to stay at Clauhemine?'

'For as long as you do—your young dragon-boy has done us a service worth more than we will owe to the fairs. We will see his gard guarded.' He grinned and clapped Van on the shoulder, 'This way I think.'

And he strode down the hill towards the clearing nearby where they had landed.

ς

CHAPTER THIRTY–THREE

G alad tried to let the excruciating pain wash through him. Knowing the many wounds were old and healed scarcely made a difference, and the confusing medley of associated remembered emotions: anger, fear, despair, desperation... threatened to overwhelm him. He shook his head as in the corner of his vision something very large and white swooped down. The mists had long been blown asunder and he was out among the Giant's Dance sprawled among the cold stones. He attempted to crawl to put his back against the altar stone and face what might be coming for him.

A shadow slipped towards him, moving through the shadows, stone to stone. Galad was going to try and struggle to his feet, but before he could make the supreme effort that would take, he heard a carrying whisper.

'Galad—it's Vandyke. I've bought Seelie wardens with me. We're going to get you out of here.'

Galad slumped back; relieved he didn't need to stand—not yet anyway.

'The Unseelie will still be here—watching.' Galad said softly. His voice rasped in an unfamiliar way, and speaking made him cough.

Then Van was crouched at his side, Galad did his best to smile, but he feared it was a grimace.

'You came back.' It seemed almost a pointless thing to say, but Galad's thoughts were still confused.

'Yes,' said Van. He lifted a fair's water-skin for Galad to drink—which he did thirstily, 'Not too much,' said Van.

The broon looked around—there was no sign of Fintan. He'd dropped the swan-man's clothing as soon as they landed and crept forward to look for Galad. Van could just see the Seelie fairs in the shadows with their weapons at the ready...

'We need to go.' Van said urgently, 'Can you walk?'

'Not fast and not far... but there's something you must do first—hide the Unicorn Blade!'

'Where? said Van with a frown. 'Not here, there is nowhere here that She can't find it...'

'There is, you just...' Galad was slurring his words, 'I cut the Veil, and you... hide it on the Otherside...'

'What?!'

'You can do this—if you're quick—I can hold the Veil. But you must be quick. I—I don't have the strength to keep it open for long.'

'Surely...' began Van.

Galad suddenly lurched forward and seized the broon by the front of his jacket, 'No! It must be here. It must be now. It must go beyond her reach!'

'If that is your wish...'

Galad nodded his head. He licked his lips, 'Help me to stand—up against that pillar,' he said hoarsely.

Van pulled at the alfar's arm and succeeded in getting him upright though it made Galad groan and Van stagger under his weight.

'Here—here will do. Stand behind me...'

Van did as he was bid, and saw Galad lift his arm to fumble at his waist.

'Do you need a hand?' said Van.

'Not with this,' grunted Galad.

Van heard a stream of water falling that seemed to take forever to stop. Galad swayed and fumbled at his waist-band again before reeling back to lean with his back and shoulders flat against the stone.

'You have no idea how much I wanted to do that!'

The alfar sighed in satisfaction... tinged with triumph— then pushed away from the stone onto his feet; he swayed. Van caught him under the arm to support him; Galad pointed back towards the central stones, 'Over there.'

They staggered back. Galad took several deep breathes to compose himself, lifted his hand holding the Unicorn Blade. He reached as high as he could and slowly and deliberately cut a rent in the Veil that throbbed with newly appearing rainbow colours and greenish mist. He braced himself between the flowing edges. It was impossible to judge what he found purchase on, but the drifting colours bent and folded at his back and outstretched arms.

'Now... now... Take the blade and hide it. Quickly—I—I don't—know...'

Van took it from his hand and leapt through the rent.

Stonehenge stood serene in the moonlight. A fast moving pair of lights charged by a short distance away across the fields, accompanied by the dull reverberation of an engine; followed quickly by another pair, and another, but no one attempted to investigate the flair of strange green light at the Henge.

'Hurry...!' Galad had slumped, his knees bent, his arms raised to keep the Veil from closing.

Van scanned the ground and saw a small gap at the base of a dark stone. He hastily dug away the surrounding earth with his knife.

'Hurry...!'

Van hacked furiously at the ground and created a shallow hollow against the stone's base, big enough to lay the Blade in snug against the stone.

'Van—please!' gasped Galad.

The broon packed the earth back and stamped it down before turning to the rapidly closing rent that was sealing itself remorselessly from the top down. Van lunged across and dived over Galad's body, now slumped almost to the ground. He turned and dragged the alfar's body back, and found Fintan at his side helping him pull the near unconscious alfar to safety. Silently the Veil sealed itself with a final furl of colour. Van shuddered to think what might have happened if Galad had been left across the boundary when it did so.

Galad was senseless on the ground, totally spent. Fintan looked around him, 'We need to get out of here.'

A flint-tipped arrow fletched with crow feathers landed nearby.

'The Unseelie know we're here,' said Fintan.

The whirr of an arrow being loosed nearby showed where their Seelie guards were,

'This way,' said Fintan, 'we need to defend ourselves.'

He bent and dragged the alfar up, holding him around the waist as he half-carried, half dragged him away from the Stones of Clauhemine and into the open grasslands around it.

'Head for the nearest trees,' panted Van, having grabbed Galad's pack that had been near him on the ground when the broon first found him. There were some small scrubby trees at a short distance over the top of a gentle slope. The thicker glade where the Unseelie kept their stolen ponies was on the other side of Clauhemine, and although the trees there were larger and offered more hiding places... they were also much closer to the Court.

Mists had begun to rise among the stones, wisps at first, but then swirling into thicker clouds of concealment.

'The Queen is summoning, she will send her wardens after us,' said the lead Seelie fair appearing at their side from the shadows. 'We can use the trees if need be to escape—but what about you?'

'You agreed to guard us,' said Van.

'But not to create a war between the Courts.'

'You took payment!'

The fair was grudging, 'We will fulfil our agreement to defend you, but we will not attack on your behalf.' He drifted back into the shadows, bow half-drawn at the ready.

'You will not have to. Aid is coming,' said Fintan.

'Aid?' said Van, trying to scan the edges of the mist to see what lurked inside.

'My sisters and brothers know. They will come.' Fintan was still supporting Galad's body, taking the alfar's full weight across his arm and shoulder.

Van looked at them. 'Can you fly with him? Leave me here—the Seelie can help me get away. You take him.'

Fintan shook his head, 'The Seelie are already among the trees, they do not want to provoke the Unseelie Queen.'

Van muttered some harsh words in Gaelic... before bursting out in frustration, 'Bow! I need a bow!'

Fintan grinned, 'Help me lay your sleeping friend down.'

Galad was anything but sleeping naturally; he was dead-weight, his face pale and drawn, his breathing rasping and shallow.

'How do you think he is?'

Fintan shook his head, 'I don't know, but I think it will take more than the waters of Hen Carreg... And first we have to get him there.'

He dug deep in his trouser pockets and produced first one pale leather strap, then another. 'It may not be a bow, but how is your aim with a slingshot?'

Van grinned back; a near feral snarl revealed by the moonlight. 'Oh, I can manage one of those...'

He scuffed the ground with his boot to dislodge the earth near the tree roots. Natural drainage had loosened the soil and made a narrow runnel strewn with loose pebbles.

'We have enough here to inconvenience them for a while—how long until your help arrives?'

Fintan stooped to gather and sort some stones. He looked up to the western sky... 'As soon as they can, they will come to us—trust me, Swanfolk stay together... you fight one, you fight all!'

ς

CHAPTER THIRTY-FOUR

Boyd felt he must have dozed off momentarily because suddenly he felt the splash of cold water against his feet as Gwynfor landed. The swan-man paddled swiftly to the shore where he waddled up the sloping shingle and allowed Boyd to slide from his back to sit on the dried mud. Gwynfor shook himself and Boyd's sodden trousers slid to the ground as well. Boyd looked around him slightly dazed; he still clutched the heavy gold neck-torc in one hand. Several of the swanfolk were sitting around the benches; two came forward holding piles of clothes, and what turned out to be two large white cloaks. One draped a cloak completely over Gwynfor. The other, a woman, waited expectantly on the jetty—suddenly there was a loud splashing in the darkness of the shallows and Finnola strode ashore illuminated by the light of the Moon.

She was completely naked, water droplets shining brightly on her pale skin and the bib of short, brilliant white, downy feathers trailing down the centre of her chest, tapering to her belly. Boyd hastily looked the other way. Under the white cloak there was movement and then Gwynfor stood up, holding the cloak loosely around his waist—he too was evidently naked, apart from his breast feathers. Boyd sat still and stared down at the ground in front of his feet.

The waiting swans handed out clothes—Boyd kept his eyes firmly fixed on the ground, but he could hear the rustle of cloth being hastily drawn over legs and bodies. He could feel his cheeks flushing rosy, but more was to come...

'Boyd,' said Finnola, 'you cannot put those wet trousers on—you can borrow some from my young brother.'

Boyd glanced up and saw that Finnola was now fully dressed, and behind her was a younger man, one of the paddlers he thought, who was holding some pale trousers. Boyd stood up and went to take them.

'You best take off your small-clothes before you dress; they need drying too,' said Finnola.

Boyd looked down at his black boxer shorts, clinging wet and cold to his lower body and thighs. He didn't move, but Gwynfor came to his rescue,

'Finnola—turn your back! Our dragon-boy isn't as used to naked bodies as we are.'

Finnola gave a snort of impatience and turned around, 'Well hurry up. We need to go to Fintan with all speed.'

Boyd stripped off his underwear as fast as he could and grabbed the loose, pale grey trousers from the waiting swan-man and pulled them on. He left the offending black boxers on the ground, feeling his cheeks flush again as the young man picked them up without a word and walked away; collecting Boyd's wet trousers as he went. Boyd noted with some embarrassment that neither Gwynfor nor the other man had felt they needed to turn around, and he was very glad that Mac and his sister hadn't been here waiting for his return.

'Ready?' said Finnola, turning before Boyd had time to answer, 'Good. Fintan needs us, we must fly to him.'

'What?' said Boyd, 'what's happened?'

'They have the Alfar, but they are trapped. Fintan can only fly one of them to safety at a time, and he will not leave one behind. We must go to him—but we need to inform the High Queen beforehand. We cannot interfere in the balance of power between the Courts, not without her approval.'

'But how do we get that? Where is she?'

Finnola looked over her shoulder as she strode away, 'With your sister and the Mannish girl.'

'What?' Boyd trotted after her, still pulling the cord to tighten his trousers with one hand as he held them up with the other, and stumbling slightly because they slopped over his bare feet.

Gwynfor put a hand on his shoulder and spun him around. He knocked Boyd's hands away and expertly pulled the draw-cords into place and crouched to quickly roll the trouser legs up.

'Many younger brothers,' he said with a grin as he stood up. Boyd was too dumbfounded to say thank you.

'Boyd! Follow me, we must make haste.'

There were lit torches burning with pale fire attached to the walls surrounding the courtyard at the well of Hen Carreg. Rag was sitting on the stone bench near the long trough that stretched out below the bank where the spring rose; her arm around Penry's shoulders as he bent forward. Mac was dipping her wide-toothed comb in a heavy glass bowl of water and combing it gently through Penry's hair, letting the excess drip to the ground. Standing to one side was the leader of the High Court fairs who had helped them. At her side were another two fairs and behind them at a discreet distance were several guards with tall lances barbed with obsidian, The Swans and Boyd arrived at Hen Carreg's enclosure.

Finnola rushed forward, 'Majesty...!'

The fair's leader turned to face her.

'High Queen—our brother is endangered. We need ask your permission—he is at Clauhemine aiding the svartalfar's gard, and Wulfric Kennetson's appointed gard for these two is with him...'

'Yes—I heard of their plan to rescue the alfar from my Sister-Queen.'

'Majesty, this boy has recovered the lost torc of our realm—Fintan's inheritance is at hand...'

'And you would not see him slain before he has worn his entitlement?'

'High Queen—he is my brother.'

'What...?' said Boyd. 'She is the High Queen?'

The fair turned to face him with a sly smile, 'Did you think all Queens do is wear crowns and fancy clothes, boy?'

Boyd stuttered to silence, and then remembered his manners and bowed. Rag had looked up and her jaw had dropped open. Mac stopped combing Penry's hair... even Penry, groggy but rapidly returning to normal, raised his head. He had taken enough in to be surprised as well.

Boyd took it upon himself to do as Van had insisted he should, 'Your majesty—our friend over there has something—a gift to you for your aid. If it will also prove worthy of you granting help to our other two friends and the... the Swan-man... we would be most grateful—as I'm sure would be our uncle.'

'If it relates to what you hold in your hand—then it is not yours to give... That is the lost inheritance that elevates Fintan Alavon to become the new Swan-lord of the Summerlands...'

'This...?' Boyd looked at the torc still clutched in his fist; the gently flickering torchlight reflected from the golden surface even though dried mud still clung to it. He turned aside and looked at Finnola. She nodded and held out her hand. As Boyd handed her the twisted gold torc, his own bracelet gave a parting pulse. He felt the torc-necklace in his hand shiver in response before Finnola received it from him.

The High Queen nodded in satisfaction.

Boyd took a breath and continued. 'Not that, majesty—something else. Penry…'

Penry looked panicked and ducked his head down, holding his jacket tightly around him by quickly folding his arms.

'Penry…!' Boyd's voice held a warning note.

'You did say it wasn't yours…' whispered Rag.

'But it's not hers either,' hissed Penry.

'You said she can cut this bind between us—and if that's what it takes, you are going to hand that thing over!' Mac caught Penry's hair in her comb, twisted it and pulled it back, dragging Penry's head up with it. She meant business.

All eyes were on Penry. Even the waiting guards had come to the ready, holding their lances with both hands. The High Queen turned to him and walked closer. She stood in front of him.

'Princeling—you have a were-price to pay me for your passing?'

Penry gulped. He struggled to find an excuse, but his mind was a blank… apart from the thought his father was going to kill him… and he really wasn't sure if that was just a rhetorical threat.

Rag gave him a hug and whispered, 'You can do this. It's the right thing…'

Penry gave a very weak smile and slowly stood up. He bowed, fumbled inside his jacket and straightened up, the softly glittering Elfstone in his hand. The High Queen gasped. Penry held it out in both hands and shakily got down on one knee to offer it up like a proper supplicant; he finally found his voice.

'High Queen... in honour of the aid you have extended to me and to my friends... I offer you this lost jewel...'

The Elfstone glistened beneath the shimmering torches, the shell-like fractures over its surface creating subtle glimmers of intense blue. The Queen reached out slowly, almost as if she didn't believe it was real—then she seized it firmly and held it aloft. The surrounding Fair Folk cheered. The Queen's face was wreathed in smiles. She quickly took the crystal to the well and carefully washed it in the spring water. An attendant fair offered her a linen cloth to dry it with, but she waved him away and dried it lovingly on her own tunic.

'High Queen...' Finnola said softly, 'We need to make haste to my brother...'

'Yes, yes—go with my blessing. Take some of my wardens with you if you will have them fly on your backs.'

The Queen's gaze was fixed on the dazzling crystal axe-head in her hands.

Finnola whirled around, Gwynfor and the others were ready to run back to the mere.

'Wait,' said Boyd, 'I'm coming too.'

Gwynfor paused and looked at Finnola, 'He has the right to be a man.'

'But he is still a boy...' said Finnola.

'Vandyke is my uncle's sworn liege-man; it disgraces me to be left behind from his rescue!' Boyd declaimed proudly, hands on hips in his best 'I-am-a-warrior-too' manner.

'Bo-yd!' said Rag.

'Ssshush!' said Boyd with a scowl, and turned back to Finnola and the swanfolk.

'Boyd...' Finnola said reasonably, 'This isn't something we do lightly.'

'Neither do I. He is our gard, we are as bound to him as he to us. It is my duty...'

'It is not a duty your uncle expects.'

'It is a duty Van deserves. He is part of my family...'

'Well, I wouldn't go that far...' Rag muttered the thought quietly, but still clearly enough to be heard.

'Rag—shut up! I'm going and that's the end of it!'

Finnola sighed, 'If you are so determined, it is a noble thought...'

'Oh fine!' Rag announced, jumping up and coming forward, 'If he goes—I go!'

'Rag—you can't. You'll be in the way.'

'I will not, and you can't make me stay!'

'Can too!'

'Can. Not!'

Rag folded her arms and eyeballed her brother belligerently. Her red hair glinted fire-bright in the torchlight and the static charge around her seemed to make her bristle with energy.

'You will get hurt...' growled her brother.

'And you think you won't?' retorted his sister.

'Enough!' barked the High Queen, and everybody turned to her. 'If the boy and his sister believe their honour is at stake they should have the chance to prove themselves.'

'Majesty...' began Finnola.

'You are taking many swans?' Finnola nodded. 'Then let them ride with the rear-guard,' said the High Queen. 'Mayhaps they may not even be landed at Clauhemine.'

The Queen signalled to her guard, and swept away, her attendants trotting behind her.

'What about us?' said Mac, 'Are you leaving us here—with them?'

Boyd went over to her. Penry had sunk back down onto the stone bench and was contemplating what sort of spin he could put on this, and how much he could get away with NOT telling his father...

Mac looked woebegone; she felt she was being abandoned. Boyd reached out, and from hesitantly patting her shoulder, took her hand and clasped it in both of his.

'We will be back. It's not safe for you. I—we—we have some experience of this world. We've had some training in what we might expect... at least I have...'

'And I have,' called out Rag. Boyd gave his sister a scowl.

'We need to leave,' said Finnola.

Penry stood up; suddenly aware he should be part of this conversation. 'I will protect you, Mac. Now I'm recovering, I can look after you.'

Both Boyd and Mac looked at him sceptically.

'I can! I know my father's court. I know how things function—we are their guests and they won't harm us—especially now we've paid them handsomely for their hospitality.' He glared at Boyd, and then softened his expression with a smile. 'Mac—we are still bound. We cannot ride apart and I don't think a swan can take both of us together. We need to ask the High Queen to break the bind and send you home.'

'At dawn?'

'Now she has the Elfstone, I think she can do it anytime she likes!' Penry said ruefully.

'Dawn is not that far off,' said Gwynfor looking to the east and the lightening sky, 'We need to go. Now.'

'We're coming,' said Boyd. He squeezed Mac's hand, 'Don't let her send you back before we have time to say goodbye properly.'

The he turned and ran after the departing swanfolk.

Rag was already walking away, 'Bye Penry,' she called, 'See you soon.'

Penry waved, 'Don't worry. We shall be here waiting for when you return.'

Mac just rolled her eyes, and flopped back down onto the bench.

ς

CHAPTER THIRTY-FIVE

Van and Fintan were making some useful hits against the gradually encroaching Unseelie by the yelps and squeals from the pre-dawn darkness. The broon's eyes were keen in the dark and he soon got the mastery of whirling a hard pebble or flake of flint in his slingshot. Fintan had a good aim too. Galad was slumped where they'd laid him against the bank below the trees and didn't stir at all. His breathing was both ragged and shallow. Van was becoming increasingly worried that the alfar's hurts, though invisible to him, were far more dangerous than they'd thought. All he could see was that the alfar's old scars, the ones visible outside his clothing, were red-raw and blotchy, as if only newly healed.

A wooden lance thudded into the ground a few yards in front of them. It stayed waving in the air, the point deeply embed in the ground.

'Oh that's not good if they are within throwing distance,' muttered Fintan, loosing off another stone that whistled through the air.

'Why don't they use their archers?' Van grunted, and flung a stone from his sling.

'I don't know—your guess is as good as mine. She obviously has some plan they're following.'

'Good job, too,' Van scrabbled on the ground for more pebbles, 'if she did we'd be ducks on a pond.'

'Maybe that's it. There's a roll in the ground out there and we're beyond it under these trees—from a distance, they can't get a clear shot...'

A flint-tipped arrow thrummed as it hit hard into the tree-trunk behind them.

'...and maybe now they're coming into their range!' Fintan ducked down, 'And it's getting lighter. It will be full dawn soon and they'll see us clearly.'

Another lance stuck into the ground some distance to the front of them.

Fintan paused as if listening... 'They are coming,' he said.

'Who?'

'My brothers and sisters.'

Out of the west they heard wingbeats, and a white-fletched arrow landed in the ground just in front of them.

'They are here!' Fintan was jubilant.

White shapes with wide wings circled down out of the sky. A High Court archer was on each swan's back. They fired arrows barbed with shards of black glass to drive back the Unseelie, down the slope and away from their quarries' meagre shelter.

Three huge swans landed heavily and flapped towards them.

'These are my brothers, Fingal and Finlay... and my mighty cousin Gwynfor!' Fintan was delighted. 'Help me get the alfar on Gwynfor's back.'

It was a struggle because Galad's body was deadweight.

'We need to tie him. He can't hold on.'

Fintan stripped off his voluminous shirt and tore it into lengths of cloth. With these they tied Galad's hands together and looped them around Gwynfor's neck.

'Take a loop through his belt and tie it around my body.' The thought came into Van's head, and he did as Gwynfor suggested.

'And we need to bend his knees and tie his ankles up so they are out of the way...' muttered Fintan.

Van could see the logic... he was only glad that the alfar was unconscious and couldn't object to the indignity of being trussed up like a roasting chicken!

Above their heads, more swans circled; the fairs on their backs loosed arrows more as a defensive barrage than in anger, to make the Unseelie keep their heads down

A swan swooped low—and Van saw a red-headed girl clinging onto its back holding a bow and quiver of their obsidian-barbed arrows, losing them off with a very determined expression.

'That's...' he gasped.

'My sister,' said Fintan.

'What?'

'Yes, she says the little fire-brand refused to be left behind, and she said if her brother was going so was she.'

'Boyd is among them too!?'

'He has done well, Master Broon, you should be proud of him.'

Van snorted. The gardmark on his arm tingled as it swirled beneath his skin... well, maybe there was something to these two after all... he thought. And Gwynfor answered his thoughts, 'Yes, he has the makings of...' and then came a swannish concept that Van couldn't quite grasp, but he knew it was important to them.

Galad was trussed and loaded, and Fintan called the swans to make a defence so Gwynfor could take his much needed long run to get airborne with his burden. The other swan, Fingal, Van thought it was, went with Gwynfor as guard.

The remaining swan looked Van in the eye. 'No, I am Fingal, that was Finlay.'

'My apologies,' said Van gruffly.

'No matter—climb on his back. Fingal will fly you back to Droithmere,' said Fintan.

'What of you?' said Van.

'I will follow,' said Fintan, 'when I have made sure all others are safely away.'

Another flurry of circling swans shielded them as Fingal made his run, flapping his wings hard as Van clung to his back and tried not to hinder the swan. As they rose, he saw a bird circle with a dark-haired youth on his back.

Boyd raised his bow in salute before crouching down again over the swan's back. Van raised his hand... and had to admit to himself a grudging pride in the lad for insisting he had a duty to perform. His immediate second thought was of facing the terrible wrath of Wulfric Kennetson should one of them fall off and break a limb! Or—Stars forefend—kill themselves!!

He spent the rest of the flight anxiously twisting his head to try and catch sight of them.

Fingal's thought entered his mind as an amused chuckle, 'The Wulf's cubs are well protected. Finnola will not let her fall. And our cousin Gwynedd flies the dragon-boy. We are all too grateful to let him come to harm.'

'Grateful for what?' said Van.

'You will see when we reach the Mere.'

They flew onwards with the light of the rising sun behind them, soon assembling into a phalanx above the two huge birds flying lower, and slower, one with the badly hurt alfar strapped to his back.

Van hunkered down and it was not that long before they landed. Most of the phalanx landed in the water and the High Court fairs jumped into their element and made their own way. Fingal followed his brother and Gwynfor to an open meadow beyond the mere's edge where they could land on grass. The swans bearing Rag and Boyd also made a landing there.

Boyd slid off the back of Gwynedd, grateful for once not to be in the water. Finnola and his sister landed nearby, Rag slid down and stumbled as her feet hit the grass,

'You ok?' Boyd called out.

'Yes—just a bit wobbly, but that was great!'

Finnola ducked her head and padded away to where some swanfolk stood with clothing and cloaks. Boyd walked over to Rag—having mentally thanked his swan, Gwynedd.

'What now?' Rag said.

'Now they change,' said Boyd quietly, 'they use the cloaks because... well they're naked when they fly—no don't look Rag, it's rude!'

'Ok, ok—I'm not looking.'

Rag stared at the ground, but caught sight of Van's feet coming towards them. She looked up. He looked cross. 'Oh not again,' she thought.

'Are you both all right?' he demanded.

'Yes, we were careful, and we are fine,' said Boyd.

'There is nothing careful about riding to battle on a swan's back!'

Van abruptly threw his arms around Boyd and hugged him tightly. Boyd was too startled to say anything. Van quickly dropped his arms and stepped back,

'Harrump... well done lad... and lass...' he nodded to Rag.

She hastily took a step behind Boyd in case there was a hug coming her way, but Van just gave an awkward affirmatory gesture that might have been a thumb's up or a clenched fist.

'My brothers have taught you well...' Van mumbled, and clapped Boyd on the shoulder as he strode past him to get to Galad and Gwynfor.

The waiting swanfolk were helping to unhook the alfar's arms from about Gwynfor's neck. The swan was clearly exhausted and crouched with his wings half spread as they manhandled Galad from his back; the alfar barely stirred. Van quickly cut the cloths that bound his knees and straightened his legs out, while the other swans cut his wrist bands. Van still had Galad's pack swung across his back. The alfar stirred a little as one of the swan-women, older than Finnola, produced a crystal bottle and waved it under Galad's nose. He stirred, turned his head and tried to ward her hand away. She nodded at the waiting attendants and they came forward with a pale green canvas stretcher fixed onto short legs.

'Lift him on,' she said, 'first we must take him to the well before we go to the Street.'

'What street?' said Rag.

Finnola, now dressed, came up behind them, 'The Street is what we call our collection of houses, our village. She is our cunning-wife; she will do what she can to help him, but first...'

The Swan-wife turned to them as the stretcher was lifted to be taken away by a swan-man at each corner, '...But first,' the Swan-wife said, '...he reeks of old hurts. We need to strip him and bathe him in the spring. He stinks of blood and death. We need to take all of his clothes and wash them too...' she held out her hand to Van and he surrendered Galad's pack, '...or the stench will remain with him.'

She handed the pack to a younger woman following her.

Galad evidently heard some of this; he made a feeble protest, '...Not my coat—leave my coat...'

'Never fear. We will wrap you in your dragon-skin, Alfar, if that gives you comfort—but we'll need to dress you in something made for Gwynfor until your own clothes are dried.'

She turned to Fingal and Finlay, now swan-men and dressed, 'Stay with your cousin until his brothers arrive. He needs to sleep to recover his strength—they will carry him back to the Street.'

Rag saw that Gwynfor was still in swan form and had tucked his head under his wing.

'Will he be alright?' said Rag.

Finnola took her by the hand, 'He just needs to sleep. Flying twice with somebody on his back has exhausted him—sleeping in his swan form will revive him quicker than changing back to his folk shape.'

Finnola led them away, turning to take a path in the other direction from Hen Carreg, 'We should let them get on with their bathing, they have the High Queen's say-so and they don't need us standing around to watch.'

'Quite!' said Van, 'So where are we going now?'

'To see the Queen. We go to the top of the Tor.'

Boyd looked at the eastern sky, the sun was peeping above the distant hills. 'It's after dawn—will the Queen be able to break the bind between Penry and Mac? It's not too late?'

'Oh I think so—time is no matter, with that crystal axe she can cut the Veil. She's at the height of her power—Midsummer's Day. And...' she turned to smile at Boyd, '...with the torc returned, we might even be able to help...'

She laughed and ran ahead of them, clearly thrilled. 'Come—follow me. We shall climb the labyrinth path to the very Gates of the High Court!'

She was laughing as she sped away. Rag, Boyd and Van had to break into a jog to keep up with her.

ʃ

CHAPTER THIRTY-SIX

When they eventually made it to the top of the Tor, a significant climb, they found the Fair Folk had dressed the plateau of the peak with bright banners and encircling silk curtains that kept the wind from the assembled fairs and swanfolk. Clearly it was a celebration day, even this early in the morning.

Attendants were circulating freely with food and drinks, and Rag and Boyd realised how hungry they were and accepted everything that was offered. Van also happily took the food—on a celebration day like this, largesse was distributed without obligation to the receiver.

The swanfolk were particularly animated, evidently knowing something was about to happen. Finnola was virtually hopping up and down, but eventually, when a single trumpet sounded a herald's call they all stilled in anticipation.

Out of the great doors at the foot of the pinnacled stone tower that was the entrance to the High Court, came attendants and guards dressed in rich blues and shimmering greens. The warden-guards wore stiffened leather armour, gilded and painted with the High Queen's devices and carried tall spears tipped with long blades of shining black glass. Another fanfare heralded the High Queen—this time she was gowned as befitted her rank, rather than dressed as a marchwarden with a bow. At her side was Fintan, dressed in pure white, with a short cape of white swan feathers about his shoulders. Around his neck, inside the cape's wide standing collar of white feathers, was the polished gold, twisted torc; it gleamed in the early morning sunlight against the pale skin of his bare throat.

The High Queen waited for silence. She held up her hand, then presented Fintan, 'Swanfolk—Behold your Liege-lord, Fintan Alavon, sworn Keeper of the Summerlands, by descent and destiny, rightful Swan-Lord of the Droithmere!'

There was a collective sigh as the swanfolk all sank to one knee and the Fair Folk made respectful bows. Boyd and Van made low bows, hand on heart.

Rag, unsure whether to curtsey or bow did a combination of both and got an eye-roll from her brother. She stuck her tongue out at him. Van cleared his throat meaningfully and raised an eyebrow at her. Rag scowled.

Then the whole crowd stood and applauded, which she eagerly joined in with because she couldn't go wrong with clapping her hands.

Fintan waved a hand in acknowledgment and strode towards the gathered swanfolk accepting hand-shakes and congratulations as he made the circuit of those gathered there.

The High Queen beamed happily and beckoned forward Penry and Mac to stand in front of her. She caught Boyd's eye and beckoned them to come forward too.

'We can undo your bind with any stone. But it is fitting we use the crystal.'

She lifted her hand and a warden stepped forward holding an elaborately carved box lined with silk; its lid was open and the Elfstone rested inside.

She took out a small obsidian-bladed knife from a concealed pocket in her gown, 'Give me your hands,' she said.

Penry and Mac held out their hands. She made a tiny nick in each of their forefingers, just enough to produce a bead of ruby blood. Then she took the Elfstone and collected a drop of blood from each of them, before she held the stone in her palms and whispered to it—too softly for Rag to hear and she was standing almost at the Queen's elbow. The blood had vanished from the stone when she returned it to its box.

She then turned Penry and Mac to face each other and had them touch the little black blade with their still bloody forefingers, and then she ran the blade down through the air between them.

'There,' she said. 'You may step away from each other.'

They both took a step backwards.

'No more than that!'

Both of them backed up then turned and walked as far apart as they could until the banners outlining the boundaries of the festivities stopped them.

Mac gave a great sigh, 'Wow—That is such a relief!'

Boyd walked over and gave her a hug, 'You're going to be ok now.'

'I know,' she said, 'bye-bye Fairyland! Not that that means goodbye to you, I mean... I can go home!'

Just then a large shadow passed over the Tor. Van's head jerked up and around to follow the rapidly moving dark shadow before it vanished. He suddenly gripped his forearm and winced.

'Y' man is here!'

'What's that mean?' said Boyd.

'Muirdoch—y' man. He has come.'

At the far edge of the assembly there was moment of flustered tussling by the guard wardens and a brandishing of lethally sharp lances...

'Your majesty,' burst out Boyd, 'He has come for us! There is no danger!'

The Queen raised her hand and the guards came smartly to attention surrounding a tall lean figure dressed in black leather.

'Ser?' said the Queen imperiously, and held out her hand.

Muirdoch strode forward, and gracefully dropping to one knee, took her hand and kissed the tips of her fingers. She nodded and he rose to his feet with an easy elegance.

'High Queen—I bring greetings from Wulfric Kennetson and his sincere thanks for your aid to his wards.'

'Ser—it was our honour. I am pleased to offer you refreshment after your... journey.'

'Lady,' Muirdoch inclined his head in acquiescence, before turning to look around him with an effortlessly benign, but imperiously regal, smile.

Rag could only think... wow, and you were the one who got in a snit and threw your porridge up the wall when you didn't get your own way!

Muirdoch's confident demeanour was impeccable, polite and gracious, as if meeting High Queen's and Fair Folk Courts was an everyday occurrence. Fintan escorted his sister over so they could both be introduced.

'Ser...' said the Queen.

'Muirdoch,' the Water-horse supplied helpfully.

'Ser Muirdoch, may I introduce Lord Fintan—newly restored Swan-lord of the Summerlands, thanks to your ward—and his sister, the Lady Finnola.'

Muirdoch gave a bow to each of them, 'I am delighted Boyd was able to be of assistance to you—surprised...' Muirdoch stared at Van who could scarcely meet his eye '...and delighted.'

The Water-horse smiled at Fintan and Finnola .

Van muttered 'Lord' and took a couple of steps backwards away from Muirdoch's scrutiny.

'Yes, Lord Fintan—you must tell me all about it,' said Muirdoch.

'Oh just Fintan will do—come and have a drink, they're serving an excellent apple-wine...'

Fintan put a hand on Muirdoch's arm—which only caused the Water-horse to stiffen for a second at the unexpected familiarity, before he allowed Fintan to lead him away.

Finnola gave Rag and Boyd a bright smile, 'Nice of him to come...' then she followed her brother.

Van slapped a hand to his forehead, before grabbing another drink from a passing attendant's tray and knocking it straight back.

'Errm... did you know he was coming?' said Boyd.

Van flexed a kink of stiffness out of his neck, and cleared his throat, before answering Boyd's question.

'No.'

The broon composed himself, straightened his shoulders and stood upright. 'The Laird will have an idea where I am because of his ward on me, and to know I'm all but in the Palace of the High Queen... doubtless, this being Midsummer Day, he expected to find you here also—and Muirdoch will have come to take you home.'

Mac had come over to stand beside them. Penry held back, he really didn't want to be noticed by *Each Uisge*.

'So soon?' she said, 'How am I going to get to Glastonbury?'

'As soon as you care to,' said the Queen who had approached them without them noticing, 'We can go to a quieter place—outside the curtains, and I can cut the Veil and let you go—but you can't take your memories with you.'

'What do you mean?' said Mac.

'You can't remember what you've seen and done—I cannot allow that.'

'What—none of it, not even us?' said Rag.

'I must know something!' wailed Mac, 'How can I explain if I don't know?'

'We can do this,' Boyd said soothingly, 'we—we can go through together.'

'No!' exclaimed Van, coming forward.

'Van—it's the best way. I go through. I know where I am. I can arrange to get back to Scotland—OK it is a few trains but I can do this...'

'But Boyd...' said Rag.

'You will be fine, Rag. You have Van—and Muirdoch to take you home.'

Rag looked like she'd just tasted something bad. Van's face was stony.

'Come on, guys... I can't just abandon Mac. And Penry can't go... where is Penry?'

Penry had stepped back from the crowd and was standing just inside the stone gateway that lead to the Glass Palace of the High Court considering his options when two swanfolk helped Galad through the surrounding sheltering curtains. He could barely stand and was completely drained of colour. Now dressed in Gwynfor's loose pale grey shirt and trews, and soft, felted slippers, he had his dark leather coat hung about his shoulders.

'My thanks. You can leave me here,' Galad's voice was a whisper. He leant back against the stonework of the outer gateway, and then slipped down to sit on the paved floor.

Penry stared at him for a moment, before giving a sigh.

'Well you're not much use to me now, are you?'

Galad's face twisted into what would have been a snarl, but he was too weary to even manage that. He just waved his hand loosely in dismissal.

Boyd spotted them and came over. 'Penry we... oh Galad—how are you?' Boyd crouched down at his side, 'Did the well water cure you?'

Galad was having trouble keeping his eyes open, '...It ... helped.'

Boyd took Galad's hand in his two hands, 'Galad—I will tell my uncle how much you helped us. I'm sure when he knows—he will do as much as he can to help you... if you want him to.'

Galad gave a weak smile and shook his head ruefully. He gave Boyd's hand a squeeze, 'Go safely, Master Boyd. Look after your sister. Family... is...' but he didn't finish his sentence before his eyes slid closed.

Boyd clasped the alfar's hand firmly in both of his and made his silent farewell. He stood up and turned to Penry.

'You are going to see he gets help aren't you?'

'Of course,' said Penry, 'I will tell my father—he will know what to do.'

'That's good,' said Boyd, 'Do you want to say goodbye to Mac? The Queen is going to cut the Veil so we can leave.'

'Really...' said Penry, 'With the Elfstone?'

'Yes, I've already spoken with Muirdoch and Van—he is going to take Van and Rag on his back—though, Rag's not keen—which is daft. She's flown on a swan—flying with Muirdoch is hardly any different.

'I think *Each Uisge* wings will be larger.'

'Is that so... I hadn't really thought about it, but then I've seen him more as a horse than a bird...' mused Boyd. 'Anyway—will Galad be ok here alone while you come and say goodbye?'

'I am sure being alone will not bother him.'

Penry was desperately trying to think of some way he might distract them enough so he could snatch the Elfstone and run... but where to ...even if he could. ...Stupid Galad to have lost his Blade—he could have cut the Veil for the two of them and they could have escaped and then hopped back somewhere else, and... and...

At which point Penry's thoughts and schemes fell apart.

Boyd and the now reluctant Penry walked through the banners to a quiet space where the High Queen waited with only two of her well-armed wardens, along with Rag, who stood a few paces away from them. Muirdoch had returned to join them; he and Van stood discreetly to one side to oversee the transit from this place to the other. Penry gave Mac a little wave.

'Look at me Miss Mackenzie,' said the Queen, 'look at me closely... Hear my voice...'

She fluttered her hand over Mac's eyes. The girl's eyes drooped closed. The Queen leaned forward; she took Mac's head in both hands and whispered in her ear... The only words that Rag could catch were ...*sleep ...no memories ... a dream* ...

Mac slumped a little when the Queen let her go, but Boyd had been warned and was there to catch her, one arm around her waist.

'It will be as if she's walking in her sleep, Boyd. Walk through and I will close the Veil behind you.'

'Good luck!' said Rag, '...See you soon.'

Boyd nodded.

The Queen took the Elfstone from the casket her guard presented to her. She took it in both hands and reached up high, eyes closed in concentration. At first nothing happened—those waiting were silent, scarcely breathing. The Queen dropped her arms, took a firmer grip on the shell-fractured surface of the stone with both hands and tried again... This time a tiny furl of colours started to peel away, almost like the thin curl of wood-shaving left behind a plane... She pushed hard, seemed to feel resistance... and then the Veil ripped silently apart like a curtain blowing open.

'Quickly now,' said Muirdoch, '...remember what I told you, get to a telephone and the Macleods will see all your travel arrangements are made—Bristol to Edinburgh by train, and we'll have Russ and Peat collect you from Edinburgh station in the car. Do *not* go anywhere else!'

'I know...' said Boyd, as he was guiding Mac through the narrow gap in the furling mist that was rapidly solidifying and sealing itself from the top down.

Then they had gone and there was no rift in sight.

The midsummer sun shone down brightly from a gorgeous blue sky onto the baked earth and grass of Glastonbury Tor. There are a scattering of tourists up at the top who didn't take any notice of the two young teenagers who suddenly emerged from the shadow of the old stone tower of St Michael's and stood blinking in the sunlight.

'Woah...!' exclaimed Mac and staggered, slipping to her knees as Boyd held her, letting her down to the grass gently. 'What... who...?'

'It's ok, Mac—I think the lack of sleep has got to you, and you're probably dehydrated...'

Mac pulled her hand away, 'What... Who ARE you?'

'It's me—it's Boyd... we met at the station at Castle Cary yesterday—and we agreed to split a taxi fare rather than wait for the bus...'

'Boyd?' Mac peered into his face, then shook her head, 'You... sort of seem familiar, but I don't remember the train...'

'I think you said you slept most of the way.'

'Did I... That's crazy, because I don't... Wait—there was somebody else here...'

'Yes, my sister Morag, and a guy called Penry, but they've gone into town now. You wanted to be at the Tower at dawn, so we walked around all night. Don't you remember? We went to the Holy Well and looked at the ruins, and then we climbed over the hedge and up the Tor the back way... and after the dawn broke—you fell asleep. You just woke up.'

'Asleep?' Mac shook her head again trying to clear her thoughts. 'That is just crazy—I had some really weird dreams about flying ... and swans... and all kinds of sh...' She hastily stood up. 'Are you making all this up? Did you give me something, spike my drink!'

Boyd got slowly and calmly to his feet, 'No. I wouldn't do that. You did have a glass of cider... but I think maybe you had too much sun yesterday. What with all the festival stuff for Midsummer Eve...'

'Yeah, we had to be here for Midsummer... I kinda remember that bit...'

'And I told you about living with my uncle, who's the laird of a castle in Scotland, how he has an estate in the Highlands, with deer, and hunting dogs, and fishing in the loch... you remember that don't you?'

Mac frowned, 'I... think I... remember something... But why did I come here? I was in Stratford upon Avon.'

Boyd shrugged and gave her a big smile 'You said you were bored and you always wanted to go to Glastonbury, and you met Penry and he said he was going, so you thought—why not?'

'I did? I did—and my mom is going to kill me! Cell, where's my cell?'

Mac searched her pockets.

'You said you lost it on the train—Look why don't we go down to the town—there's bound to be somewhere you can make a call. And we can get some breakfast... I'm starving, aren't you?'

He took her hand and led her towards the winding path down the Tor and on to Glastonbury town.

After several minutes they were near the bottom of the Tor. Standing there was a tall, hippy-looking young man dressed in white, with one pure white wing-feather pushed into his long blond hair. He was busking for the tourists, playing a guitar. He sang well, his head bent over as he plucked intricate notes from the strings.

As they passed, the man looked up.... and Boyd looked into his striking blue eyes. That's when the youngster recognised him, and spotted the large twisted gold torc around the blond man's neck. Boyd stared in amazement. He pulled up short and was going to speak, but Fintan winked; he gave Boyd a wide grin, and shook his head, then carried on playing an archaic sounding folk-song.

Mac was in a hurry to find a public phone and pulled Boyd along after her... and when he looked back, Fintan was walking away from them, still singing...

5

CHAPTER THIRTY–SEVEN

The High Queen gazed at the barely disturbed air in front of her and sighed; she beckoned the guard with the casket and carefully placed the Elfstone inside. The guard withdrew.

She turned around, but before she could speak to her guests there was a furore on the far side of the gateway beyond the surrounding banners that shielded the gathering. There was a blare from a brass horn...

'My father...!' Penry gulped and fled the Queen, pushing his way through the hangings, anxious to distance himself from the fairs.

The horn sounded again, but closer.

'How dare he...!' snarled the High Queen, '...Here. Of all days! Wardens!'

At her command Fair Folk wardens rushed to surround her, almost seeming to appear out of nowhere—so it seemed to Rag, who certainly hadn't noticed them before. The Queen strode towards the commotion in front of her gates. Rag hurried after her. Muirdoch paused momentarily; he waved to Van to stay behind them.

'Watch our backs Vandyke,' he muttered before he strode after Rag.

The surrounding banners and attendants had been pushed aside by the entourage of the Svart Lord. He stood at the head of his guards—a very tall imposing figure, his long black hair flowing loose down his back; he was dressed in complicated robes under a cuirass of dark leather studded with tiny gold rosettes. He slowly looked about the gathering with a sneer on his lips he didn't try to conceal.

The High Queen swept forward to take her place in front of her personal banner. The two stared at each other in a silence that dragged on everybody's nerves. Eventually the Svart Lord drew a deep breath, and spoke; his voice was beautiful, melodious, but there was a tang of steel beneath his seemingly amiable tone.

'I have come for my son.'

'We do not detain him.'

'Good. Where is he?'

'He shall be found—in the meantime, since you are here, I invite you to partake of my hospitality without fear...'

The Svart Lord snorted in derision, but the High Queen ignored it,

'...Or expectation.'

She clapped her hands. Behind her the inner gates opened revealing glimpses of the glassy pillars and fantastically carved translucent archways that led down into the heart of the Tor, to the fastness of Droithglarma. Attendants carrying trays of sparkling wine served in cut crystal goblets surged out and came forward to serve the unwelcome guests.

Penry had circled around the Fair Folk to approach his father from behind—in the hope of disassociating himself from awkward questions as to why he was there. He failed; one of his father's personal guards took him by the shoulder and firmly escorted him forward.

'Penry!' his father's beautiful voice carried, and any idle conservation hushed for a moment. 'A word.'

Penry smiled sweetly, shook off the guard's hand, and came forward. He gave a slight bow, 'Father—you're here.' Which even to him sounded lame, but he was still trying to claw back some dignity from being pushed towards his parent like a naughty school-boy.

'I am.' His father accepted a proffered glass of wine. 'And so are you.'

Penry took a breath and prepared to lie his way out of this mess. 'Yes, Father, but...' he began.

His father held up his hand for silence, before turning to the Queen, 'Might we have a brief moment? I would like to speak to my son.'

The Queen nodded and the fairs withdrew, some re-entering the gates, others, from what Rag could see, almost melted out of sight, she couldn't make up her mind how... they just seemed to fade away. She was far enough away she couldn't hear what was being said by Penry, but as she took a pace forward, Muirdoch grabbed her by the elbow.

'Not one step further...' he said very quietly in her ear. Rag frowned and folded her arms across her chest, but stayed put.

'Father...' began Penry, the words tumbling out in a rush so as to avoid awkward questions, 'I did my best—I managed to discover where the fairs of Arden had hidden the Elfstone, and I had it in my hands... and kept it safe for you... until... until we came here and the High Court Queen took it from me.'

'She took it...'

'Yes, Father. I was injured. I couldn't help myself... then it was in her hands...'

'She took it...?' His father looked grim. The delicate stem of the crystal goblet he held in his fist snapped with a loud *crack*.

Rag saw Penry jump at the sharp sound, before he nodded his head vigorously. The Svart Lord whirled with a flurry of silks and leather, threw the ruined glass to the ground, and strode forward to confront the High Queen.

Suddenly all the vanished fairs re-appeared, and more beside them, both archers and lancers—the space around them bristled with black-tipped spears. The Svartalfar guards had their hands on their sword hilts and a dreadful slithering noise of metal being drawn susurrated through the near silence.

'I believe you have something of mine...' The Svart Lord's voice was silky with hidden threats.

'Your son is free to leave...' the High Queen said calmly.

'More than that!' The words were almost spat out by the furious lord. 'The lost Stone is mine!'

'The Elfstone was freely given to me as a were-fee—in return for my aid and hospitality,' said the Queen.

There was a gleam around the Queen's silhouette that Rag hadn't noticed before... and it seemed to be increasing...

'Penry!' His father's bark was almost as fierce as any potential bite.

'I... I... didn't know what I was doing... I had a head injury,' Penry pleaded.

The Svart Lord scowled, but a quick glance around him at the glowing High Queen, now at the height of her Midsummer powers, her warrior guards armed to the teeth and ready to fight, and Muirdoch—now standing between him and Rag, and looking equally fearsome. The Svart Lord struggled to bring his temper under control; slowly his face cleared to the stony neutrality Rag knew so well from Van's face ...especially when he didn't like doing something he had to do, she thought.

'High Queen, perhaps I was overly hasty—you have aided my youngest son in his time of need... Of course you should accept The Elfstone as my gift... freely given.' He gave a slow bow of the head.

The Queen acknowledged his retreat graciously and bowed slightly in return, 'Come, my Lord—you are a guest in my house, as is your company. Let us enter my halls and we will seek refreshments suitable for this occasion.'

She held out her hand, and to avoid looking sullen, the Svart Lord was forced to take it formally and escort her through the gateway.

He paused when he saw Galad slumped against the stonework, barely conscious.

'Madam—permit me to speak to my son's gard. I shall follow in a few moments.'

The High Queen nodded and progressed forward with her attendants about her. Muirdoch, who was escorting Rag, and with Van staying a step back behind them, paused; Penry was hanging back as well, keeping out of his father's line of sight.

The Svart Lord kicked Galad's foot hard to rouse him, 'Your usefulness is over—for all the good you ever were. Tainted you were and tainted you remain...'

He snapped his fingers and pointed at Galad's arm; his trusted guard swept forward and stooped, grabbing Galad's arm roughly, dragging it up to be within reach of the Svart Lord. The lord waved a hand impatiently and the guard pulled Galad's shirt sleeve back so roughly he tore the fabric. The intricate black knots of gardship writhed under the exposed skin of Galad's forearm in angry agitation that mirrored the Svart Lord's temper. He passed his hand over it slowly and the gard-mark drained from Galad's pale skin in a fine mist of black droplets that dissipated on the wind. Galad mumbled in discomfort. The Svartalfar turned away with a sneer, as the guard dropped the alfar's arm and followed his master.

Muirdoch paused, 'Van—see to him. I hope the Queen will agree to shelter him for a few days at least.' He walked on through the gates.

Rag hung back, wondering if she could do anything without knowing what or how. She could see Galad was drifting in and out of awareness—it reminded her of her father.

Van, was scowling with anger as he knelt at Galad's side; he gently pulled the torn sleeve down, tucking it into its proper place.

'You know...' Galad looked at Van and said with an effort, '...you and his-high-most darkling have a very similar look about you when you're cross...' Galad chuckled at his little joke, but the effort made him cough, which evidently hurt his chest and ribs as he had to grip himself with his hand and arm.

'And what would you know?' Van said gruffly. 'Here, give me your arm—the Swans kept your pack with them. They said they'd bring it back along with your clothes tomorrow. I dare say the fairs will find you a bed and a blanket for the night. Let me get you up...'

Rag stepped forward to help.

'We don't need you here...not now,' said Van brusquely. 'Best follow Muirdoch quickly before you get lost.'

Rag bit her lip and went to walk through the gates, but she was stopped by the sudden appearance of the High Queen returning with just her two closest guards. Rag shrank back against the wall of the gatehouse to give them room.

Van strained to haul Galad to his feet, but had to lean him against the wall for support. The Alfar did his best, but only managed a half-bow towards the Queen before slumping back against the stonework.

The Queen laid her hand on his arm, 'You fought bravely against my Sister-Queen's Wynter Knyght—he thrives on darkness and despair and few ever gain the mastery of him. Thank your stars you were called to confront him at the nadir of his powers... Your bravery saved us all, from what I can gather... We are grateful and you may have our hospitality, but not for too long... I cannot risk the balance of power shifting between our Courts. There is a woman due to pass through these realms in the next weeks on her way to the coast—a salt trader. You should go with her. I believe she will be willing to take you at my request, and you will have time to recover away from this discord.'

'Thank you, your majesty—I am happy to accept—your generous offer...' Galad spoke with an effort, having to catch his breath, and then muttered softly to himself, 'Ah... Melleth...' he slowly shook his head, 'Don't you just get... everywhere...'

The High Queen waved her two guards forward. Between them they took Galad's arms over their shoulders and followed her, walking him down through the glittering galleried paths into the heart of Droithglarma.

Van and Rag watched their departing backs in a moment of silence—then Muirdoch stepped out from between the glassy pillars.

'We should be going too. I can fly both of you on my back, but you'll have to sit close together and hang on to each other.

'No!'

314

They both spoke emphatically at the same time. Muir-doch looked puzzled.

'I should stay with Galad.' said Van. 'When he's fit to travel, I think the Salt Woman and her crew will agree to take him when they take ship for the South. I've met her before, briefly. She's helped others who were injured or in trouble; her own men were once slaves who escaped from the galleys of the southern corsairs. And with the Unseelie Queen out for blood it is better we're all well out of her way.'

'Will you go with him?' Muirdoch was surprised by Van offering to stay.

The broon shook his head, 'I'll only wait here until the Salt Woman comes. With the Queen's favour I think the Swans will house us.'

'Ok,' said Rag, 'If he's not going—then I will ride with you. When do we leave?'

Muirdoch rolled his eyes, 'Come then—back and say our farewells.'

Rag followed him, but Van dawdled behind them both.

After they'd all three passed through the gate-way, a pair of Fair Folk wardens appeared out of nowhere and pulled the heavy gates tight shut to keep the ancient secrets of Droith-glarma hidden from prying eyes.

ς

EPILOGUE

Across the open fields, a car's headlights could be seen cutting through the darkness; its engine reverberated between the hedgerows, but nothing stirred among the gigantic stones of ancient Stonehenge. It was well after midnight, and a golden Harvest Moon sailed serenely through a black night sprinkled with distant stars, before dipping down towards the horizon.

Suddenly there was the sound of enormous wings beating against the late summer night air as something huge and black dropped to the ground. Shortly afterwards, Muirdoch and Van crept forward out of the darkness and entered the stone circle and looked around them.

'Well?' said Muirdoch.

'A moment,' said Van, turning slowly in the moonlight. 'Yes—it was over here.'

He hurried forward and scrabbled at the dried ground at the base of a Blue Stone, and from the shallow hollow he retrieved the Unicorn Blade. He held it up triumphantly for Muirdoch to see, before pausing to stamp the disturbed earth back into place.

'Hurry up,' said Muirdoch. 'The High Queen's agreement is to meet us on top of the Great Tor at dawn to cut the Veil again for us and we can return through it.'

'I'm ready,' said Van. 'The Salt Woman arrived several days ago, and now she's anxious to be off.'

'And Galad?' said Muirdoch.

'He's still weak, but he can travel.'

'Will he come back here when she returns to her trading?'

Van shrugged, 'I don't know. But he seems to know her. Her crew weren't that keen to see him though. Behind her back—one of them, a big black man without a voice—he pointed at her, then him and signed to me like this...'

Van made a heart shape out of his forefingers and thumbs, and then clenched his fists and made a breaking gesture. '...Then the man made a whole lot of vulgar finger signals that made it perfectly clear what he thought of Galad. And I do mean clear!' Van added with a grimace.

'As bad as that?'

'Oh yes—her men don't like him.'

Muirdoch gave a bitter chuckle, 'That should make for an interesting voyage. But come—Droithglarma isn't that far for me, but dawn is coming quickly.'

They two walked back into the darkness, and shortly after, the sounds of giant wingbeats broke the silence of the night...

A silence that quickly returned to shroud the ancient standing stones, as the strange visitors flew high and away towards the west, back towards an entrance to their Other-world.

The following evening in Scotland, Boyd was just shutting down the computer in their sitting room when Rag walked in. She threw herself down on the little sofa.

'So how's Mackenzie?'

'She's fine,' said Boyd.

'It's not really fair that you can talk to her online and we don't hear anything from Penry.'

'We?'

'Well he's your friend to,' said Rag.

'Yeah? And after you told me you'd heard him slagging us off to his father—how he was only making out we were all friends because we were Uncle Wulf's wards and he thought he could spy on us?'

'Well he explained about that,' said Rag. 'He told me he only said that to his father so he wouldn't do anything to us.'

'Like what?'

'I don't know... anyway, I like Penry. And he told me he really liked me.'

'Mmmmm...' muttered Boyd. 'Anyway, even if Mac can't remember anything that happened, I've asked her if she wants to visit us next year—her mother is coming over again for another conference, and I told her to lay it on thick about Uncle Wulf being Scottish nobility...'

'Is he?' said Rag.

'Whatever... he has a big castle, and land, and servants... I'm sure it will impress her mother enough to say yes.'

'What has Uncle Wulf said?'

'He said, after all the smoothing down the MacLeods had to do, persuading somebody to tell the police chief down there that Galad was just an over-zealous secret service bodyguard—somebody looking out for Mackenzie...

'Did they buy that?'

'Muirdoch said they "used their channels", whatever that means. I think they made out Galad was probably CIA or something and it would cause a diplomatic incident if they tried to find him, so word went down from on high to let it go.'

'Useful that—scary really... not quite, you know...,' said Rag thoughtfully.

'A bit like Penry's dad would do?' Boyd shrugged. 'What else could they do?'

'So did Uncle Wulf say she could come?'

'He said she could stay for a week, but we have to be very careful about... everything.'

'You can say that again!' said Rag, stroking Pookie, the friendly, little dragon-cat that had come to curl up beside her.

THE END

ACKNOWLEDGMENTS

I'd like to thank Helen, for the inspiration and loan of her ex-house, and for the many, many chats as I bounced ideas off her.

Thanks to Rachel, Dawn, Kathy, Seath and their book club ladies for ongoing encouragement, and their desire to read more about Rag and Boyd and their adventures.

Thanks to John Lord, for making an inspirational 'elf-stone', a neolithic hand-axe knapped from medieval stained glass; and for knapping some quartz projectile points, and making a great obsidian dagger: www.flintknapping.co.uk

Thank you to Charlotte Mouncey for her delightful and skilful book cover designs.

And thank you to Cheryl and Wizard's Tower Press, I am grateful for all the help in bringing my story to print.

ABOUT THE AUTHOR

Helen Brady lives in a small, ancient town in Warwick-shire. *The Elfstone* is the second in a series of fantasy novels about sister and brother, Rag and Boyd—of their growing up, coming of age, and their travels and adventures in the Otherworld, beyond The Veil. An avid life-long reader of science fiction, fantasy and history novels, her longtime influences are Alan Garner, Bernard Cornwell, JRR Tolkien, and the too numerous to name authors of old-school sci-fi short stories that she lapped up in her teens and twenties. She has two grown-up children, and when she's not writing she's a volunteer as Head of Wardrobe at her local independent theatre.

www.ingramcontent.com/pod-product-compliance
Lightning Source LLC
Chambersburg PA
CBHW021033030726
47496CB00006B/1510